Intriguing

Lord Adelaide

WENDY MAY ANDREWS

Sparrow Ink
www.sparrowdeck.com

ISBN - 978-1-989634-42-4

www.wendymayandrews.com

Stay in touch with Wendy May Andrews
and forthcoming publishing news.

Sign up for her biweekly newsletter

She's a wallflower debutante—and his best friend's sister. But one dance could change everything.

Lady Amelia Courtenay's debut has been less than successful—despite her generous dowry and pretty features. If only she could learn how to navigate society from one of her treasured textbooks. In the midst of her embarrassment, Amelia completely loses her senses and lies about a promised dance. Lucian is her brother's friend. Surely, he will take pity on her, even if he has never looked twice.

As the heir to the Earl of Everleigh, Lucian, Viscount Adelaide, cannot enlist as a soldier as he'd truly like to do. Instead, he secretly serves as an agent for the Home Office. To hide his true intentions, he must masquerade as a lazy gadabout. Discouraging the debutantes is another side benefit of the lie.

Unfortunately, Amelia's own mistruth jeopardizes Lucian's mission and puts her in grave danger. His friendship with her brother is the only thing that prevents him from throttling her. It's also one of the many reasons he cannot possibly have feelings for her.

Intriguing Lord Adelaide is a clean standalone Regency romance with perfect chemistry, memorable characters, a hint of intrigue, and a satisfying happy ending.

Dedication

In *Intriguing Lord Adelaide* Amelia thinks she can't fit in and is unhappy during her debut. But a change of attitude changes everything. This is so often the case. It might be hard but a new perspective can often turn around an unhappy situation. Here's to you if you're in the muddy middle of just such a situation. I hope enjoying a happy ending helps you get to the sunny side of your situation.

XO, Wendy

Acknowledgements

First and foremost, Mr. Andrews deserves to be recognized for his constant support of my writing life as well as the non-writing life. It feels like he knows the Amelia and Lucian almost as well as I do, as he's lived with these characters along with me. Thanks for helping me work out the bugs in the storyline and for taking me for long walks when I needed to get out from behind the screen.

My parents, always my biggest fans, enjoy following the adventures of my characters and offer me so much love and support throughout it all. Thank you for a lifetime of that. I couldn't be where I am without you.

My beta team, Alfred, Monique, Suzanne, and Christina, are so supportive and helpful in finding any plot holes as well as helping me out all along the way. Thanks so much for your story help as well as your friendship and love!

My gorgeous cover is thanks to the artistry of Envision Literary Photography and Les at GermanCreative. I'm thrilled with the results of this collaboration.

My editing team, Jenny Proctor of Midnight Owl Editing and Julie Sherwood, are experts in their field. I am grateful for their input. The characters' goals and motivations have certainly deepened with their help as well as ironing out the kinks in this story, and putting in all the commas that I always leave lying about. Any remaining mistakes are entirely the fault of the author.

Chapter One

L
ord Lucian Darius Northcott, Viscount Adelaide, was waiting for his father to die. It was the most lowering situation in which to find oneself. He didn't wish his father ill in the least. And yet, the entire purpose of Lucian's life was to replace his father as the Earl of Everleigh one day. In the meantime, he waited.

Of course, the extended purpose of Lucian's life was to produce an heir, who would then wait for *him* to die. It was a rather disheartening thought. And one for which he had very little enthusiasm, despite the fact that he dutifully participated in the Marriage Mart each year. He had important things to accomplish before he set up his nursery. Dangerous things. He couldn't very well do those with a wife in tow.

Despite his feelings, no one could rightly accuse the Viscount of Adelaide of shirking his duties. His utter boredom with said duties, on the other hand, was legendary. Even though he was a popular guest with Society hostesses, Lucian was always very careful not to allow any one young lady in particular to get the idea that he might actually be interested in wedding her. Until he was finally ready to accept his fate and become a married man, he at least had the sense not to allow anyone to entertain hopes that would go unfulfilled.

He knew enough about unfulfilled hopes that he had no desire to be responsible for them in someone else. But he also held out the faintest glimmer of hope that one day, he would meet a lady who would make him change his mind and take a chance on marriage, no matter his involvement with the Crown. That heir to await his death wouldn't produce himself.

While he had never felt love other than the filial variety, he had witnessed the fortunate happenstance of a couple of his friends' marriages that appeared to be truly happy and loving. It wasn't the norm, one might even say it rare, thus he had no idea where his hope sprang from, but he continued to hold out that tiny bit of hope that he might one day attain that blessed state for himself.

But waiting was becoming a dead bore.

With an inward roll of his eyes toward his own foolishness, Lucian pushed himself away from the wall he was leaning against indolently. He supposed he ought to do his duty toward the female guests and dance with some of them. With a quick glance around he ascertained that his earlier impressions were correct as to who was in attendance. He would easily be able to dance with both the Season's most popular debutante as well as one of its most persistent wallflowers. That should keep the tongues from wagging too specifically. And please his hostess.

He was going to ask Lady Charlotte, the Earl of Metcalf's daughter, to stand up with him for the next dance. She was that Season's most successful debutante and not a dreadful companion. Lucian had been surprised the first time he was introduced to her to find that she wasn't the simpering ninny he had expected her to be. But before he got near enough to speak with the girl, he was assaulted by the bundle of annoying energy that was his friend's little sister.

Lady Amelia Courtenay never failed to set his teeth on edge. Because of Lucian's friendship with her brother, Baron Hastings, he didn't feel he could give her a set down, but he was sorely tempted many times.

"Luce, you must save me," she declared with her usual flare for drama.

"Save you from what?" he scoffed. "I haven't noted a single ferocious beast present this evening."

"Well then you clearly haven't had your eyes open," Amelia replied drily. "I wouldn't have involved you, but it was simply unavoidable. Don't be a beast, Lucian. I need your help."

"What you needed was an extra year in the schoolroom. Then you might have learned that you shouldn't be addressing viscounts by their Christian names while you're about in Society."

"My lord, your eminence, please do me the utmost favour and dance the next waltz with me."

Now Lucian stared at her in consternation. While the young woman never failed to irritate him, there was always an unexpected current of *something* he experienced when he was unable to avoid dancing with her. He didn't want to deal with that something tonight. But how could he refuse what should be a simple enough favour?

Before he could come up with a suitable excuse, the orchestra struck up the opening notes of the next waltz. With Amelia looking at him with such a determined, expectant expression plastered on her face, there was nothing for him to do but offer her his elbow and escort her onto the dance floor.

One thing Lucian could say for Lady Amelia was that she was an excellent dancer. And when she kept her mouth closed, she was even a pleasant companion. But she inevitably ruined things by speaking or rolling her expressive eyes over something he said. It never ceased to annoy him. He rather thought the relationship would be similar if he'd had a sister. Though he supposed he'd spent enough time in her home with her older brother as a youth, Lady Amelia was very much like the little sister he never had. He stifled his sigh and started a conversation with her, despite knowing the risks.

"Tell me why dancing the waltz with you was such an urgent matter this evening, Button, and perhaps I'll consider helping you with the matter."

"Don't call me Button," she began, "and you've already helped me by dancing with me, so I don't really have to tell you."

Lucian stared at her with the haughty expression that had never failed him in the past. Or rather, it had never failed him with anyone except the chit in his arms.

"And don't bother trying to whither me with your noble glare, Luce. You know I've been immune to it since I was about twelve."

"Which was what, last year?"

Finally, the girl rolled her eyes even as she relaxed into the steps of the dance. For a moment, Lucian actually relaxed, too. Dancing with this annoying young lady never failed to put him into a sense of home. It was the strangest sensation. But he supposed it was because he had done it so often when she was a child. And her home had always felt more like a real home than his, despite the love he had for the noble old pile that was Everleigh.

Allowing his mind to drift, Lucian wondered why it was that Hanley House, Lord Hanley's comfortable estate, was more home-like to him than his own. He suspected it was because there were no expectations of him at the Courtenay home, other than to be a well-loved guest, which was how Jeffrey's family had always made him feel. On the other hand, at Everleigh, the expectations of him were unending and heavy. Which was why he had spent so many of his school vacations as far away as he could.

His father had never stood comfortably for that, of course, and had insisted that he come home at least some times. So, while Lucian did have particularly complicated feelings toward his birthright, he loved it nonetheless and felt a great deal of respect for the role he would one day take on. In the meantime, though, while it was still in his father's possession, he made sure to spend ample time elsewhere.

"Lady Fanny was making fun of me for being a wallflower."

Lucian was almost startled from his contemplation by his companion's words. She had become so quiet, he had nearly forgotten she was there, which was most unlike her. When the meaning of her words sank in, he had to swallow the profanities that immediately rose to his mind to keep himself from expressing them.

"I beg your pardon," he finally managed to say. Even he could hear the hauteur in his tone but fortunately, the girl realized it wasn't necessarily directed at her and she managed to muster a grin.

"Which part are you questioning, Luce?"

"First of all, Button, you really ought to be calling me lord while we are in company. For another, why would that dragon have the nerve to make fun of you? And why would she be so ridiculous as to call you a wallflower?"

"She might be a dragon, but she isn't wrong." Now Lucian was surprised to note that the girl would no longer meet his gaze.

His eyebrows rose. While he prided himself on his keen skills of observation, he had to admit that he had avoided keeping too close an eye on this particular lady. He had no interest in examining why that might be. But since she had made her debut, he had spent very little time with her. Now that he was finally looking, he noted multiple changes in her, obvious even in just their short time together. Lucian wondered if the girl he knew had matured into a different sort of woman or if there was something else going on.

"What do you mean?" he asked with a frown. "You couldn't possibly be a wallflower."

"Why not, Luce?" she demanded with an answering frown of her own before she corrected herself. "Apologies — my lord," she added at the end with a slight grin.

"I wouldn't think your brother would stand for it, for one thing, nor your sisters. For another, you're quite lovely and surely have a decent dowry. I would have thought you'd be extremely popular."

Lucian watched a variety of emotions that he couldn't quite pinpoint move across her expressive face. She was obviously gratified that he thought her lovely but took exception to the rest of his words.

"What is Jeffrey supposed to do about it?"

"Threaten anyone who makes you feel like a wallflower, for one thing."

He was gratified to see genuine amusement finally trickle into her expression.

"I'm certain that would surely make me very popular," Amelia countered sarcastically while continuing to follow his lead perfectly. Lucian could see that they were drawing the admiring gazes of many of their fellow guests. "While I don't really think threatening anyone would be in keeping with Jeffrey's inclinations, he hasn't come to Town for the Season yet. And for various reasons, mostly involving increasing their own families, my sisters haven't been able to join us, either. They have each repeatedly written flowery messages of best wishes and instructions, but I'm not finding it much help beyond the abstract. I appreciate their thoughtful words, but they haven't actually been of assistance."

She never missed a single step of their dance but looking into her expressive eyes, Lucian realized that her distress was very real, even more so than her light banter was letting on. He tightened his grip on her for a moment, wishing he could offer greater comfort.

"Have I not danced with you enough, Button? It seems to draw attention."

"Don't call me Button, *Luce*," Amelia returned, placing determined emphasis on the name he had admonished her for using. "And no, you haven't danced with me since my come out."

"Really? I thought for certain that I had."

"Well, you haven't," she insisted. "Apparently, I would find it more memorable than you would. Not that it would necessarily make that much difference," she added with a sigh. "The fact is, I just haven't taken."

"Why not?"

Amelia's grin did strange things to his equilibrium, leaving Lucian to wonder if he had drunk too much of the watered-down punch.

"I appreciate the fact that you're probably trying to make me feel better, but retelling the facts isn't going to do that."

"But how can I help if I don't understand?"

"Why would you bother?" Her question wasn't belligerent; she seemed as though she genuinely didn't know.

"You're one of my people." The statement made sense to Lucian but not to his companion, if her furrowed brow indicated anything.

"I'm reasonably certain we aren't related, Lucian, despite the fact that you spent half your childhood at my house."

"I didn't say we're related, my lady, I said you're one of my people. Did Jeffrey never tell you about our people, our kin?"

"He did not."

Lucian sighed. How was he to explain the tight bond he and his friends felt? His brothers were included in that kinship, of course, but sometimes, some of his friends, like her brother, felt more like his brothers than his siblings did. "It started when we were very young, our first year in school together. We banded together and made our own little family to stand up to the older boys. I'll tell you more about it some other time. Right now, you need to tell me how you could possibly be unpopular during the Season. Even if you don't feel like telling me. I promise, it will make you feel better."

"Just because you will it, my lord, doesn't make it so," Amelia countered in a quiet voice, barely discernible over the orchestra and the constant hum of the conversations whirling amongst the assembled guests.

"Just get it over with. I shan't allow you out of my sight until I've had a full explanation."

Amelia gusted another sigh, but this one sounded more resigned than irritated. "I don't think there's enough time left in the waltz to explain it all, Lucian, my lord."

"Then I'll take you driving tomorrow. You can tell me then."

"I don't think you should, my lord. It wouldn't be kind to my mother."

Lucian prided himself on his superior understanding. He had excelled at Oxford, despite his penchant for getting up to all the shenanigans that boys of his background enjoyed at that age. He had managed to find the perfect balance of success and indolence. He could surely understand the words of one young woman who was speaking the same language he had been born to. But he couldn't understand this one.

"Have you run mad, Amelia? Why would your mother mind? Your mother loves me."

"That she does, Viscount Adelaide," Amelia replied pointedly, seeming to imply that he should know exactly what she was on about. When he continued to stare at her as though she had lost her mind, the girl sighed dramatically and explained. "Luce, think about it. We're in London for the Season. In other words, I'm in the Marriage Mart. You are a highly eligible bachelor, whether you're actually interested in matrimony or not. If you were to turn up to take me for a drive, it would put ideas into Mother's head."

"No, it wouldn't," he said with a scoff. "Don't be ridiculous. I've been visiting your family since I was a child. Surely, she would be more bothered if I don't turn up to take you for a drive. In fact, I would argue it's the polite thing to do."

Lucian watched as the girl he had known since she was in pigtails stared at him with the most mature expression he'd ever seen on her face. He felt for a moment as though she were reading his thoughts, and he quailed.

Finally, she nodded. "Perhaps you're right. In any case, even if it gives her ideas, it probably can't be worse than the despair she's suffering over my lack of success."

Before Lucian could demand further explanation, their dance was coming to an end. As she curtsied to him and took her leave, Lucian had to ask himself which dance this qualified as. He had intended to dance with one of each—a Diamond and a Wallflower. He would have classified Amelia as a Diamond, but she assured him she was a wallflower. Could he say he was finished since he had done both at once? The thought was tempting, but it would set tongues to wagging far more than he was willing to endure if he was noted to have only danced with one partner.

With a sigh, he decided the only opinion that mattered was his own, so he would count his friend's sister as the Diamond and seek out a wallflower. But not an awkward one. Not that he would know whether or not she was awkward from appearances. His eyes quickly scanned the assorted guests.

Miss Daisy Alcott would do, he supposed. He had spoken with her at least once or twice and knew she could carry a conversation and didn't giggle excessively. She was another one that seemed not to have taken so well in her debut. And for poor Miss Daisy, it was now her second Season. It was a lucky thing for her that her father's pockets were far from shallow.

Chapter Two

The Season was the most disheartening thing Amelia had ever experienced. It was also the most boring thing she had ever experienced. Which might explain why she was failing at it. It seemed the other young women dancing through the Marriage Mart were enjoying themselves immensely. They seemed to like talking about frocks and seamstresses and who was seen talking with whom and who had danced with which nobleman. She only hoped they were noting her in Lucian's arms, as it was the first time, she was actually enjoying a moment of it. The very worst, though, was when they started talking about the size of potential gentlemen's holdings.

For one thing, Amelia was rather horrified that they were privy to such information. Should that not actually be considered a confidential matter? She shuddered to think that the size of her dowry was being bandied about amongst her so called friends. Not that she really considered many of these people her friends. They all thought she was strange because she didn't really care whether the best colour to match with ochre was puce or whatever the giggling misses were speaking about. On more than one occasion she had walked away from a conversation, leaving stunned silence in her wake.

It was on one such occasion that she had run into Lady Fanny, who had said something about her having no dance partners. Amelia had felt her control snap, and she had claimed that she was promised to Lucian for the next dance. It had been a foolish claim. One that would have made her a complete laughing stock if the viscount had refused her.

But she had always known she could count on Lord Lucian Northcott, Viscount Adelaide. Even his name sounded solid and dependable. Amelia was well aware that Lucian had developed the reputation of being indolent. But seeing as she had known him since she was in short skirts and pigtails, she knew he could work harder than anyone, if he put his mind to it. She had even seen him help with the sheep shearing one time when she was a girl. He just didn't choose to do so for some reason she couldn't quite fathom.

The workings of his mind were none of her concern, Amelia reminded herself once more. He was merely her brother's friend. And really, she shouldn't have forced his hand. But there was no one else she could have asked.

Not that she *had* asked, she thought with a grin, as the viscount expertly guided her around the dance floor, avoiding collisions like the skilled professional he was. She ought not be contemptuous of the gentleman. She had demanded that he dance with her, after all. Part of the reason was his skilled dancing, so it was rather hypocritical of her to judge him for that very skill.

In all actuality, she didn't judge him for being a good dancer. That was just practice and natural talent. But she rather thought at times that Viscount Adelaide was a waste.

His handsome face was a waste on such an indolent fellow. Or perhaps it wasn't. Who would have him if not for his beauty?

But she couldn't respect a man who was so very lazy, Amelia reminded herself. He was just her brother's friend doing her a favour. *But is he truly lazy?* It was often hard to tell. It seemed he presented a different face to Society than she was sure was really him.

As her hand rested on his shoulder, she felt the flex of his muscles even through his coat. She didn't think anyone could come by such obvious strength by being truly lazy. A frown began to furrow her brow as she thought about what a contradiction Lucian was. She fought the desire to study him that mounted in her chest. He wasn't one of her books that she could pore over for hours on end. It would cause a nasty scene if it were noticed that she was staring at the man like he was a specimen of some sort.

Then again, another glance around the room as they circulated amongst the other dancing couples told her that she would be far from the only one staring at him. And the fact that she was his dance partner would probably absolve her of impropriety. But since she was so very awkward herself, she couldn't be sure, so she made an effort to keep her eyes to herself, or rather to allow them to roam around at will, just anywhere but staring at the actual object of her fascination.

Because she truly was fascinated. The Viscount of Adelaide was handsomer than he had a right to be, in Amelia's estimation. Did he really have to be both rich and beautiful? And she couldn't forget how graceful and articulate he was. It was mortifying when she herself was none of those things.

Of course, she had a mirror and knew she wasn't the ugliest woman to ever grace the shores of England, but she was far from a Diamond of the First Waters. And while she had been well trained by dancing instructors and thus was unlikely to trip over her own feet while performing the steps of the dance, she didn't have inherent grace like Lucian did. And articulate?

Forget it. She could make a short story long any day of the week with all her digressions and additions. It was why she tried not to open her mouth in public anymore. Not only were the topics of her best conversations not the most popular, but once she got started, she couldn't seem to stop herself from rambling on.

"Did that harpy really bother you that much?" Lucian so interrupted her thoughts with his question that she was uncertain what he was talking about at first. She stared at him and blinked, which he apparently found amusing. "You haven't changed so much, have you, Button?" His question so enraged her that her confusion turned to fury in the blink of an eye.

"I don't know why I bothered to ask you to dance with me, Luce, as you're the most annoying creature in Creation."

"You didn't ask, Ames, you demanded. And I will tell you, I'm shocked that you allowed such an impolite cretin as Lady Fanny to disturb your equilibrium in such a way."

"I wasn't so disturbed, Luce, I just didn't want to stand for the abuse a moment longer."

"Then why are you being so quiet?" Lucian's frown was ferocious and yet still appealing, making Amelia wonder if she had been struck on the head and not realized it.

"I'm being quiet so I don't bore you to death."

"Methinks your logic is flawed, Button."

Amelia sighed. She so hated the nickname Lucian and her brother had come up with for her as a child. She rather thought it sprung from someone saying she was as cute as a button. That should be considered a compliment, she was sure, but she couldn't find it in her heart to consider it one. She didn't want to be cute. She wanted to be beautiful or stunning or magnificent. Anything other than cute. Cute was for kittens and lambs and perhaps babies, although she was careful to never use the word in such a way. But it set her teeth on edge whenever Lucian used the old expression. She was well aware that her reaction was precisely why he continued to use it so frequently. Another thing she needed to learn to control better. She dragged her attention back to his question, trying to ignore the pesky irritation.

"If my silence bores you, you can fill it with your own thoughts. My words would surely bore you, but there'd be nothing you could do to overcome it if I was filling all the space with my blather."

Now Lucian was truly looking at her as though he thought she were an imbecile.

"I can see we're going to have a lot to discuss during our drive tomorrow," Lucian said as he gazed at her quizzically. "You have now brought up several things for which I will expect a much more thorough explanation."

Amelia tried valiantly to ignore the flutter of excitement that was generated in her midsection by his words. She had an appointment with Lucian Northcott. He was taking her for a drive. Probably at the fashionable hour. She had told him that it would be unkind to her mother, but now she had to have a stern discussion with herself about her growing excitement. Perhaps it was *really* going to be unkind to her own weak heart.

Because Lucian Northcott, Viscount Adelaide, was decidedly not for her.

Handsome, fashionable, powerful, bored. She wasn't sure why the mysterious nobleman was suddenly taking an interest in her affairs, but she was reasonably sure it had something to do with her brother. Lucian probably thought it was his duty as a gentleman to look after his best friend's little sister. Amelia fought the urge to roll her eyes. He clearly didn't think of her as a woman, nor had he considered the consequences of taking her out for all the *ton* to see.

She really ought to refuse the invitation. Not that he had worded it as an invitation, come to think of it. But she had no business getting herself tied up in a knot over the handsome gentleman. She really ought to find some kind gentleman farmer from the wilds of the north and settle down to a boring life herding sheep or some such.

Not that she knew a single iota about sheep or farming or anything like that, but she was confident that a gentleman like that would consider her an asset to his life. Someone like Lucian would only consider her an obligation. She had no interest in being anyone's obligation. And she had less than no interest in putting herself in a position of being ridiculed by her noble peers of the *ton*.

Having said that, she didn't hate the sensations that fluttered through her as the last strains of the waltz rang out in the large, crowded ballroom and Lucian whirled her around the room with a flourish. For a moment, she felt almost beautiful and fashionable. Amelia was down to earth enough to know that it was merely an illusion. But it was an illusion she would enjoy until it was over.

Lucian brought Amelia back to the same spot where he had collected her. They bowed and curtsied to one another, and he took his leave after extracting her promise not to keep him waiting when he came to call on the morrow.

And then he danced with her friend Daisy.

Perhaps he had decided to do the world a service and only dance with wallflowers. Amelia tried hard not to watch them too closely. Daisy Alcott was a lovely girl, and one Amelia would have called a friend up until the moment she was seized with a wave of jealousy when

Lucian left her only to lead out her friend in the next dance.

It was foolishness beyond all bearing. She had always had a tendency to consider Lucian Northcott to be her own personal property; not wanting to share him only further compounded her insanity. She had already explained quite clearly to herself why Lucian wasn't for her. She had done so frequently through the years. It didn't matter in the least that she had given him her little heart when she was still in pigtails.

She pursed her lips and reminded herself one more time. Lucian Northcott was not for her, so it didn't matter who he danced with.

With a firm nod to reinforce the thought, Amelia turned her back on the dance floor and went in search of the refreshment table. Perhaps a drink would restore her equilibrium.

When she was a child, Luce had barely acknowledged her existence. She really ought to have gotten over him by the time she had turned fourteen. But somehow her adoration of him had only grown with each summertime visit. It had been hard when Lucian's father, the earl, began insisting that his heir visit his own home upon occasion. But really, Amelia reasoned, Luce should have wanted to go home anyway. With how close he was with her and her siblings, she was surprised he had been able to tear himself away from his own brothers. Amelia's own brother would never have absented himself for as many holidays as Lucian had seemed to.

Of course, her brother had also visited some of his school friends from time to time. Her sisters, too, had gone for visitations with distant cousins or other acquaintances. Amelia had always hated those times. She was happiest when the entire family was under the same roof. Those times were becoming few and far between these days with all of them getting married off.

It was another unpardonably foolish thing to be wishing that wasn't so. No amount of wishing would be able to stop the march of both time and reality. None of them were children anymore.

And thus, she had been forced to make her debut. If only Amelia had managed to be popular, she thought with despair when she had once again grown bored of her own company. It was the loneliest feeling in her experience to be in such a large crowd of people and still feel all alone. Amelia wished wholeheartedly that the Season business had never been invented.

Chapter Three

Despite the apparent sweetness of Miss Alcott, Lucian could not say that his interest was engaged in the least. It took every ounce of his considerable self-control to pay at least a modicum of attention as the chit babbled on about something. He only hoped he made the appropriate comments whenever she stopped for breath.

It was completely unlike him to be so distracted. But he couldn't get his thoughts back in order after his abbreviated conversation with Amelia. How was it possible that his friend's beautiful little sister was a wallflower? It made no sense to him. Had she been hoping for a compliment? That was the only explanation he could think made even a little bit of sense. But as he took Miss Alcott through the familiar steps of the minuet, he couldn't see Amelia anywhere on the dance floor, despite knowing how much she loved that particular dance. In fact, now that he gave the matter some thought, he hadn't seen her on the dance floor much at all during the weeks they had been in Town.

Lucian made it his business to attend the events of the Season despite how boring he found them. It was at the balls and routs and other nonsensical events that all the best information could be gleaned. Despite his irritation with life in general of late, he took his responsibilities seriously. His duties as Viscount Adelaide, as well as the heir to the Earldom of Everleigh, meant that he needed to know what was taking place politically and socially in the realm. For the politics, he needed to associate with his fellow well-born members of Society. For the social concerns, he had entirely different tactics. He wasn't so foolish as to think the concerns of the wealthy and titled few were anywhere similar to those of the vast majority of the residents of the land.

Despite feeling like a wastrel as he waited to inherit, he had managed to find a way to make himself useful. The Home Office had managed to find something of note for him to do despite his being a viscount. The role made him feel more fulfilled than awaiting his father's death. If only it didn't involve flitting about Society.

It irritated him that he was so well known as a lazy lout. A fashionable and accommodating lazy lout, but lazy was the last descriptor that truly applied to himself, even though he cultivated it studiously. And because he cultivated the reputation, it was ludicrous that it irritated him so. He almost shook his head but stopped himself in time. He needed to keep his wits about him. He always kept his wits about him, even if no one knew he had any wits. It was one of the reasons he was such a successful agent.

He wasn't as powerful as some, nor was he in a position of advising the king, but Lucian knew how to involve himself in what was necessary to get the things done that he considered important. It was for that reason that he was surprised that something so significant as his dearest friend's young sister failing at her debut came as a shock to him. He would get to the bottom of it on the morrow, he assured himself as he bowed over the hand of his dance partner and took his leave of the ball. He couldn't bear to be there any longer.

~~~~

Lucian nodded his approval at the servant who hurried to take the leads of his team as he pulled up in front of the Courtenays' townhouse. It was a mark of their prosperity that they had a servant designated for just such a duty. And it was one more reason why it made little sense that Amelia hadn't taken well for her Season. He shoved the thought aside. He really ought to leave it to her brother and mother to sort out. But loyalty to his friends and a firm belief in his own superior intellect convinced him to take a hand in the matter.

The fact that she was so beautiful should make it easy to assist her. Of course, as his best friend's little sister, he probably shouldn't even notice that she was such a pretty young woman. But it mattered very little what he thought of her appearance. When he went looking for a wife, it surely couldn't be in the family of his own best friend. That would be a little too familiar.

When his breath caught in the back of his throat when she appeared in the doorway of the room he had been shown to, Lucian put it down to the air being dry. It certainly had nothing to do with how fetching the girl looked with her hair all tied up in some curious fashion with her hat perched on top, framing her inquisitive face perfectly. And it certainly didn't mean he thought the light blue of her spencer brought out the grey in her intelligent gaze. Lucian quickly got to his feet and met her in the middle of the room.

"You are remarkably prompt for a woman of Society, Button," he commented, watching in amusement as the fury that filled her face brought a pleasant pink to her cheeks, even as she tried to swallow her reaction.

21

"I knew you wouldn't want to keep your horses waiting," was all she bothered to say in response, as she swept past him toward the front door.

Lucian watched, a little surprised, as she paused to smile at the footman who was holding the door for her. He knew she was always polite, but most of the debutantes he had met seemed to consider the servants to be a part of the landscape, someone to take for granted and utilize but not actually acknowledge. It was refreshing and one more thing to appreciate about his afternoon companion.

As he handed her into his curricle, Lucian was again surprised, this time over her slight stature. He rather thought it was the energy she seemed to exude that made him think she was bigger than she actually was. There was a reason he and her brother had started calling her Button all those years ago, and it had nothing to do with the negative response it never failed to generate in her but everything to do with her diminutive size. He had almost forgotten that as they had all grown.

"Now out with it, my lady. Why were you placing yourself amongst the wallflowers last night?"

The deep sigh of discontent that came from his companion almost made him falter as he guided his matched pair of horses into the stream of traffic. His eyebrows inched toward his hairline, and he turned a questioning expression on her, even as he kept half his attention on the traffic around them.

"Luce, don't make me tell you. I never should have agreed to accompany you."

"Well now you can't weasel out of it for certain, silly chit," Lucian countered with a chuckle. "But perhaps you'd best wait until we get into the Park, and I can give you my undivided attention. I had my suspicions last evening that there was something afoot, but now that I know it's a serious matter, I need to concentrate."

Despite her evident discomfort, Lady Amelia laughed lightly. "I ought to feel flattered that you are giving the matter your time, shouldn't I? And a part of me does, but the rest of me doesn't want to face the humiliation that is sure to arise from telling you of my folly."

"It's a lovely day we're having, though, isn't it?"

Amelia laughed again, and this time it sounded genuine. "Very well, Lucian, we'll chatter about the weather until you feel ready to talk about it. But that really should be my excuse not yours," she concluded with another tinkle of laughter. "I'll give you a hint, though. The fact that I'm not so great at chattering about the weather is part of my problem."

Lucian had no idea what she was talking about but was relieved to hear the lightness in her tone as she continued to comment about the pretty landscape they were approaching as they neared the Park and the mild temperatures they had been enjoying. They finally entered through the Park's wide gates, and she turned to him with a superciliously raised left eyebrow.

"Now can I unburden myself, my lord? It was dreadfully unkind of you to demand an explanation that I don't really want to give you and then tell me I had to wait. Surely you can understand my desire to get the unpleasantness over with quickly."

"My apologies, B—" he started to use the offending moniker and caught himself. "You are quite right. It was poorly done of me. But in my defense, I truly didn't realize it was a matter of actual concern. I honestly thought you were jesting last night. Now, out with it."

With a little more squirming and huffing her obvious displeasure, the girl finally launched into her explanation. Lucian had to consciously loosen his grip on the reins to prevent his reaction from transmitting itself to the horses. It wouldn't do to cause a scandal by creating a carriage accident while the fashionables were taking their promenade. That certainly wouldn't improve the lady's prospects, he thought with a grimace.

"I don't know how to gossip."

She said it in a flat voice, as though she were confessing a heinous crime.

Lucian's frown started to gather, as he tried to understand what the girl was telling him.

"And I hate gossip. Actually, it's probably because I hate gossip that I never bothered to learn how to do it. And talking about nonsense makes me feel as though I'm about to develop hives. Truly, who cares which mantua maker anyone went to? We all pretty much look the same. And we all dance the same. We all paint and play the pianoforte and speak all the appropriate languages. Why can't we discuss something that would stimulate our minds a little more? Like the scientific method. Why doesn't anyone think I could be interested or know anything about that?"

"Have you been reading Immanuel Kant, Button?"

Hot colour splashed across her cheeks, and this time, Lucian didn't think it was anger that caused the blush but embarrassment. But then Amelia lifted her chin in a display of defiance.

"Sapere aude," she said with a flourish, causing a grin to spread across Lucian's face.

"I didn't know you read Latin, my lady," he said with a note of respect creeping into his own tone. "And what exactly are you daring to know?" he asked, translating her phrase.

"Well, Latin for one," she countered with pride.

"And what else?"

He grew uncomfortable under her stare as she contemplated her answer. Finally, she shrugged.

"That's really not the point, Luce. The point is, as a debutante, I'm expected to be satisfied with fashion and watercolours. The other debutantes are beyond boring, except perhaps the other wallflowers, except for the ones who really don't want to be wallflowers in the first place. And I don't want to marry a gentleman who wants a wife who is only interested in fashion and watercolours. What kind of a life would that be?"

Her voice was nearly a wail by the end of her question, but she managed to keep the volume low, so they remained undisturbed by nosy gossips awaiting a juicy tidbit. Lucian was impressed that she even managed to keep most of her emotions from displaying themselves across her normally very expressive face.

"Surely it's not as bad as all that," Lucian finally said.

She lifted her eyebrow once more and stared at him in disbelief. "Really, Lucian? Tell me honestly, how did you feel when you realized I know Latin? Would you want a wife who possessed intelligence and actually wanted to use it?"

Lucian shifted in his seat, uncomfortable with her question, as it made him think about things he wanted to leave in the abstract.

"We aren't talking about me, Amelia."

"No, but you are representative of your species, are you not? A wellborn nobleman of an age to marry. According to my family, one of your peers or contemporaries is exactly who I ought to be aligning myself with. How *you* feel could be considered representative of how your peers will feel."

"The scientific method, Amelia? You want to bring science into finding your husband?"

"Why not? We're really just a higher animal, aren't we?"

"Not according to Scripture," he countered, watching her eyes as they changed from grey to blue and back again, as she entered into the spirit of her argument.

"Well, yes, of course, but humans are humans. And gentlemen of the *ton* really seem to be all alike, and not really displaying the sort of qualities Scripture says they ought to."

Lucian laughed. "I can't really argue with you on that point. But in defence of my fellow noblemen, I would argue that most of them want someone with the appropriate social graces to be able to host their entertainments."

She again tried to whither him with her disgusted glare. "Entertainments are occasional, but a wife is forever. Doesn't she need to be of more use than as a hostess?"

Heat filled Lucian at her question, but he ignored it, knowing full well Amelia didn't know what she was implying. "Would you say your mother is more than a hostess?"

"Yes, of course."

"And what about other older women you know, like your aunts or grandmothers?"

"Well, none of them want to discuss science or philosophy with me, but yes, they seem fully cognizant. Far more so than the other debutantes, in my opinion. Perhaps the ability to reason ended with the previous generation."

Lucian laughed at her dry comment but didn't allow himself to be distracted. "Well, then, using your powers of reason, doesn't it seem likely that the conversations the other young ladies have been having are just because they're excited to be in London? And they're young? That doesn't mean that you will be condemned to a life of shopping for the rest of your days."

She stared at him for a full minute before finally answering him. "I can see your point, but that doesn't change the fact that I don't know how to have these conversations. And if the gentlemen are, as you said, looking for an appropriate young woman who can hostess their entertainments, then that would explain why I am failing so miserably on the Marriage Mart."

"Perhaps," Lucian agreed with her in a cheerful tone. "But let me ask you this: is it that you cannot, as in, you are incapable of having a reasonable conversation about fashion, or is it that you simply don't want to? I would think someone who prided herself on her intelligence should be able to carry on a conversation on any topic, wouldn't you?"

Lucian watched as the girl tried to absorb his words even as she objected to them. Finally, he saw her accept them with a nod, though discomfort filled her features.

"I suppose you aren't wrong, my lord. But it seems such a silly, frivolous thing to talk about fashions and gossip."

"So then your pride is the issue, isn't it?"

Now anger chased the embarrassment from her expressive face.

"Are you the pot or the kettle, my lord, to be calling me out on such a topic?"

"I am not the subject of our conversation, my dear, nor am I the one claiming the inability to talk about frocks. I am knowledgeable enough that I could probably tell you who your dressmaker is just from examining your gown, so I could certainly discuss the matter with you, if you'd like. I'm also not saying there is anything wrong with pride. In fact, I am glad to note that you have some. But you shouldn't be allowing it to interfere with succeeding at something you claim to want to accomplish."

Chapter Four

Amelia fought the urge to squirm in her seat as she sat next to the powerful and fashionable Viscount Adelaide. She had been half in love with him since she was a child, even though she knew it was beyond foolishness. He was practically a member of her family, for one thing. For another, she hadn't been fishing for compliments when she told him she was a wallflower. It was an unfortunate truth that didn't only stem from her lack of socially acceptable conversation.

Lucian Northcott was destined to wed a beautiful Diamond of Society. And that was perfectly fine and appropriate, Amelia insisted to herself. She didn't want to fill the role of viscountess, let alone be the eventual Countess of Everleigh. How could she possibly raise a future viscount and earl with her lack of social graces? No, despite the thrill that never ceased to shiver up her spine whenever she laid her eyes upon Lucian, he was not for her. Far better would it be to find herself the gentleman farmer she had been imagining of late.

Amelia allowed her gaze to wander around for a distracted moment to survey the other carriages driving along the same route, as well as the many fashionable members of Society vying for each other's attention. She was surprised to see a strange, slightly unkempt man walking along at the side of the fashionable route. There was something about the way he watched everyone that caught her attention. She wondered if he were thinking to rob someone. She was torn about whether or not she ought to point him out to Lord Adelaide but then dragged her attention back to their conversation.

Perhaps Luce could be put to better use than pointing out uncomfortable truths.

"Do you know any gentleman farmers?" she demanded in an inelegant change of subject, putting the strange man out of her thoughts.

"I beg your pardon. What does that even mean?"

Amelia had to laugh at the supercilious tone Lucian used, as though the very concept were below his elevated notice.

"You know what I mean, Luce, you're just being difficult. I mean a gentleman of good birth who isn't in line to inherit some great title but has land and is perfectly comfortable and happy raising sheep or some such."

Amelia was proud of the fact that she was able to gaze out at the other members of the *ton* who were milling about, seemingly ignoring the haughty stare of the handsome man beside her, never revealing the tiny deaths she was subjecting herself to in an effort to hide her reaction.

"You don't even like sheep, Button," Lucian finally replied, his haughtiness hidden by his confusion. Amelia was gratified by his obvious effort to understand.

"What would make you say that? How could anyone not like sheep?"

He just looked at her with his left eyebrow elevated as though questioning her sanity. Amelia tried to stare him down or at least not cave in too quickly. Finally, she let a light laugh escape.

"Very well, my lord, you might not wish for a quiet life in the country, but surely you can accept that there are many people who do."

"No, I can accept that there are many people who *lead* a quiet life in the country, but I cannot accept that is what they all wish for. In fact, I would surmise that most of them would wish for a little more excitement than they have."

"Based upon what do you make such an assumption?" Amelia demanded. "Because I can tell you that I, for one, very much wish for the quiet life of country gentry. That life, I know how to do. I know how to make friends in the country. I know how to visit the tenants and visit the vicar's wife and dance at the assemblies. I miss those people."

Again, she suffered through Lucian's haughty stare, the one she was certain he must have perfected in the mirror when he was fifteen, as he had always been able to whither her with it. But not this time. She knew what she was talking about, and she wasn't about to cave in.

"My dear girl, you only think you wish it because you have never really lived it."

"Surely my childhood was idyllic."

"Lady Amelia," Lucian began, emphasizing the lady of her address. "The very fact that you aren't a miss tells me that you haven't the first idea what it is like to not be noble."

Amelia sighed. "What of it, Luce? I know for certain this isn't what I want. Why must you be beastly about it? Could you not just offer some help?"

His expression softened. "Of course, I could, but surely you realize I truly must torment you a little first."

When she laughed in response, the viscount finally seemed to relax beside her.

"I must ask, though, why have you not had this conversation with Jeffrey or your mother and father?"

"I've tried, but they didn't believe me either," Amelia answered with another soft sigh. "Jeffrey's not in Town yet, despite Mother's decree that he accompany us, so I haven't really been able to discuss it with him. I even wrote to both of my sisters, but you know how they can be. They weren't of much help either."

Silence descended between them for a moment, but it was the companionable sort that one might experience with a good friend. Amelia savoured it, as it was so rare, and almost hoped that it would remain uninterrupted. But Lucian was always the sort to power through and since she had asked him a question, he was sure to have an answer for her soon.

"One of my brothers might be what you're looking for," he answered almost hesitantly. "Not that any of them are acceptable for you, and none of them are really properly set up yet. But they are untitled gentlemen of noble birth." Lucian paused for a moment, likely thinking about his four brothers. "Apparently, I've taken to thinking aloud. You have twisted my intellect, Button," he complained with a smile. "But someone along those lines. Ash and Rod are way too young for you, and I don't think Gilbert or Foster could be considered worthy of you, but that's what you mean, right? A younger brother of someone?"

Amelia nodded hesitantly. She supposed it was what she was thinking. "Or perhaps a country squire. He might be more in a position to have lands. None of your brothers have property, do they?"

She couldn't interpret the expression that very briefly displayed itself on his usually impassive face, as it was there for such a short period of time. But she rather thought he was displeased with her words, even though they were in harmony with what he himself had just said.

"It matters little whether they have lands or not; they wouldn't be right for you, Button. I cannot fathom what made me even suggest them except that a part of their circumstances align with what you claim to want for your future." He paused for breath and perhaps for thought, and Amelia found herself awaiting his next words with bated breath. "I think perhaps you ought to rethink your position on the Season and what you are searching for in a mate. I cannot imagine you tucking yourself away in the wilds of Cornwall, content to be a shepherdess for the rest of your days."

Amelia shrugged but avoided meeting his gaze. "Perhaps you don't know me as well as you think, my lord."

"I've known you well enough since you were a child. I know you as well or better than Jeffrey does. So, I know you like a brother knows a sister. Which means I know everything there is to know."

Amelia looked him full in the face and laughed. There was no way that was the least bit true. But somehow, it warmed her heart to think he thought so.

"Very well, Luce. I'm not prepared to set aside my intentions just yet, but I am prepared to listen to your arguments to the contrary. Tell me what sort of husband you think I ought to be looking for. Or do you think I ought to go against every convention and set up my own household?" She paused as he stared at her in disbelief. "Don't look so shocked, Lucian. I am intelligent enough to be a scientist or a philosopher or some such. Just because I wasn't allowed to go to school to learn more about those things doesn't mean I couldn't read everything. I read every single one of the books Jeffrey brought home from school, I'll have you know."

"And did you understand it all?" he demanded; his tone incredulous.

"Not everything, but you boys had the advantage of having a teacher explaining it. Whenever I asked

Jeffrey, he would say it was too much for my feeble mind."

Lucian laughed at her aggrieved tone. "What he really meant was that it was too much for HIS feeble mind, especially if it was mathematics or chemistry. Those were not his strongest subjects."

"You probably did well in them. Could you explain Pythagoras' Theorem to me?"

The viscount laughed again, careful to keep it low enough to not draw any more attention to them than was necessary.

"I certainly could, but that is a conversation for another day, my dear. The purpose of this drive is to determine why you are not enjoying your debut. And you still didn't tell me why it would pain your mother for me to take you driving."

"For all you think you're so wise, you should be able to figure that one out on your own, Lucian Northcott," Amelia exclaimed with chagrin, as she didn't really want to explain herself to the handsome man. But never one to back down from a challenge, she answered him promptly. "And I actually did explain it to you, almost immediately after I said it. If you weren't paying attention, that's your fault," she declared with alacrity. "You know you're the most eligible bachelor in the kingdom. It would set any fond mama's heart to palpitating if you were to come calling."

Lucian grinned at her words but only shook his head. "Your mother has known me since I was barely out of the nursery."

"So, you'd think she'd be sensible enough not to want to tie her daughter to you for life? Is that what you're saying, Luce?"

After casting her a darkling glance, Lucian steered his team toward a hitching post. "Shall we stroll for a bit? I feel a trifle confined in the carriage."

"Really, my lord? I thought you were born to drive," Amelia teased, enjoying herself despite the topic they'd been discussing.

"Not when I'm trying to speak with a demented girl child," he countered.

Amelia, far from offended, just laughed and allowed him to hand her down from the high carriage he had driven that day, trying to ignore the shivery sensation that ran from where his hands rested on her waist to her extremities, hoping that it didn't shut down her brain on the way. She had hoped these sorts of reactions were a thing of her youth, but it would seem her one-sided fascination with Viscount Adelaide was still alive and well. As usual, she chose to ignore it. He was her friend, and she wanted to keep him as such. If he ever had an inkling that she had developed any sort of warmer feelings for him, she was certain he would run far away from her, at least figuratively if not literally. But she wouldn't put it past the viscount to suddenly decide it necessary to check on his father's holdings in the Scottish Highlands or some such in a legitimate effort to distance himself from an uncomfortable situation. So, Amelia ignored the shivers, however pleasant and intriguing she might find them, and dragged her thoughts back to the topic at hand.

"Why demented, my lord?"

"You would rather be a spinster than a lady of the manor?" He countered her question with one of his own and then glowered at her when she merely shrugged.

"Why not? It is likely to be far more pleasant."

"You think being a spinster would be pleasant," he repeated with a frown. "I thought you said you considered yourself to be intelligent. Have you never met a spinster?"

"I've surely met plenty."

"And you learned from those introductions that those ladies or women were delighted with their lot in life?"

"Yes," Amelia said as decisively as she could, despite the fact that his incredulity was making her question her conviction. "Don't you think it is better for a woman to remain in possession of her own self rather than become the property of a nobleman?"

"Only if the nobleman is a dastard. In all other cases, it would be far better and safer for a young woman to align herself with a gentleman of means. Do you not consider your parents' marriage to be a partnership? Your mother helps your father run his estate and plan for the future of his line. She has always seemed quite content with the arrangement to me. I don't understand why you are so opposed to it when it has been working quite comfortably for generations of your family."

"But those generations just did what the ones before them did. Without thought, it seems to me. I am convinced that some thought ought to be put into the matter."

"The scientific method, as you said," Lucian added without rancor. "But that should still lead you to the conclusion that it works well."

"If that's what you think, then why aren't you setting up your nursery as we speak instead of flitting about Town as England's most eligible bachelor and wasting all the brains you've been blessed with?"

Lucian appeared much struck by her words, to Amelia's surprise. Finally, he sighed. "We have much to discuss, little one. I don't see how we're going to get it all sorted in one afternoon."

Chapter Five

L ucian took some satisfaction in watching Amelia's chin drop down in shock.

"You agree with me?"

"I'm not saying that. I'm saying we will examine the matter using your favourite method and come to our conclusions. I agree with you that it would be foolish to do something just because our parents and grandparents did it. But I don't think dismissing it out of hand is any less foolish. So, we will examine the matter. And you haven't distracted me away from the other matter of your disdain for gossip and fashion. Will you be in a great deal of trouble if we are late returning from our drive?"

"I shan't be in any trouble, but my mother might be preparing to have the banns read," Amelia replied with a giggle.

Lucian thought she was being ridiculous, even though he enjoyed hearing her laughter. There was no way her mother would want her to wed him; he was sure of it. Amelia was certainly exaggerating when she claimed he was the most eligible bachelor of the *ton*. While he was sufficiently arrogant to know he was a welcome guest to most hostesses and many matchmaking mamas coveted his deep pockets and future title for their daughters, Lucian was sufficiently confident in Lady Hanley's knowledge of him to not have any desire to align her much loved youngest child with him.

With a shrug, Lucian dismissed her words and returned to their matter of discussion. "Which do you want to sort out first? Whether or not you ought to marry a nobleman? Or how to deal with Society conversations?"

For a moment, he fought the urge to shuffle his feet and forced himself to glance around casually at the gentry passing by while his companion stared at him as though wishing him to perdition.

Finally, she sighed melodramatically even as she rolled her eyes.

"I am being quite ridiculous, am I not? I ought to be thanking you for your assistance rather than glaring at you for making me choose between two uncomfortable topics." She sighed again, but gently this time, as though fortifying herself for an ordeal to come. "Very well, let us be logical on the subject. In a certain way, this really isn't two separate topics. Especially if you were to manage to convince me that I ought to truly consider marriage with an active member of Society. If I were to do that, I would absolutely have to deal with Society, wouldn't I? So, let us start there. Tell me, my lord, why should I consider marriage to a nobleman?"

Lucian smiled at the small woman strolling at his side. It was hard for him to reconcile the child he had known with the woman she had become. When he had first met her, she had been such a little thing, with great big, attentive eyes, watching everything he and her brother got up to and desperately wishing to be included. She was still small but not at all childlike anymore, despite the big attentive gaze she still possessed. He wasn't certain if she still wished to be included. In fact, he rather thought that was exactly her problem. She didn't wish to be involved in Society activities. Or rather, as he had pointed out to her, her pride had been pricked when she wasn't included, and so now she wished to reject the very society that she feared had rejected her.

"For one thing, my dear girl, you have the experience of an entire lifetime of association with noblemen that should make the experience seamlessly easy."

"That argument won't wash, my lord. That reasoning would mean I ought to be enjoying my Season, and as I already explained to you, I am not doing so in the least."

Lucian laughed. "Very well, Button, I'll grant you that point, but with your father being an earl and your brother a baron, you've grown up in the circles of the *ton*. You know exactly how to go on."

When she made to protest, he held up his hand to stem the tide of her words. "I know you claim to dislike it, but you cannot truly expect me to believe you don't know how, Amelia. I've seen you. You know exactly what is acceptable or appropriate on any given occasion."

She didn't bother to reply verbally, merely offering him half a shrug and a lopsided smile that he found excessively endearing.

Now it was Lucian's turn to sigh. "Very well, Button. I think you were right. We need to discuss your issues with not enjoying yourself in company. If you truly detest it, whether or not you are born to the role is a moot point. I think you would make a marvelous countess or marchioness or even a duchess. But if you would hate every moment of it, that hardly seems like a satisfactory life. So, tell me what you think would be so enjoyable about marriage with your country gentleman."

She tapped her chin in thought, just as he had seen her do countless times before. He had never found it so appealing. Lucian began to wonder if he had been exposed too long to the sun. A quick glance, though, assured him it was overcast. He dismissed the thoughts and tried to remain focused on the conversation at hand while putting far from his mind the sudden desire he felt to pull Lady Amelia into his arms. He had never wanted to do such a thing with a Society woman.

Lucian reminded himself that it mattered very little how Lady Amelia might appeal to him. She was his friend's little sister. Somehow, it felt as though he would be betraying his friend if he were to have warm feelings for the young woman. He also reminded himself that he was not yet ready to be setting up his house. He loved his father but was very resistant to the thought of pleasing him so completely. The old earl had been pressing him to produce grandchildren for a couple of years already. Lucian had a history of resisting his father's dictates. While he had every intention of giving in to this one eventually, now was certainly not the time. He was only six and twenty, after all.

Besides all these concerns chasing themselves around his head, there was also the matter of service he needed to attend to. No one knew about his association with the Home Office. That was as it should be. It helped that most weren't even aware of what the Home Office was or what its role was in the security and economic prosperity of the nation. Amelia wasn't wrong when she claimed that most people weren't overly interested in anything beyond their own affairs. That served his purposes quite well most of the time. But now he had to convince his young friend that she could trust that people would think more deeply than the latest item of gossip.

Amelia interrupted his thoughts. "It would be just like life at home rather than life in Town. I'm quite good at visiting the tenants and directing the staff and planning the menus. You are right; I know next to nothing about sheep or wool or whatnot, but I'm far from daft. I could surely learn. But a gentleman who must take his seat is an entirely different matter altogether. Surely you must see that, Luce."

"I do see that it's a different matter, but what makes you think you wouldn't excel at that, too?"

The way she elevated her eyebrows at him as though to indicate she thought he were a simpleton made Lucian want to laugh out loud, but he again regained his composure quickly. The chit was far too lively for his peace of mind.

"Have you not been paying attention, my lord? I have already mentioned multiple times that I'm not doing so well in that arena." She rolled her eyes at him. "This is the most circular conversation we have ever had."

Lucian grinned but managed to politely answer her. "My apologies, my lady. I should have been more clear. What makes you think you could not learn to excel at *tonnish* ways?"

She again sank into silent contemplation, but Lucian was relieved that this time it was short lived.

"I suppose it's because I do not wish to," she finally admitted. "It's deadly dull to my estimation."

"Have you not given thought to what takes place in the House of Lords, my dear? How important those activities are? And the fact that it is actually around those activities that the Season revolves? Or are you like every other debutante who thinks the Season is revolving around her and her quest for an advantageous husband?"

Lucian was being harsh with the girl, but he was curious to see how she would react to it. Understandably, her first reaction was anger, and it brought roses blooming in her cheeks, but she managed to hold onto her tongue and think through his words before she reacted verbally.

Finally, with a sheepish wince and an adorably wrinkled nose, she admitted, "I suppose I'm like all the other debutantes, Lucian. I haven't really thought about what takes place in the House. But you're quite right. The Season does revolve around the sitting of the House, at least in its timing. If Parliament closes abruptly or resumes unexpectedly, the social whirl is impacted in one way or another."

"So, isn't it possible that important things are taking place in the House? Things that a gentleman might be in need of a good wife in order to accomplish?"

Again, she wrinkled her nose at him. "It's possible, Luce. Are you trying to tell me that it is fact? Or merely suggesting that it's a possibility I never took the time to give thought to?"

Lucian laughed. "You are far from daft; you just didn't think about it. And yes, it's a fact. The Lords sitting in the House is far from a social occasion. Most of the social events peripheral to the sitting are where many of the important matters are discussed and decided. But it's deadly serious business."

He watched in some amusement as Lady Amelia's eyes widened as she contemplated his words. Her expression again turned sheepish.

"I'm embarrassed that you have had to point this out to me, Lucian. How could I have been saying goodbye to my father every autumn and not given thought to why he was going?"

Lucian shrugged. "We do have a tendency to take our families for granted."

"But I'm the one who would like to think that she's more intelligent than the next girl." Amelia's dry tone made Lucian smile. "So, tell me, what do they do in the House, if it's not all cheroots and port all the time?"

Lucian chuckled at her words. "I can assure you, it is never cheroots and port. The Grand Chamberlain would have apoplexy were you to even suggest such a thing."

Amelia frowned at him. "Is it really so serious?"

"It actually is. I don't take it as seriously as I probably ought to, but I do take my seat from time to time. I have a steward attend in my place when I cannot be there in person."

Her frown was now one of concentration, as though she were trying to take all the new information in. "And your father and my father and all the lords are there?"

"Not all lords have a seat but yes, your father and my father are certainly there. Or rather, they are always represented. Your father seems to take it much more seriously than mine. He is almost never missing. It's extremely rare that he sends a representative. Even when your family was in mourning. Since, as I said, it is not a social event, he wasn't necessarily breaking protocol by being present. Most considered it noble of him to be so dutiful."

Amelia sniffed a little. "My mother didn't see it that way. She thought he was disrespecting her mother by leaving us alone to mourn."

"Do you think your attitude toward nobles might stem from that event?"

Amelia shrugged slightly. "It's possible." Her tone was one of reluctance. "That wasn't the only time something like that happened. "As you said, my father is very faithful to his seat. There have been times when Mama didn't appreciate that faithfulness. She felt his allegiance should be wholly with our family. And since I was certain he was having a fine time with his cronies, it is possible the two circumstances have coloured my perceptions."

Lucian laughed at her delicate phrasing. "I would certainly say your perceptions were coloured," he agreed with a low chuckle. "But the fact that the matters debated in the House of Lords are serious doesn't negate the fact that your father clearly enjoys his time there. While it isn't rightly termed a social event, some of the gentlemen thrive in the environment. Perhaps that is why he is so very determined to be regular in his attendance, regardless of his family's circumstances."

He watched as Amelia stared off into the distance, mulling over his words, even as she kept a steady pace beside him as they strolled in the waning afternoon sun.

"Thank you for explaining this to me, my lord. I think it will take some more thought to decide how I feel on the matter. And I would like to know more about what really happens there before I make my final decision."

"You could always attend a session or two."

"Truly? I thought it was an environment exclusive to gentlemen."

Lucian chuckled again. "Is that what your father said?" he asked even while nodding. "He wasn't wrong. Only gentlemen take their seat, of course, but there is a visitor's gallery where journalists and politically minded women and ladies can listen in to the debates."

Now her eyes were widened with excitement.

"When can I visit?" Her voice was almost breathless with her newfound excitement, making Lucian's lips twist with amusement.

"The leopard has suddenly changed her spots." Lucian teased her even though he found her enthusiasm charming and actually looked forward to seeing her reaction to visiting the House. "I will find out which topics are to be debated when, and you can choose what might be of most interest."

She was still wide-eyed as she contemplated his words but nodded her agreement.

"So, what you're saying, then, my lord, is that I might be able to assist my future husband with the running of the country? That sounds far more exciting than sheep," she concluded with a small laugh.

"I would have to agree with you. Although, in the middle of a damp, midland winter, I do appreciate the wool, so someone has to raise the sheep, but I don't think that is the life for you, little one."

She was too caught up in her own thoughts to take exception to his use of the diminutive, and they strolled along in silence for a time.

Chapter Six

Amelia was enraptured with what Lucian had just told her. Rather, he hadn't really told her much at all when one reviewed the matter. But the thought of having something important to contribute to the future was thrilling beyond all bounds. It was why she had thought to retire to the country, really. Surely raising animals was more important than going to balls. But if there could be something purposeful involved in the social whirl, she just might consider trying to improve at it. That thought had her turning back toward Lucian, eager to discuss the matter.

He was staring quite fiercely off to the side, and Amelia found herself straining to see around his shoulder in a quest to know what he was looking at so intensely. She didn't see much. A few fashionable people she knew slightly milling about and that same scruffy individual, who appeared to be watching everyone in a strange way.

"What has caught your eye, my lord?" she asked with laughter evident in her voice. "Is it Lady Francis's overlarge bonnet? Even I, who knows so little about the fashion dictates, know that isn't the best choice for someone of her stature."

"I beg your pardon, Button, I wasn't attending."

Amelia frowned, but it wasn't in response to his use of the pet name. It was most unlike Lucian to be distracted. And it was very unlikely that it was something so trivial as an ugly bonnet that would do it.

"What were you looking at, Luce?" she asked him in a low voice, instinctively knowing it was somehow an important matter.

"Nothing," he quickly responded. So quickly that it reinforced to Amelia that there was something somewhat suspicious involved. But then he added, "Were you asking about fashion, Button? I'm impressed." Perhaps she had been mistaken and he really was looking at Lady Francis. Amelia allowed the conversation to turn, at least for a time.

"I don't care how much you might admire that bonnet, it is not for you," Lucian persisted in a droll tone, leading to a peel of laughter erupting from Amelia's throat. She quickly clamped a hand over her mouth to stifle the abrupt noise. She didn't want to put herself beyond the pale now that she had finally found something about the Season to interest her.

"No, you looby, I did not admire that bonnet. But now that you bring up the topic, you did promise to help me find a way to be more successful at my debut. Before you start that, though, could I ask you another adjacent favour?" At his frowning nod, she continued. "Could you point out to me who you would consider to have good politics? If I'm going to wed someone in an effort to help them run the country, I want to be sure that I'm backing the right side of matters."

"And you'd trust me to know which is the right side?"

"Of course," Amelia responded immediately. "Who could I possibly trust more?"

She was surprised when pink briefly touched Lucian's cheekbones, as though he were touched or embarrassed by her words. She hoped it wasn't embarrassment. That would be beyond awkward. He cleared his throat, and his expression returned to its normal impassivity.

"I will have to think about it, little one. It's an important side of a very serious matter. I never thought to advise you on such a thing. I wouldn't want to point you in a misleading direction. But yes, I promise to think of a few potential options for you to consider."

"Thank you, Luce," she replied with a smile as she tucked her hand more tightly into his elbow and they continued their stroll. "Now tell me how to gossip and not sound like a fool."

Lucian's grin made a flock of butterflies take up a fluttering residence in her belly, which Amelia promptly dismissed as being nonsensical. Even if she were going to try to learn how to coexist with the jabbering debutantes of her Season, she had no intention of actually turning into one of them.

"Do you suppose it's because I am older than the other young ladies making their debut this Season, Luce?" She blurted out the question even though he hadn't yet answered her first dictate.

Lucian frowned. "You really must learn to not be so free with my name, Button."

"Really, Luce? And yet you never cease in calling me by a childhood pet name. How is that any better? Besides, I would never do so in company, and well you know it. Now quit being evasive. I've now asked you two different things, and you've yet to answer either of them."

"Well, one of them was hardly a question, more like a demand." He chuckled when she rolled her eyes at him. "Very well, my very dear Lady Amelia. No, I do not think you are different from the other ladies just because you are a little older. For one, you are barely older than any of them. You've only delayed your debut by two years, so you've barely reached your twentieth summer. That's hardly a great, old age. And I think whether you were sixteen or twenty-five, you would still be your very own, unique person. And I also think you quite like being unique. I think, even if you adored talking about fashion, you would find something else to interest you just so you could be interesting and different."

Amelia's frown furrowed her forehead fiercely, making Lucian laugh. "Be careful that your face doesn't stick that way."

That made her relax somewhat, but she still wrinkled her nose over his words. "Do you really feel that I'm such a contrarian, my lord?"

"Do you disagree?"

Amelia puffed out a laugh. "Now you're answering questions with questions. You truly can be beastly, Lucian Northcott. But no, I don't think I'm a contrarian. Not like that. I don't pride myself on being difficult or different."

"Don't you, though? Don't you think you're better than the other young ladies because you know more about science and such?"

"Well, yes," she stammered. "Not better, just more intelligent. I'm sure the other young ladies have fine, redeeming qualities."

"If you thought that, wouldn't you have spent a little more time looking for those qualities?"

Heat and confusion suffused Amelia as she contemplated his words. Was it possible that he was right? She would hate to think so.

"Do you think I'm beastly, Lucian?"

"Not in the least, my dear. I think you are a darling. But I think you forgot to use that wise brain of yours when you took one look at the other debutantes and decided they were beneath you. And therein lies your solution. By realizing that they are not necessarily the

48

absolute dullards you decided them, you will find something to interest you in conversing with them. You can recognize that they might be an expert in something you haven't taken the time to excel at – fashion and gossip. Now you needn't necessarily learn to do it yourself, you just need to express an interest in what interests the other ladies, and you will have a foundation for becoming friends with them and not hating every moment of the interaction."

Amelia stared at her brother's friend with something akin to awe. "I thought I was intelligent, but your wisdom makes me feel like a babe in arms."

Lucian patted her hand where it lay in his crooked elbow. He even bowed slightly to her. "I am thrilled that I could be of service."

When Amelia lapsed into silence beside him, though, Lucian prodded her into speech a few minutes later.

"Have I offended you completely, my dear?"

"Not at all, my lord. You have just given me a great deal to think about. I wish I had spoken with you before I had even come up to Town."

"That might have been awkward," he replied in a dry tone. "And you wouldn't have known how you felt anyway." He paused, and his tone shifted to one of a much more bracing nature. "Don't let it trouble you, my dear. You haven't put yourself beyond the pale in any instance. And from what I can tell, you haven't permanently ruined any potential relationships. Now that you have a different perspective, you can begin anew."

"Ought I to apologize?"

"To whom? Every young woman you've met? Emphatically no," he replied before continuing in a gentler tone. "That would be the kiss of death for your social life, for certain. Admit nothing," he concluded with a light laugh.

She joined his laughter. "Very well, my lord, I will make my best attempt." She paused for a moment, casting her gaze around, and was almost distracted from what she meant to say next when she noticed the same man she'd seen before watching them very intently. It wasn't so uncommon for her or Lucian to draw the attention of their noble counterparts, but the average citizen rarely took notice of them unless they were hoping to benefit in some way. So, it was decidedly strange that the scruffy man would be staring at them so intently. But Amelia dismissed the thought and turned her attention back to the viscount. It was likely the unkempt man was hoping to beg from Lucian, or perhaps pick his pocket, but she was confident the groom accompanying them would be able to dispose of the problem, so she needn't say anything. She remembered what she was going to ask before she was nearly distracted. "Could we meet again in a few days to review how I'm going on? And then you can tell me which sessions of the House I ought to attend."

"That sounds like an excellent idea. How many days do you want to experiment before we review? Three? Five? An entire se'en-night?"

Amelia wrinkled her nose in thought. "Let us say five. I cannot think at the moment which events are on my calendar, and we aren't home again until the fourth day, so I will have more to discuss if we wait five days. I don't want to put it off for an entire week in case you have some adjustments to suggest."

Lucian laughed again as he patted her hand. In a rather avuncular way, Amelia thought, surprised by how disappointed she felt in the pit of her stomach. She shook her head slightly to dispel the distaste. This was Lucian, her friend, nothing more. Her disappointment turned to a thrill of attraction as his hands engulfed her waist when he handed her up into the carriage. It seemed to her that he had lifted her much slower than necessary. It had almost felt as though he were going to embrace her. The thrill of that sensation was a little harder to ignore, but she firmly dismissed the unwelcome thoughts.

Chapter Seven

L ucian could have hissed his displeasure, but he couldn't allow Amelia to be disturbed by his problems. And he most definitely had problems. For a moment there, he had thought the beautiful young woman on his arm had noticed they were being observed, but aside from when she asked him what he was looking at, she hadn't remarked further. He only hoped he had managed to fob her off. With her quick mind, it was entirely possible she had seen something and would think about it later. He would never forgive himself if she were to be pulled into the quagmire of his work for the Home Office.

Because it surely was a quagmire. It stank like the foul matter that it was. And there could be no association of it with someone as pure as his best friend's little sister.

Reminding himself of her role in his life was one way to keep his feelings for her in their proper place. And yet another reason why he could not allow himself to be drawn into a personal relationship with a gently bred female had just made itself known. The villains of this piece would not hesitate to involve her if they thought it could be to their benefit.

Even though he had promised to meet with her again in five days, he wasn't sure if it would be wise for him to keep that appointment. Or perhaps he now had a deadline for ensuring this matter for the Home Office was closed by then. Either way, he could not allow it to touch Amelia. Of that he was more than determined.

He was grateful for her ability to carry an intelligent conversation without a great deal of input from her companion as he was having a hard time concentrating on the traffic, his concerns about the ruffian who had been following them, and her, so he wasn't the best conversationalist as they drove back to her home.

When he realized she was waiting expectantly for a reply from him, he had to review in his mind what she had been talking about.

"Yes, my dear, I promise, I will remember to explain the mathematics we discussed next time we meet. I will just need to brush up my own recollections before we do so," he concluded with a grin.

"Are you trying to tell me you don't remember?"

He appreciated her incredulous tone, as it implied she expected him to be as intelligent as she considered herself to be. He probably was. But he hadn't been using mathematics much since he'd left school.

"Don't worry, Button, I'll make sure you understand it fully by the time we're through."

She stared at him a moment longer, and the back of his neck grew warm from her scrutiny, but he was reasonably sure he managed to maintain an inscrutable façade.

"You seem distracted, Luce," she suddenly commented quietly, as though not wanting anyone on the sidewalk they were passing to overhear. Or maybe she didn't want the groom hanging off the back of the carriage to hear. He appreciated her discretion but not her observation.

"Of course, I'm distracted, my lady. Have you noticed the amount of traffic around us?"

A gurgle of laughter came up from her throat, and Lucian had to smile over it despite his discomfort. She sounded carefree and delighted in that moment. It wasn't like her usual, over-thinking self. He liked it too much.

"You, my lord, are a very good prevaricator. Yes, I did notice the traffic. But it isn't much different from the traffic that was in place when we were on our way to the Park. And from the tales I overheard you and Jeffrey telling when you were up at your college, you have experienced far worse in the way of traffic and successfully navigated it. Blindfolded, even, if your tales were to be believed." She tapped her chin while she watched him as though she were examining a specimen for flaws. "There has been something a little off about you since we saw Lady Fanny. You aren't going to pursue her, are you? I understand that, as a widow, she has a slightly different expectation from Society, but I truly think she isn't for you."

Lucian blinked at her as his brain tried to process what she had just said. He wondered if he ought to go along with her supposition or deny it hotly, as was his first instinct. It might be better if she thought he were pursuing a dalliance with the fast widow if it kept her from pursuing the matter further and arriving closer to the truth.

"Lady Amelia Courtenay," he began in a scolding tone. "You are not to acknowledge any familiarity with widows and their proclivities. And whether or not I wish to pursue anyone is none of your concern, is it?"

For the briefest moment, the chit appeared as though he had slapped her, and Lucian felt a qualm of guilt. But better to hurt her feelings a little than to have her step into his problems. Pulling her into his life had a far greater possibility of injury to her.

"I thought we were friends, Lord Adelaide," she answered stiffly and formally. "As such, I thought it

54

fitting that I warn you off a potentially troublesome situation. But you are quite correct; it is not my place to do so. I do thank you for the drive and the information this afternoon. I shall wish you a good day."

If he didn't stop her, Lucian suspected she would jump out of the carriage even as it was moving. But he quickly reached over and clamped his hand firmly around her wrist as she was gathering her skirts.

"Don't be a simpleton, Amelia," he said, calm but stern even as anger seethed in him. How could she be such a fool?

She sniffed but settled back into her seat, uncomfortable probably because she knew she had been acting just as he said. He shouldn't have called her names, but jumping from a moving carriage was stupid enough when you were a teenaged boy in the countryside let alone a young lady in copious amounts of skirts on a teeming street in the city.

"What has gotten into you?" he demanded.

"I haven't a clue what you're talking about."

Lucian couldn't help being a little impressed that she was going to try to brazen it out. He allowed it to pass for the moment, even though she ought to be reprimanded even more for being so foolish. Her lack of moderation was always getting her in trouble.

He softened his tone. She was right. They were friends. They had been since she was barely out of nappies.

"My apologies, Amelia. I shouldn't have snapped at you. But you needn't be so sensitive that you would jump from a moving carriage just because you don't appreciate something I've said. If you're going to carry on like that, you shan't find much success in Town, I must say."

"But what of my husband's political career?" she demanded with an innocent expression, causing Lucian to chuckle.

"You are an outrageous bounder, Lady Amelia. If you are to be a political wife, all the more you will need to control your tongue and your reactions. There is bound to be any number of things that you'll overhear if you turn your attention to such matters, and you can't give it away or it will ruin everything."

This obviously caught her attention as she stared at him with fascination gleaming in her rounded eyes.

"Tell me everything, Luce," she demanded breathlessly, making Lucian wish he could do just as she asked.

"We are nearly to your home, Button, so it will have to wait for another day."

"Can't you come in?"

Lucian grinned at her eagerness, a part of him wanting to do just as she begged. But he knew trouble lay in that direction. He could not start giving in to her demands. He could not allow himself to soften in her presence. And he absolutely could not allow his heart to become entwined in her affairs. She was his friend; that was the extent of it. Not even that, in fact. She was his friend's little sister. It could never be anything more. She was far too innocent for him, and he would not compromise her safety.

"You have too much to think about, my lady, and I have other appointments I must keep."

"I thought you were a gadabout, Lord Adelaide. Surely you don't have anything truly pressing at the moment."

"That is where you are wrong. And this is where you can start practicing the control and reserve you will need to cultivate if you truly wish to promote your husband's political career." It took effort, but he managed to keep his amusement to himself when she turned such a woebegone expression upon him. "I shan't be moved by your hangdog looks, my dear. I grew immune around the time I turned sixteen."

This brought a giggle to his companion even as he pulled his carriage to a halt in front of her townhouse.

Lucian cast a practiced eye over the front of the property. Her father was clearly managing not to empty the family's coffers if the size and upkeep of the large building was anything to go by. It was evident that maintenance was being done. There were no telltale signs of genteel poverty that some of the other well born families were subject to. He was glad to see it. He would hate to think his friend was going to inherit empty titles.

But it also made him wonder at the lack of beaux chasing after Amelia. With the family so well heeled, it would be expected the young lady would have a generous dowry. That coupled with her good looks, she ought to have been the toast of the *ton*. Surely, she couldn't have been so awkward as to have ruined her chances. He resolved to keep a closer eye on her when their paths crossed socially.

"You won't forget that we are to go driving again, will you, Lucian?"

"Not if you'll remember that you ought to be more formal with me, my lady."

Her grin did not display repentance, but she bowed her head submissively anyway.

"Thank you for the lovely afternoon, my lord." She was very proper in her leave taking as she dipped into a curtsy and then flitted up the stairs to the already opening door. The servants were clearly attentive. The chit was not so proper, though, that she didn't turn on the doorstep and offer him a small wave.

Lucian drove away with a knot in the pit of his stomach. He didn't want to care about Lady Amelia. And he definitely didn't want her involved in his problems. He tried to reassure himself that she couldn't have seen anything and even if she did, she certainly wouldn't have any understanding of what she had seen. But that didn't really set his mind at rest.

What had Terrance been doing in the park anyway?

After leaving his carriage back in the mews of his own London townhouse, he hailed a hackney and was quickly settled in at White's to ponder his problems. He spread the paper wide in front of him with a snifter of brandy at his elbow, hoping that would afford him a degree of privacy.

It worked wonders. Other gentlemen left him to his own devices as they must have considered it evident that he was occupied. Except for one interfering gentleman.

"You haven't turned the page in over fifteen minutes, Adelaide. That tells me you're pondering. There's no use sitting here hiding behind the paper. Out with it. What's eating you?"

With a roll of his eyes, Lucian slowly lowered his paper, grateful that the scoundrel who interrupted his solitude had at least had the forethought to keep his voice down. Jasper, Viscount Lonsdale, had been at school with him and Jeffrey. As such, their friendship was deeply rooted. He was one of the few people who would know such a thing about him. "For your information, I was reading an engrossing article summarizing everyone's arguments from the House yesterday."

"I read that article. It doesn't take that long," Jasper scoffed. "You will recall we went to school together, so I know it couldn't possibly have taken you so long to read it."

"I was pondering the author's commentary as I read," Lucian argued, but he couldn't keep his features hardened under his friend's steady stare. With a sigh, he folded his paper and took a sip from his glass.

"That's the other way I knew you were faking," his friend declared. "There's still something in your glass. If you really were reading rather than trying to work out some sort of problem, you would have finished and called for more."

Lucian frowned. Was he so very obvious?

Jasper laughed softly. "Don't worry, no one else would know. But you've had this tactic since we were boys. Those who know you well would have been able to read you like the open book you used to be." The other man sighed. "I liked that open man," he added with a small laugh.

"So, what is so urgent that you needed to interrupt whatever I was doing?" Lucian had nearly come to his own conclusions anyway, so he didn't really resent the intrusion. Jasper had always been a good friend.

The other gentleman shrugged. "I wanted to offer you my assistance," he said with a smile.

"I beg your pardon. Your assistance with what, pray tell."

"Whatever has you holing up behind the paper."

Lucian allowed a chuckle to escape him even though it brought the eyes of others to their conversation. It was well known that Viscount Adelaide and Jasper Blakely had been good friends since they went away to Eton. Jasper was another member of the pact he and Jeffrey had made as boys. Along with Lucian's brothers, they called their family and friends their kin.

"I appreciate your concern, but there's nothing I need assistance with at this time," he said, dismissing his friend's offer. Not accepting his dismissal, though, Jasper continued to stare at him.

"Well, if you truly must make yourself useful, there is a small matter," Lucian said, finally yielding to his friend's concern. "I'm actually somewhat surprised that you haven't already involved yourself."

Jasper settled himself back more comfortably in the armchair next to Lucian's and watched his face closely. "In what have I been remiss?"

"It's Lady Amelia."

Suddenly Jasper was much more attentive. "What about Lady Amelia?"

"She seems to not be taking."

"How is that possible?"

"That is exactly what I wanted to know. I might have already solved the root cause of the problem, but the girl could use a little attention if you encounter her at any events. She has allowed herself to become a wallflower."

"Amelia a wallflower? Surely you jest."

Lucian shrugged. "As I said, it might be solved already, but do ensure you partner her in a dance the next time you're at the same ball."

Jasper chuckled and nodded elegantly as though to bow to his friend. "Something tells me this is not what had you hiding behind the paper, but if you aren't ready to share, I suppose I'll let you get back to your thought process. Just keep in mind, if you have need of assistance, I am never far away and always ready."

"I appreciate that," Lucian answered with a serious nod of his own, hoping his expression wasn't overly heartfelt. He opened his paper back up to cover his awkwardness. He didn't really want Jasper to know just how very much he might eventually need the other man's help. One of the matters he had been tasked to look into might be more in Jasper's area of expertise.

The Home Office was concerned about stirrings of industrial unrest. It was something they were trying to keep a close eye upon, but it was impossible to be everywhere at once. And the most restive often weren't interested in what the government might have to contribute on the subject. But the government very much had an interest in what was going on. Lucian only hoped they would be able to hear about it before any true conflict arose.

Sadly, some of the larger landowners, generally those with titles, were not looking favorably on the advancement of technology. It was such a short-sighted viewpoint, in Lucian's opinion. But it was one that was shared by most of his acquaintances, including his father. It made for some interesting conversations on the rare occasion that everyone was home at Everleigh, since some of Lucian's brothers were going in the industrial direction.

It was good that this thought had crossed his mind, Lucian noted. He would have to write to his brother Foster to see what he might know. He was the brother most interested in the mechanical inventions of the day. Not that Frost would be quick to share if he thought Lucian was on the verge of interfering. With a sigh, Lucian folded his newspaper back up. He had done enough pondering. Writing to his middle brother wouldn't do. He would have to speak with him in person. With Terrance in Town, it was obvious something must be afoot. The man was a known menace who specialized in stirring up trouble in the industrial factions. Lucian would have to set someone to the task of ascertaining where exactly his brother was staying these days. It was never a certainty. But he couldn't delay if matters were getting urgent.

Chapter Eight

A melia pondered her reflection as her maid twisted her hair into a fashionable series of knots upon the top of her head. Even as she thought about all that Lucian had discussed with her that afternoon, she was impassively examining her features.

She knew they were appropriately placed to be considered attractive even if she didn't necessarily agree with the common convention. In her estimation, her colouring of blonde hair and blue eyes were as interesting as dishwater. But it was considered fashionable. With a shrug, Amelia concluded there was no accounting for taste.

The difference she noted in her appearance, though, was that her cheeks were finally rosy. Up until now, whenever she was preparing for a *ton* event, she was pasty pale as though she had caught the ague. It certainly wasn't a good look even if her features were even and her hair and eyes the accepted fashion. This evening, there was every possibility she just might take. And she had Lucian to thank for it. He was correct. All it took was a change of perspective. Now, she was eager to learn from the other debutantes. She wanted to hear what everyone had to say. She wasn't certain she was convinced she would learn anything of a political nature in Lady Ashtonby's ballroom, but Amelia was prepared to keep her ears open for the possibility.

And she had so much to learn!

Just the cursory reading she had been able to do between the viscount leaving her at the door and the time she had to begin her preparations had shown her there was an entire world of which she knew nothing.

Amelia couldn't believe she had allowed an entire field of study to escape her. It made nerves jump in her belly. What else had she not realized she didn't know? She couldn't think of that or she would become derailed for certain. For now, she had the entire matter of governance to learn about.

She had been interested to learn that it was the eighteenth parliament of Great Britain currently sitting. Amelia wondered about the previous seventeen. She quite loved that all that she was learning was triggering even more questions. But she wasn't certain where to find the answers. Amelia hoped Lucian would be at the ball that evening so she could find out if he knew yet which sessions she should attend. If he hadn't yet determined it, perhaps she wouldn't bother waiting. She suspected she would be fascinated by the experience whatever might be under discussion. And surely there wouldn't be anything she might be present for that would put her beyond the pale. Amelia prided herself on being sufficiently forward-thinking that she wasn't put to the blush by any topic. She knew that wasn't entirely true. Many things put her to the blush. But she was certain knowledge was valuable no matter if it were an awkward topic.

And the fascinating topic of governance was going to fill her days with wonder, she was certain.

As she ruminated, it finally came to her attention that her maid was speaking to her.

"My apologies, Sarah, my mind was elsewhere. What were you saying?"

"Nothing terribly important, my lady." The maid dismissed Amelia's concern with a gentle laugh. "Certainly not as important as whatever had you so deeply preoccupied. I was just remarking that you seem to be quite in your looks tonight. And that you seem different somehow. But you being so deep in thought makes me think you aren't so very different after all," she concluded with another small laugh. "No offence intended, though, my lady."

Amelia laughed, too. "None taken, Sarah. I'm well aware that I have a strong tendency to get stuck in my thoughts. It's good that you point it out, though, as I have been informed it is something I ought to make an effort to overcome."

The faithful maid bridled at her mistress's words. "Never say so, my lady. No one should tell you that you shouldn't be thinking your thoughts."

Amelia grinned at her maid's reflection, deeply appreciative of the servant's loyalty. "I agree with you wholeheartedly, as you know. But I don't completely disagree with the one who advised me not to become so absorbed in them. At least not when in company. It could be deemed quite rude."

"Never say someone has accused you of rudeness, my lady."

Amelia smiled again even as she shrugged. "Not necessarily to my face, but wouldn't you agree that it could be considered rude to be more absorbed in my own thoughts than what others are discussing around me?"

The maid shrugged. "They should make sure they're more interesting if they want you to pay attention."

Amelia laughed. "Thank you, Sarah. I appreciate your confidence in me." As the maid stepped back from her, Amelia turned her head this way and that in order to see as much of her hair as possible. "As usual, you have done wondrous things with my appearance."

"Get on with you, my lady." Sarah bashfully dismissed her mistress's praise, and Amelia reached out to grip her hand tightly in a gesture of familiarity. "I would tell you not to wait up, but I'm not certain I'll be able to undo myself on my own."

"Well, even if you told me not to wait up, I wouldn't be able to listen, my lady, so it's just as well that you don't. The housekeeper would send me packing if I was so lazy."

Amelia laughed again even though she momentarily felt badly for her servant's obligations. While she was well aware that it was the usual order of things, Amelia felt uncomfortable with it anyway. She shook her head to dismiss the unhelpful thoughts, careful not to dislodge the carefully arranged locks. Gratefully, they were locked in place with a network of pins.

After another careful perusal of her reflection, Amelia decided she was as ready as she was ever going to be. A deep breath to steady her nerves, and she was on her way to join her mother in the receiving room. Amelia was more nervous than she had been even at her first official event as a debutante. She tried to assure herself there was nothing to be nervous about, but her mind wouldn't listen to her reasoning. Because she was going with an entirely different attitude, it felt like a whole new experience.

A glance in the mirror over the mantel assured her that her inner turmoil wasn't displaying itself on her face. But as Sarah had noted, her colour was much higher than on previous occasions. She was in her looks that day. It was going to be a good night. Even her mother agreed.

"Amelia, you look lovely," Lady Hanley said in a rather lukewarm voice. Amelia ignored the lack of enthusiasm and dropped a light curtsy in response.

"Thank you, Mother. As do you. We shall be making a splash this evening."

Lady Hanley's aristocratic eyebrows rose and her nostrils pinched a little. "No cant, my dear."

Amelia hid her amusement. Despite her mother's acceptance of Jeffrey's friends into their home whenever her brother saw fit to invite them, the poor woman had never really gotten over her fear of being incorrect at any moment. Her mother tried hard to be loving, but it didn't come easily to her. Having met her grandparents a couple times, Amelia fully understood where her mother's reserve came from. But it was one more thing that had made her not want a Society marriage for herself. She had forgotten to mention that to Lucian. Amelia wondered if a political man would have to be as correct as her mother. A knot formed in her stomach before she assured herself that she could ask Lucian later.

There was a bustle of activity as the servants announced the arrival of their carriage and then bundled them into it. They didn't have terribly far to travel, but it would take a while to get there given the congested streets. Amelia thought to practice her newfound interests on her mother.

"Do you follow the happenings in the House of Lords, Mother?"

Again, her mother looked at her as though surprised by the utterances coming from her. Amelia had to laugh a little. She supposed her mother must consider her a changeling at times.

"Not very closely, no," she finally answered. "Your father tells me things occasionally when he feels particularly pressed by a matter."

This sparked Amelia's interest. "Do you enjoy it when he does so? Are you able to help him? What sorts of things?"

Lady Hanley shrugged slightly. "I don't pay too much attention. You'll have to ask your father. He is much more interested in those matters than I am. I have devoted myself to the care of you children, not to the cultivation of his political pursuits."

Amelia nodded but felt confused. "Do you think they are incompatible interests?"

"For me, they were. But mostly because I wasn't in the least interested in who said what or which bill they were arguing about."

"So, if you had been interested, there might have been room for both?" Amelia was still trying to understand and form her own opinions.

"Surely one makes room for what interests them, Amelia. At least you've always done so, haven't you?"

Amelia's laugh was genuine even though she tried to keep it genteel. "That is very true, Mother. Thank you for saying so."

"I didn't necessarily say it as a compliment, my dear," Lady Hanley said, but there was a teasing glint in her gaze. Amelia knew her mother loved her even if the older woman didn't understand her. "Why the sudden interest in your father's affairs?"

Amelia shrugged. "It isn't necessarily *his* affairs that interest me as much as the entire political arena."

"Of course," Lady Hanley remarked drily. "I should have realized." After a soft sigh and a low chuckle, she added, "You should still ask him, as I truly know very little. And I'm certain it would tickle him to discuss it with you." Lady Hanley's gaze shifted to the window, even though there was little to see in the gathering darkness. "I hope you won't find it as disappointing as you did your pursuit of education, Amelia. I truly wish for your sake that you were a more comfortable person. I wish you enjoyed all the things that are considered appropriate for females. But it often seems to me that you've been born in the wrong age."

Amelia stared at her mother in the flickering light of the carriage lantern.

"Whatever do you mean?"

"Even I have heard the rumblings of discontent amongst women wishing for more access to the world of men. I cannot even fathom why they would want it, for the most part. But watching you struggle with your strong interests and desires for things that are out of the usual realm, I can see what they mean. I know you don't wish to be a man, but you deeply wish that you could access some of the things that are denied to you because you aren't."

Amelia reached out and clasped her mother's hand, grateful to be somewhat understood by the older woman for what felt like the first time in her life. Something shifted in her heart in that moment. It felt to her that having her mother's acknowledgment put a piece in place that had been missing. She was well aware that her mother still considered her to be a strange creature, but she tried to understand that strangeness, and it made all the difference.

"So, by saying I was born in the wrong age, does that mean you think it will one day be different?"

"I am certain of it, my dear. With strong women like you trying to expand the confines of your role in life, it is inevitable, really. I only hope you are happy with what you find when you accomplish what you are after."

Amelia shrugged. "I might have found a way to be satisfied without actually changing the world around me," she told her mother with a grin that widened as her mother smiled in genuine pleasure.

"Really, my dear? Is this realization somehow tied to you questioning my support of your father's aspirations in the House?"

At Amelia's nod, Lady Hanley grew thoughtful. "I can see how that might work for you, my dear. I'm happy that you've found a direction. And you seem much more eager to enter the fray this evening. Might I ask, what prompted this sudden interest and change of heart?"

"Lord Adelaide explained a few things to me this afternoon while we were driving."

"I see," Lady Hanley answered mildly, but Amelia could see her expression turning crafty.

"Don't get any ideas about Viscount Adelaide," Amelia began, using Lucian's title in an attempt to distance him from herself. "I don't think he's the man for me, even if he's been a good friend."

"If you say so, my dear," Lady Hanley replied, her peaceful smile doing nothing to quell Amelia's concern.

"I'm serious, Mother. You cannot get your hopes up about a match in that quarter. Lucian is far too opinionated for me. Just imagine the fights we'd have. Surely you wouldn't want that for me." When her mother didn't look moved by this argument, Amelia added, "Besides, he isn't in search of a wife at this time anyhow."

"That means almost nothing, my dear. No well-heeled gentleman is ever truly in search of a wife. It's only the fortune hunters who are. The rest need to be caught."

Amelia turned rounded eyes upon her mother. "Are you suggesting I ought to pursue a gentleman? That sounds hardly genteel."

"I am suggesting that gentlemen need to be encouraged to get themselves to the altar. One would never want them to think it wasn't their idea."

Amelia laughed suddenly, though she tried to keep it to a gentle titter for her mother's sake, but she was truly impressed with her mother's craftiness. "I had no idea, my lady."

"You've been a trifle too preoccupied with your own thoughts, my dear. I am pleased to see that you have gained a broader understanding. It will serve you well."

Amelia had no response to that, merely lapsing back into her corner to ponder her mother's words. She couldn't fathom pursuing Lucian. While he was far more handsome than he ought to be and there were occasionally delicious little shivers in her midsection when she was in his company, she didn't think he would be at all a comfortable husband. He had far too strong a presence for that. And with her own determined personality, Amelia was reasonably certain it would be a recipe for disaster.

But despite that, she was impressed with her mother's thoughts. Especially since they tied in with what Lucian had been saying. He had advised her that she shouldn't discount the other women in her life as being less thoughtful than she was even though they didn't seem to wish to pursue an education. Clearly her mother gave at least certain things far more thought than Amelia had suspected. It made her feel badly that she had misjudged her mother and made her again question if she had done the same to others.

She sighed quietly. Lucian was right. She would have to widen her mind even more than she had already. It was a little humiliating for someone who thought she was so thoughtful to find out that she had disregarded a great deal of valuable information.

When they arrived at their destination, Amelia was still deep in thought. She tried to pull her attention back to the matter at hand, but she wasn't certain if she was going to be successful. The ball this evening, and the crowds attending, were all wrapped up in the things she was pondering. It was a bit of a jumble. Thankfully, she had been raised from the cradle as to what was acceptable behaviour, so even though her thoughts were preoccupied, she knew she wouldn't put a foot wrong. Or rather, she used to think she wouldn't, but now she was no longer so confident.

With concerted effort, just as they were being announced, Amelia brought her full attention to the spectacle before her, and her senses were nearly overwhelmed by the sights and sounds that confronted her. And the odours, she thought with a slight smile as she nodded and curtsied to various acquaintances. With the expected poise and elegance, she and her mother descended the grand staircase into the ballroom.

In a detached sort of way, Amelia admired the architecture even as she observed the ebb and flow of the heaving masses below her. They were late enough that the room was already crowded, but not so late that their hostess wasn't still receiving. For a debutante, it was the exact right time to arrive, and Amelia was forced to admire her mother's skill as chaperone. She supposed Lady Hanley had already had practice with her older daughters, Amelia's sisters, who had debuted and wed five and two years ago respectively. Still, it took considerable forethought to arrive at this precise timing. And Amelia hadn't even noticed. She curbed the impulse to remark upon it to her mother and merely made a mental note to speak of it later.

The three ladies bobbed curtsies to each other as Lady Hanley and Amelia stopped at the bottom of the stairs in front of their hostess, the notorious Lady Gretchen Ashtonby. Amelia's lips twitched as she thought of the lady's reputation as a fearsome hostess. She didn't look so very intense, but Amelia was aware the woman was known to have the ability to slay one with just a glance.

"Lady Hanley, Lady Amelia, I am delighted that you could attend."

"It is very much our pleasure, my lady," Amelia's mother answered politely. "It was kind of you to invite us."

"Not at all." Lady Ashtonby waved Lady Hanley's words away. "It is always a pleasure to support the debutantes. I must say, it amuses me." She turned to Amelia and assessed her. "I do declare you are a taking little thing, aren't you? It surprises me you didn't get snatched up in your first week."

Amelia wasn't completely certain how best to answer such a statement. She merely smiled as her mother handled it for her.

"One wouldn't want to be overeager," Lady Hanley murmured.

Chapter Nine

L ucian didn't think he would ever see the time when he would be watching for a woman's arrival to an event. Not unless she were a source of information. But while Lady Amelia Courtenay was a font of knowledge, she was certainly not one of his sources. And yet, here he stood, trying to appear nonchalant even as his ears were constantly on the alert for the major-domo to announce her.

When Lady Hanley and Lady Amelia were finally called, it took all he had not to rush over to the bottom of the stairs to ensure he partnered her for at least one dance that evening. He refused to make a cake of himself, but it was a close run thing. After she had explicitly explained to him that she was a wallflower, it was particularly ridiculous that he would be concerned that her dances would all be spoken for.

Watching from the side of the ballroom though, Lucian realized that he had been correct in his first assessment. It would be impossible for Lady Amelia to go unnoticed. Before his eyes, he watched as gentlemen who had never seemed to note her before practically flocked to her side. There was almost a queue forming of eager gentlemen awaiting an introduction. Surely, they had already met the chit. Lucian scoffed under his breath as he thought of cutting the line and claiming her for himself.

Restraint won out. If worse came to worst, he would do it later. Still, he watched with a jaundiced eye as Amelia was swept out onto the dance floor by some baron Lucian couldn't remember by name. He was surprised by how animated Amelia appeared. She had been much more reserved when they had been out that afternoon. He tried not to be jealous, but it was nearly impossible to suppress the feeling.

Rather than standing by and watching like the lovesick puppy he most certainly was not, Lucian asked another lady to join him in the dance. It was a little late to do so, but she didn't object. He tried not to allow his lips to twist in derision. Who would object to an invitation to dance from Viscount Adelaide?

"Are you enjoying the Season?" Miss Easton was a pleasant enough young woman, or so he had thought when they had met previously.

"I am, my lord, thank you for asking. Might I ask the same of you?"

"Do you mean, am I enjoying the Season?" At her vigorous nod, Lucian fought a chuckle. "I suppose it is a far different experience for gentlemen than it is for ladies."

She tilted her head inquisitively but didn't respond immediately. He would have previously thought that he enjoyed it when a person thought about their response before they blurted out the first thing that came into their head, but he found himself impatient for her answer. Involuntarily, he found his gaze seeking out the one woman who he found most likely to blurt, but Amelia wasn't within easy glancing distance.

"Do you mean that gentlemen's enjoyment of the Season is different because they are involved in different activities?" the young woman asked, making

Lucian frown as he tried to recollect what they were talking about.

"Yes, that's right," he said with relief as he remembered. "This is far from my first time in Town, for one thing."

She nodded but continued to look at him in question, as though waiting for him to say more. Lucian sighed. He supposed he set himself up for that by his wording. By saying for one thing, it was expected there would be more.

"For another, I am kept quite busy with my seat."

The girl nodded as though she understood what he was talking about, but Lucian still found himself longing for Amelia's constant questions. How was that possible when he had always found her unending questions to be an irritant rather than a pleasure?

Lucian was used to young ladies chattering his ears off during the dance, and he barely had to make any effort to ensure a conversation flowed during the few minutes of their time together. But not with Miss Easton. She was a curiosity. Lucian wondered if his friend Jasper would enjoy her company. That thought brought a grin to his face that again prompted an inquisitive lift of his companion's eyebrows but no verbal questions.

"My apologies, Miss Easton. I merely remembered something about a friend which amused me."

She nodded but continued to look questioning. Lucian chose to ignore her expression. If she couldn't be bothered to put her question into words, he shouldn't feel obliged to answer. Blessedly, the end of the dance could be heard approaching with a flourish. Lucian hoped his relief wasn't evident as he bowed to his partner and escorted her back to where he found her. He then went in search of Lady Amelia.

There was still a crowd of young men around her, but Lucian easily cut through them and claimed Amelia for himself.

"That was skillfully accomplished, my lord," she remarked with laughter sounding in her tone and sparkling in her gaze.

"To what do you refer?" Lucian tried to appear innocent, which prompted a low gurgle of laughter from her, much to his delight.

"You know very well, but I shan't upbraid you for it as I was hoping to speak with you. And seeing as this is a minuet, I shan't have to put up with changing partners at the very least."

Lucian's lips twitched at her words. "What did you have an urgent need to discuss with me, then, Little One?"

She smiled at him. "While I don't really appreciate reference being made to my diminutive size, that expression is far better than Button."

"I don't see why Button bothers you so much."

"A woman wants to be thought of as beautiful or alluring, not cute, my lord. Surely you realize. Cute is for kittens, and puppies, and lambs."

"And young ladies one has known since she was little more than a kitten."

Another gurgle of laughter slipped from her, and Lucian found his grip on her waist tightening fractionally. He had to force himself to relax as to not draw attention to them.

"Never mind your ridiculousness, my lord. I did have something specific I wanted to ask you about, and I shan't allow you to distract me from my purpose."

"Very well, I hadn't meant to stop you. What is this burning topic?"

"I wanted to ask if it would be acceptable for someone to visit the House whenever they wanted or if you need to make an appointment. Do I need to wait until you tell me the topics and I pick one, presumably so that you could arrange for my entrance? And did you get a chance to consider who might be the most interesting gentleman for me to cultivate a conversation with?"

Lucian's lips twitched at her turn of phrase even as part of him wanted to reject the thought of her cultivating anything with another gentleman.

"My apologies, again, my lady. I didn't realize you would take to the topic quite so vigorously and therefore didn't prepare the list for this evening. But never fear. I will have a footman deliver it to you first thing in the morning."

"Well, I didn't mean to make trouble for you, Luce, but it has taken my fancy, and I cannot help but pursue the topic."

"I can see that. And I can see that the excitement has created a force about you that others are responding to."

The chit grinned. "That is the same thing Mother said. Do you know, you were quite right about her, as well? It does turn out that there is much more going on in her thought processes than I would have given her credit for. I am quite ashamed of myself, to be perfectly honest. Here I thought I was such a great specimen, and it turns out I'm a selfish lout."

"Never that, my dear," Lucian said as he swirled her in the dance. "But it is charming of you to think so."

"Why ever would you say that?"

He was surprised to hear her sound horrified.

Lucian shrugged. "It means you are willing to admit when you are wrong, which is a rare trait to be sure."

She didn't look convinced, but she at least stopped staring at him as though he had lost his mind.

Lucian turned his mind back to her original question, as he still hadn't answered it.

"No, I haven't yet thought of who you ought to, as you said, cultivate. But I promise to give it some thought. As well, you can attend the House nearly any time you want. There are occasions when the session might be closed to the public, but those are rare. The only thing I would warn you of is there might be topics that could put you to the blush or bore you to tears, which is why I thought it best that you have a list so you could choose."

She was listening and nodding in that endearing way she had, and again, Lucian's grip tightened upon her, causing her gaze to fly up to mesh with his.

"Is everything all right, my lord?" she gently questioned.

"Perfectly," he answered without acknowledging what he had done, merely directing her in another theatrical circle. The gesture drew more eyes toward them but seemed to delight her.

"You are a most excellent dancer, my lord," she complimented.

Lucian could actually feel the heat creeping into his cheeks at her words, much to his further embarrassment. Since when had the innocent compliments of a debutante made him blush? Lucian didn't think he had been put to the blush since he was thirteen years old. It was awkward as all get out. To make it worse, the many gazes upon them only made his embarrassment intensify. If any of his friends noticed, he would never be able to live it down.

"As are you," he replied mildly, doing his best to bring his impulses under control. Blushing like a schoolgirl was unacceptable for the heir to the Earl of Everleigh. Lucian couldn't even fathom what his father would say were he to see him.

As though she were a mind reader, the girl asked after his father, and Lucian's eyebrows nearly collided with the unruly fringe of his hair that never managed to stay in place.

"What prompts you to ask after the earl?"

Amelia blinked at him. "It is a usual question, isn't it?" She started to frown. "Why? Is something actually wrong with him? I just thought it was the polite thing to ask." She sighed heavily. "Have I transgressed already?"

Lucian broke through his own preoccupations in order to reassure her with a gentle chuckle. "No, no, nothing like that. It is my fault, not yours, my lady. I was just thinking about the earl, and then you asked after him. It was a strange coincidence is all."

Lucian wouldn't meet her gaze as Amelia stared at him with a studious but puzzled expression. "You are being a trifle odd this evening, my lord," she finally commented. "But I don't mind being puzzled, so don't let it trouble you. I'm relieved that he is well."

It took effort, but Lucian managed a relaxed smile, or he hoped it appeared relaxed, at any rate. "In his last letter informing me of all the duties I am slacking on, he seemed his usual self. I am certain that I would be informed if his health were in decline."

Amelia's frown was filled with concern. "Why would he consider you to be slacking in your duties? It seems to me that you are reputed to be quite dutiful despite how indolent you always seem to be. It is the strangest contradiction." She glanced away, staring into the distance over his shoulder before bringing her assessing gaze back to his face. "Although, truth be told, it did seem a trifle undutiful that you always spent most of your school breaks at my house rather than at your own."

Lucian returned her smile. "I suppose that was. It is from where his constant harping springs, anyway. But you are right; I certainly care for my responsibilities to the best of my ability. I just choose to do it from afar. Besides, Gilbert is happy to take up wherever I am lacking, I am sure."

Amelia's frown returned. "Does Gilbert appreciate that role?"

Lucian stared at her and nearly faltered in the dance steps. "I beg your pardon?"

"I've always thought that being the second son must be a terrible position to be born into. Second sons are rarely titled, nor do they inherit much of anything, as everything must stay with the estate. But they grow up in the same environment as the firstborn and must always feel like a spare just in case something happens to the heir. It must be a little dreadful. Or a lot dreadful, in fact." She laughed a little while Lucian's frown creased his forehead. "While I'm sure Jeffrey didn't appreciate having multiple little sisters, I've often thought it was a blessing he didn't actually have a brother to fret about. And his friendship with you seems to have filled that need that I'm sure boys have for a childhood companion. Though he might have enjoyed having a playmate when he was too young for school, I think the benefits of being the only son outweigh the possible drawbacks."

Lucian laughed. "That is a unique perspective, my dear. I don't think most families would agree with your assessment."

Amelia laughed gently. "No, most people don't agree with most of my assessments."

Again, Lucian's heart cramped a bit as he thought of the young woman's sweet challenges. "So, you are determined to pursue a gentleman with a political bent, are you?" he asked to turn the subject and then was surprised when discomfort coloured her features.

"Well, I wouldn't term it quite like that, as I still think it's exceedingly vulgar to pursue a gentleman even though I know many of the ladies consider it acceptable. My mother says the goal is to be clever enough to make the gentleman think it is his idea."

"See, I knew your mother was a knowing one," Lucian remarked with a smile that she answered with one of her own.

"That she is," Amelia answered. Her tone was mild, but Lucian could hear the wonder in it, as though she were surprised by the discovery. He thought to question her on it but stuck to the matter at hand.

"So, what have you been pondering about the political ideas?"

"Well I still know so very little, to be honest. I spent what was left of the afternoon after we parted in my father's study reading as much as I could find out about governance, but since he wasn't home, he couldn't direct me to which books would be best. But what I did find out intrigued me to the point that I think it might be the best option for me." Despite how energized she seemed by the concept, she still sighed a little disappointedly. "I think you were right; the sheep farmer from northern parts might not be the best match for me."

Lucian chuckled over her words. "I'm sorry if that disappoints you."

When Amelia's gaze met his, it was dancing with laughter. "It was a disappointment, it's true. But far better to find out before I even met the gentleman than after I was already ensconced in his home."

Lucian shook his head. "You are delightful, Lady Amelia."

Her eyebrows suddenly reached toward her curls again. "Truly, Luce? I thought I was just a burden."

"Never, Button. Why would you think that?"

The girl shrugged, which wasn't much of an answer, but then her frown turned more puzzled than usual.

"Lord Adelaide, I don't wish to alarm you, but it seems there is a strange gentleman watching us."

"Of course, there are gentlemen watching us; you are a beautiful woman."

"Don't be daft, Luce, I'm serious. It's someone I've never met before. In fact, he looks like he borrowed someone's clothes to get into the event. As though he's trying to look the part of someone who belongs here but he isn't quite fitting in. Do you know what I mean?"

Lucian knew exactly what she meant. A quick turn of the woman in his arms, and he was sure of it. They had followed him. And now Amelia would be in danger. Or perhaps not if he could dance with enough other women to hide her in the crowd. But if it was the same man who had been following him in the Park, they would have been seen together there, too. It took all his self possession not to colour the air with the foul language that was filling his thoughts. He managed to swallow down his vitriol.

"I think you must have been reading some gothic novels while you were doing your research this afternoon, my dear," Lucian told her in a bantering tone. "It isn't kind of you to question someone's acceptability just because they haven't retained a good valet."

When Amelia stared at him as though to challenge his statement, Lucian continued. "Are you questioning our host's ability to screen his guests?"

Amelia searched his gaze, and Lucian had to fortify himself to withstand the scrutiny, unsure what she would see, as it felt as though she could see right to the depths of his soul.

"I'm not saying that at all, my lord. I'm saying this is a very large house with multiple entrances and a big crowd milling about. It wouldn't be the least bit challenging to gain entrance on a night like this, even if you hadn't been expressly invited. And I'm wondering why someone like that would take such an interest in you."

Lucian refused to allow his glance to flicker back to the man she had spoken of. "What makes you think it's me he's interested in? Perhaps it's you."

She opened her mouth as though to answer but then shut it to look back at the man under discussion before turning back to Lucian with a frown.

"I suppose you could be right, my lord. I cannot explain to you why I think you aren't. It's just a feeling I have, and that's not in the least bit logical. So never mind about him. Perhaps I was imagining things."

Lucian could tell from the expression on her face she didn't actually believe that she had imagined it, but he appreciated that she was making an effort to brush her concerns aside. He appreciated it even though he was afraid she ought to be even more concerned than she had been, as he was very much afraid she was now going to be in danger. This was just one more reason why he avoided well-born women. He would always have to be concerned for their safety as long as he remained with the Home Office.

With a sigh, Lucian realized he would now have to speak with his superiors about Lady Amelia. In his five years working for the Home Office, he had never found himself in this position, unlike some of the other noblemen and peers with whom he occasionally worked. It was sure to be awkward. But it couldn't be avoided.

Chapter Ten

A melia, as always, enjoyed dancing, especially with Lucian. They had been dancing together since she was a little girl when he would visit her brother. But she hadn't danced with him so very much since she'd made her debut, so tonight was a special thrill for her. Despite that thrill, she couldn't forget about the man who had been watching them. It was a different sort of watching. Amelia knew what it was to be watched in an admiring sort of way. That wasn't what the man was doing.

A shiver slithered down her spine. It was not the delicious sort that she had experienced when Lucian had handed her down from his carriage that afternoon. This shiver was of the fearful sort. And she had no idea why. Amelia also couldn't understand why Lucian was trying to dismiss the matter. He had eyes in his head. Surely, he realized the man was watching them. Worry seized her. What if someone was after Lucian and he didn't realize? What could she possibly do about it?

Taking a deep breath, Amelia tried to dispel the unaccountable worries from the back of her mind. It wasn't going to accomplish anything except put her back in the odd category. She was determined to leave that behind. She wasn't odd. She was a debutante, and she was going to be a successful one if it was the last thing she accomplished.

Amelia was proud of herself for her new determination, but she was still slightly distracted by the thought of the watchful man at the back of her head. She resolved to think about it later when she could no longer enjoy being in Lucian's strong arms as they circled the dance floor.

She would have to think of some way to protect him. *Jeffrey*, Amelia resolved. She would talk to her brother about it. She would have to have a servant track him down, of course, since he still hadn't shown up for her Season. But since Jeffrey was Lucian's friend, he could be counted on to advise her in this matter. And that thought allowed her to get on with enjoying her evening.

And enjoy it she did. Curtsying and laughing and dancing throughout the night. Amelia suspected she might actually dance a hole in her slippers. She had heard of this happening, but it had never been her experience. Perhaps this was to be the night for it.

She even took some time to get to know some of the other debutantes and discovered that they weren't as awful as she had thought. Amelia had already made friends with the other wallflowers. They were each unique in their own way and had made her feel welcome from her first Society event. It was the more socially adept debutantes who were more of a challenge for her. And it was these ladies to whom she had made overtures that evening.

"Your gown is lovely," she'd complimented one young woman.

"Thank you." The other lady had simpered in a way that had almost set Amelia's teeth on edge but then the smile turned into a grin. "I actually got to have an appointment with Madame Celeste."

Amelia returned the debutante's grin. Even she, with her lack of interest in fashion, knew that an appointment with Madame Celeste herself was a coup of epic proportions.

"Did you have to promise her your firstborn?"

"Nothing quite so dire. But I suppose the depths of my father's pockets didn't hurt my chances."

Amelia laughed. She didn't think that was the only reason. Nearly every young woman present and even most of the older ladies would be willing to pay whatever price the exclusive modiste named. But Madame Celeste was extremely selective about who she would take on. After looking the other girl up and down, Amelia had to admit to the truth.

"I think it was more the look of you than your father's pocketbook. You could grace the doors of any dressmaker and look wonderful in anything they could make you."

"That is very generous of you to say." The other girl had an expression of confusion on her face, as though she couldn't understand why Amelia would say something so nice to her. Amelia merely shrugged. While she was becoming more comfortable with all this Season business, she was well aware that she was unusual. Offering an honest compliment was one of those cases. It shouldn't be unusual, but the young woman was clearly surprised by her candor.

"I'm sorry we haven't been introduced yet, which is unusual. One would think we'd be familiar with everyone at events such as these."

The other girl let out a titter of laughter that sounded nervous to Amelia's ears, and she wondered at it.

"I've barely been introduced to anyone," the other girl replied. "I'm not really one of you."

Amelia's frown must have translated clearly to the other young woman.

"My aunt is Lady St. John, but I'm not gentry. I'm only here on sufferance."

"If Lady St. John is your aunt, wouldn't that automatically mean you are, in fact, gentry?"

"She isn't even really my aunt, to be honest. She has been dearest friends with my mother since they were little girls, so she offered to take me around, but there's no blood relation."

Amelia blinked as she tried to process the information the other woman was providing. With a smile, she put out her hand to grab the other woman's.

"How do you do? My name is Lady Amelia Courtenay. My father's an earl and my brother's a baron, but you're still the one who was welcomed by Madame Celeste, so it all comes out in the wash."

The other girl stared at her for a moment before a wide grin stretched her face and she dipped into a curtsy. "It's a pleasure to make your acquaintance, Lady Amelia Courtenay. My name is Miss Caroline Smith, the most unfortunate name in all the realm, but I'm happy to meet you."

"Well, Caroline is a lovely name. And the whole point of being here is to change the last name, is it not? So, it shan't matter much longer."

"I suppose you're correct there. Although I'm not sure if my father's business acumen will be able to find me the right husband. Papa is determined to buy me a title, but I don't want it just for the sake of it even if he does. I want a husband who's at least tolerable. Surely that shouldn't be too much to ask."

Amelia frowned again as she gazed at her new friend. "I would think you ought to set your sights a little higher than tolerable, Miss Smith."

"Oh, please, do call me Caroline. And I suppose you're right, but I do hate to be disappointed."

Amelia sighed to herself. Once again, she had befriended someone who couldn't help her with her social predicament, but while she was trying to be more open minded, she didn't intend to change herself entirely. She put her hand through Caroline's elbow and steered her toward the refreshment table.

"Let us get a glass of lemonade and discuss what you might be searching for in a better than tolerable mate. Even though this is my first Season, I know nearly everyone here because my sisters have debuted and wed already, so I could probably direct you toward a few possibilities."

Caroline squeezed Amelia's hand to her side but still looked at her quizzically. "Why would you be willing to help me? Am I not someone you would consider your competition?"

Amelia frowned and glanced around the room. "I suppose that is the prevailing attitude, isn't it? That all the young ladies are competing for the few available gentlemen. But look around the room. There seems to be a nearly equal number of gentleman and ladies. And I really only need one. From what I understand, it wouldn't be legal for me to wed more than that. So as long as we are not both being courted by the same gentleman, I don't see how we could be competitors with one another. Now, if we are going to discuss having a footrace or some such, then I will gladly compete with you."

Caroline's laughter that followed Amelia's statement seemed much more genuine than previously, and Amelia filled with delight. Perhaps she could manage to have the best of both – make friends and have gentlemen display an interest in her. She found her gaze searching for Lucian as though to share her joy but was surprised to see him in conversation with the man who had been watching them. Or rather, it looked to be an argument rather than a conversation. Averting her gaze, Amelia tried not to become preoccupied with his whereabouts. Despite her insistence to Caroline that they were not in competition with one another, Amelia did feel that she had a purpose for being in Town, and she needed to concentrate on seeing it through.

She did not have time to become obsessed with the whereabouts of Viscount Adelaide.

Chapter Eleven

L ucian stared at the clerk in consternation.
"What do you mean you didn't know
Terrance was in Town? I thought you had
people tracking him at all times."

"I'm sorry, my lord. We lost track of him."

Lucian made every effort to swallow down the retort
clogging the back of his throat. It wouldn't help
anything to bellow at the young man in front of him.
And getting on the wrong side of the clerks could
actually hinder any help he might need from them in
the future, so he always did his best to restrict his
reactions in their company. But this was beyond the
pale.

"Did you not think it would be helpful, even wise, to
keep me informed of the fact that you'd lost track of
him?"

Lucian took some small amount of satisfaction in
watching the clerk swallow nervously as his eyes
flickered about the room, as though seeking assistance
from some other source.

"My lord, again, my apologies. You ought to have
been informed. But we did just learn of the fact that
we'd lost track of him. It's entirely possible that a
message has already been sent to you."

"It hasn't. My servants know where to find me." He took another deep breath to maintain control of his ire. "Never mind that. Terrance is in London, and I have seen him twice, I confronted him at a ball he had snuck into. Even when I threatened him with violence, he refused to give me any explanation. His presence at the ball leads me to believe that he is watching me. I would like to know why. Rather, I would like to have a reasonably informed idea as to why before I confront him again on the subject. Do you have any ideas or do I need to give you some time? I don't know why you don't just arrest him and throw him into Cold Bath Fields or send him off to one of the colonies. With the trouble he keeps stirring up, why is he allowed to carry on? And what ought I to do about it all?"

Again, the clerk swallowed nervously, and Lucian started to become suspicious that there were things afoot within the Home Office that he was not being kept informed on. Clearly the clerk was hiding something. And Lucian didn't think it was guilt over not telling him about Terrance.

"I will have to speak with my superiors, my lord, before I could hazard a guess."

Lucian grinned although he was far from amused in the traditional sense. He watched the other man blink in confusion. The viscount liked to keep others guessing.

"See that you do so. I will return after first light."

"First light? But my lord, that's only a few hours away."

"Well then you'd best get busy, hadn't you?" Lucian had intended to remain cordial with the clerk, but his patience was quite thin at the moment. Not only was it unacceptable that the Home Office would manage to "lose track" of someone they were supposed to keep a very close eye on and not tell Lucian about it despite his very personal involvement, but on top of that, now, the fact that Lady Amelia might be in danger . . . Lucian had no intention of allowing the matter to slide. And the entire staff at the Home Office needed to be well aware of that or he would take the matter as high as necessary. He would only bother the king as a last resort, but it wasn't out of the question if the matter wasn't resolved quickly and to his satisfaction. Lucian didn't care if he was being fanatical at this point. It was important. Amelia could be at risk. And the nation, of course.

Even as he scowled, Lucian had to chuckle at himself. Never had he been more concerned about anything than his efforts for his king and country. But here he was lambasting a clerk, even if in the politest of terms, and he knew full well that it had nothing to do with his sovereign. But he couldn't find it in himself to change direction. Amelia was family. She must be protected.

That was just a fact. It was no indication that he had developed any sort of warm feelings for her, he assured himself firmly as he strode from Whitehall in the direction of Everleigh House. As he walked, he made a mental list of all that he would need to accomplish even as he kept his eyes and ears alert to any possibility of attack. While this was a fine area, especially in the daylight, nowhere could be considered safe when one was walking about alone.

Lucian couldn't decide if he was relieved or disappointed when he reached his destination without incident. He rather thought that a violent encounter would have allowed him to vent his pent-up agitation. But he wasn't so foolish as to think his own success was guaranteed. At any moment, a ruffian with a blade could do more damage than he could handle. It was that thought that made sleep elusive every night.

This would be another night during which there would be little sleep. But at least he was now aware that

Terrance was on to them. Lucian shook his head. Someone had certainly showed a remarkable level of incompetence. He would have to speak with his superiors on that subject as well as on the subject of Lady Amelia. It was a bit of a relief. Even though he ought to have been on top of the matter, he felt slightly exonerated knowing that he wasn't the only one who had done a less than stellar effort. It hadn't been his assignment to watch Terrance at all times. He had provided the information that had caused agents to track the man. The fact that they had not done so could not be blamed on him.

If he repeated that fact several more times, perhaps he would accept it. But it mattered very little whose fault it was. If something were to happen to Amelia, he would never forgive himself for his involvement or for his lack of control over the situation.

Lucian had thought the matter of Terrance was closed. He had been looking into a series of accidents at some factories on the outer edges of London. It had been easy to pose as a potential investor, as he actually was one. Not in those particular factories, but he could have been. Terrance was involved in stirring up the workers about their work conditions. Lucian couldn't really blame them, but sabotaging the factory wasn't the way to go about it. He had been told the case was closed and the matter was handled. Now here was Terrance following him about, showing up at a ball and while he was escorting a lady in the Park. That wasn't to be borne.

Taking a seat at the small desk he had installed in his room, Lucian quickly wrote out the list he had prepared in his mind. It was at moments like this that he wished he had taken his own lodgings. He wished he could take over the library here in the family town house but Lucian could never forget that it was his father's. While the earl never bothered with coming to

Town anymore, it would be beyond presumptuous for Lucian to start using it as his own. Even though he was essentially awaiting his father's demise, he wasn't doing so gleefully and had no intention of taking the role before it was time.

Besides, his father would have apoplexy if he ever found out what his firstborn son was really doing.

Lucian had always wanted to be a soldier but because he was the heir, it had been forbidden. Working for the Home Office was the closest he was ever going to get. There was nearly as much danger and none of the acclaim, but it perfectly suited him. At least most of the time. Now that he had inadvertently involved someone he cared about, he had to question his choices. Perhaps he ought to contact his brother. Gilbert was involved in all the same things Lucian was. It was a twist of irony. Gilbert had been born the spare. It was the worst position Lucian could imagine, just as Amelia had said, but his brother seemed to take it all with aplomb. Their father had never wanted Gilbert to enlist, either, but probably would have allowed it if the young man had insisted with a little more enthusiasm. Lucian had been surprised when Gil had accepted their father's edict on the matter. If Lucian hadn't felt a sense of duty to his title, he never would have allowed their father to gainsay him. But then Gil had shown up at the Home Office one day.

"What are you doing here?" Lucian had demanded with a mixture of anger and embarrassment.

Gilbert only shrugged. "You're only so good at keeping secrets, Adelaide," he had drawled, knowing how much it irritated his older brother to be so addressed by a sibling.

"How long have you known?"

Again, Gil shrugged. "Longer than you," he had answered with a self-satisfied grin. "It was me who recommended you."

Lucian's usual control had kept his jaw from flapping open, but inside he had been filled with shock. That had been a few years ago. Now their third brother, Foster, was also involved, as well as several friends. Probably their fourth and fifth brothers would also be working for the Home Office but Ashford had gone to sea at the tender age of fifteen, and their fifth brother was still in school. At times Lucian envied the both of them, especially Roderick, since he was still at school. Lucian had frittered away his own school experience.

Raking his hand through the thick waves of his hair, Lucian sighed. Not that he was so very old himself, but he often thought that youth was wasted on the young. Then he laughed. The memory of Gilbert's statement as well as his recollection of being jealous of the youngsters lightened the difficult night he was having.

He gave his head a vigorous shake. He needed to get his concentration focused and figure out what Terrance could be thinking. Why would he make such visible contact? Clearly, he wanted Lucian to know he was there. But why? And what did it mean for Amelia? Did he have to worry as much as he was? Lucian hated the feeling of inadequacy that was dogging his thoughts. It happened to him upon occasion. Or it had when he had first signed up with the Home Office. It had started after Gilbert had informed him so gleefully that Lucian had been approached at his suggestion. And then whenever he hadn't really known what to do in a given situation no matter that others' lives depended on the decisions he made. Thankfully now, more often than not, he knew what to do, or at least his instincts were better informed.

But he was definitely experiencing that unwelcome feeling now, and he knew full well that it was because of Amelia. If he thought it would help, he would abandon her completely and have no further contact. But there was no guarantee that would keep her safe.

If he thought it was possible to convince her mother to take her home to their estate, he would choose that option. Unfortunately, he didn't think Amelia was the sweet, biddable type who would meekly retreat, at least not without being told more than he was able to tell her. And who could blame her? He wouldn't do so either.

So, he had to find out what was going on, and he had to do it all whilst traipsing through the *ton* and appearing as though he hadn't a single care in the entire world. Normally that was second nature. This time it didn't feel like that. Lucian shoved aside the unhelpful thoughts.

Going through his list, he glanced at the clock on the mantel. It was nearly the time that the servants would be stirring so he wouldn't be disturbing them too excessively when he awoke the various footmen he needed to send out with messages. He grimaced. He ought to be abed himself. If he were going to have his wits about him, at least a modicum of sleep would be required. After another glance at the clock, he assured himself that he would snatch a few hours of sleep after sending out his messengers and before returning to Whitehall.

Within a few minutes of a vigorous pull to one bell, there was a small contingent of bleary-eyed men standing before him awaiting instructions. Lucian smiled with satisfaction. He liked knowing he could count on his men. He quickly distributed his instructions, and everyone but his assistant filed out.

Thaddeus watched him similarly to how Amelia had, as though he were a specimen he was trying to understand. Lucian tried not to squirm under the examination. He raised his eyebrows in inquiry.

"You seem particularly invested in this investigation, my lord. More so than usual, that is to say."

Lucian stared at his assistant for a moment before answering, "What makes you say that?"

Thaddeus shrugged. "You never involve quite so many messengers. And I've never seen you rouse the men before daybreak."

Lucian shrugged but didn't bother answering further. He didn't have an answer to offer. He *was* more invested, but he couldn't explain the reasons. This one seemed more important or urgent than any other investigation he had yet been involved in.

Lucian hated the tingle warming his cheeks that told him a blush was trying to rise. He brazened it out, staring at his assistant with his eyebrows elevated in a haughty fashion. He was Viscount Adelaide. He needn't explain himself to the likes of Thaddeus Martin.

Thad stared back at him, unblinking for a moment before a grin broke across his face.

"You are being a right bounder, Adelaide, and well you know it. You needn't put on your airs with me, my lord. If you want to take this matter extra seriously, who am I to tell you otherwise? I was merely venting my curiosity. And I have to say, your reaction has not made that dissipate."

Lucian joined the other man's laughter.

"I can see why it wouldn't, Thad, but I haven't an answer for you."

"Which is no doubt why you tried to slay me with the Northcott stare. But never mind, I shan't tease you about it any longer. It doesn't really even matter why it matters so very much to you, in all honesty. Whatever your reasons, Terrance is still a traitor who needs to be stopped however we can. I don't understand how they could have lost him."

"He's a slippery snake, to be sure."

"And wily to boot. What are you going to do?"

"That's the imperative question, isn't it?" Lucian countered with a sigh. "We thought his trouble at the factories was to interfere with supplies, but his connections with France couldn't be proven. We need more information. I need to have at least an inkling of what the rat is after before I confront him. Or rather confront him again, since I did actually demand what he was about while at the ball this evening. He was less than helpful. But the fact that he has so brazenly shown himself tells me he's up to something and very confident of his success."

"Will you speak to the king about it?"

"Not if I can help it," Lucian replied with a laugh that lacked mirth. "His Majesty has no interest in accepting that his brother's associates are trying to destroy the progress we're making. I would really rather it be someone more important than me who has to take on the task of explaining it all to our sire. And I'm quite sure we'd all rather just deal with the matter than to involve the monarch anyway."

"Of course," Thaddeus accepted with a slight bow. "What would you have me do?"

"You have as many or even more contacts than I do. Find out what you can. And coordinate with the others as to their findings. I want as much information as possible by this afternoon."

Thaddeus's watchful gaze searched Lucian's face. "Why the sudden urgency? If you know anything that might be of use, I do wish you would share it."

Lucian stifled the foul language that threatened to erupt from his throat. "That is the problem, Thad. I don't know anything of use. And Lady Amelia might be involved."

"Surely not." Lucian appreciated that his assistant didn't ask useless questions such as *which Lady Amelia?* "Her ladyship's loyalties could never be in question."

Lucian's grin held true amusement this time. "I didn't mean she might be involved with Terrance, you numbskull. Terrance saw her in my company twice. I'm worried he might read too much into that."

"I see." By the man's tone, Lucian was afraid that he really did see, far more than he was comfortable with. He only hoped his face was as impassive as it was reputed to be.

"Don't you bother reading more into it than necessary, either," he admonished. "As Jeffrey's sister, I owe it to her to ensure she is safe."

"But why would you suspect Terrance would even think anything of her?"

"I am never in the company of the same chit more than once."

"And why were you this time, my lord?" The laughter evident in Thaddeus's tone set his teeth on edge, but he couldn't fault the man for his amusement. If it weren't himself in the current dilemma, he'd probably find it amusing, too.

"Like I said, she's Jeffrey's sister." Even he could hear the bite in his tone, but he didn't much care.

"Very well, my lord. I will get right to work." He paused for a moment with another one of his thoroughly searching expressions. "If I might be so bold, might I recommend that you get a little rest before you carry on?"

"Looking a little peaked, am I, Thad?"

His assistant merely grinned and nodded. "You'll be of much more use to yourself if you aren't too tired."

"I cannot argue with you there." Lucian nodded, and the other man left the room. After his assistant left the library, Lucian slumped back in his chair, exhaustion overtaking him. The other man was right; he needed to rest.

Chapter Twelve

Amelia stared unseeing out the window of her father's carriage, listening with only half an ear as her mother chattered about Amelia's sudden success on the Marriage Mart. She was aware that a half smile was playing about her lips. She wasn't disappointed by her success that evening, to say the least. But she was too distracted by her concern for Lucian to really appreciate it.

She bit her thumb as she tried to puzzle it through. Having danced half the night away, Amelia was painfully aware that her powers of analysis were probably not as keen as usual. But she ought to be able to put her finger on what was bothering her so much about that strange man who had been staring at them while she danced with Viscount Adelaide. With a sigh, she realized she couldn't concentrate sufficiently with her mother's chatter buzzing in her ear. Usually, she could manage to do both at once quite nicely but not this night. She supposed her head had been turned just as well as the next debutante.

Turning to her mother with a grin, Amelia finally interjected.

"Yes, Mother, it was all quite delightful, you are absolutely correct. But I am far too wound up and yet excited to be able to concentrate on what you are saying just now. I know it is quite important to consider the matter of portions and all that, but for tonight, I just want to savour the experience, if you don't mind."

Lady Hanley blinked and stared at her daughter as though she didn't quite understand what she was saying, but then she finally returned Amelia's smile.

"Quite right, my dear. Of course, you ought to enjoy the moment of your success. Don't mind me and my fidgets. I'll try to rein in my excitement."

"I appreciate your excitement, Mother, truly. But I had no idea dancing could be quite this tiring."

Lady Hanley's affectionate smile grew. "I am happy for you to have finally found it enjoyable, my dear. You did enjoy it, didn't you?"

"Immensely, much to my surprise."

They both laughed and then blessedly lapsed into silence for the rest of the short drive. They had been amongst the last to leave the ball for the first time in Amelia's experience. As a result, the streets were far less busy than usual. Amelia rather suspected that the sun might be about to rise. She tried to swallow the yawn that threatened to burst forth but wasn't completely successful.

"Never fear, my dear. It is not a faux pas to yawn in front of your mother. I've seen you in nappies, after all."

Her mother's words surprised a sleepy chuckle out of Amelia even as her mind churned away at her concerns.

"But you were the one who told me never to be caught yawning," she protested around another of the sleepy gestures.

Lady Hanley smiled gently. "That was for Society, not family, and well you should have known it."

Amelia bobbed a nod at her mother. The older woman was right. She ought to have known it. She was so often far too literal about things. Amelia supposed it was a by-product of being of a scientific bent. But if she was going to get herself involved in the trickier side of politics, she was going to have to cure herself of that tendency.

But first, she needed to figure out why the man at the ball had so offset her equilibrium. It hadn't marred her enjoyment of the evening. She was still grinning over just how many times she had danced that night. But memories of the man's watchful gaze had tickled the back of her mind even as she had amused herself by dancing the night away. And now, even though she was on the verge of falling asleep, she couldn't shake the feeling that she ought to know more than she did.

As they pulled up in front of her father's townhouse, Amelia gave her head a shake. She was far too tired to puzzle it out tonight. She would figure it out in the morning, she assured herself as she followed her mother up the stairs and was delivered into the care of her lady's maid.

"I do apologize for keeping you up, Sarah."

Her maid merely snorted. "Milady, it's right ridiculous for you to be apologizing to me seeing as it's my job to take care of you."

"But we don't usually stay out quite this late," Amelia protested sleepily.

"I can only guess that means you were enjoying yourself for the first time, and I cannot be disappointed."

"You are too good to me."

"Not at all. Now sit down before you fall down, and I'll get your curls brushed out and into a plait so you can sleep comfortable for the night."

"Nothing will interfere with my sleep this night. I'm just that tired."

"That may be, but you won't be thanking me in the morning if your hair is a bird's nest of snarls, will you?"

Amelia giggled but protested. "Please, not a hundred strokes tonight."

"Of course not."

Since Amelia and her maid had played together as small children, there was little formality between them. It was a comfortable situation for the daughter of the house to have as her maid the housekeeper's granddaughter. But it occasionally struck Amelia as strange that her childhood friend was servant while she was served.

"Are you happy, Sarah?"

"What a strange question, my lady. Did you get tipsy at that ball of yours this evening?"

"Not in the least. I simply want to know. Are you happy?"

There was barely a hitch in the rhythmic strokes as the maid continued to brush her mistress's hair.

"Are you getting all philosophical again, Lady Amelia? You were wont to do that when we were girls on occasion."

"And I'd like to know why you're avoiding my question."

"I'm not avoiding it — I'm wondering what prompted it. Are you worried about me being your servant all of a sudden?"

Amelia lifted her shoulder in a lopsided shrug, which her maid took as an affirmative answer.

"You are just as ridiculous as ever you were, my lady. I've never wished to be more than I was. It was fun to be your friend when we were girls and you would filch cakes from the kitchen for us and we'd climb trees and such. But I always knew where I was headed. And to be honest, I don't think my lot is harder than yours. Seems to me you have far more rules to keep track of than I do. And we have great fun below stairs. Perhaps even more than you do at your grand balls and events. So yes, I suppose I'm happy. I just don't think most people go about wondering about their happiness."

Amelia saw her sleepy grin in the reflection as Sarah finished with her hair. The servant was right; Amelia was thinking too hard about everything. And it wasn't resulting in any good when she was so very tired. She would have to leave it until the morning.

Sarah helped her up into her high bed. Amelia was nearly asleep even as she was snuggling under the warm covers, but then her eyes popped open. Her brain had figured it out without her. She had seen that man before. That was why he had bothered her so much. It was the same man who had been watching them in the Park. But why?

She would have to investigate. A thrill shivered up her spine. How exciting. She loved to make investigations.

As she had thought, she would need her brother's help on this one, since it was obvious to her that Lucian didn't want to talk about it. There was no way he hadn't put the two incidents together. So, it was evident that he was keeping it from her for a reason. Even as she was falling into slumber, she had to sleepily admit that he was under no obligation to confide in her. But she truly wished he would. She would have to think about that strange encumbrance in the morning.

What felt like the blink of an eye later, Sarah was delivering Amelia's chocolate, and late morning sunlight was streaming around the edges of the drawn curtains. She threw back her bed clothes with a grin and sat up.

"Oy, my lady, I never meant to wake you."

Amelia's grin widened. "Then why are you here with my chocolate?"

The maid returned her smile. "Well, I did think it about time that you would be waking. It's unlike you to sleep this late."

"Well, I also never stay quite that late at any ball or event. But whether you meant to wake me or not, I'm pleased to be awake and am fairly certain I've slept enough. I have remembered what I was thinking about as I fell to sleep last night and have much to do."

"Well you shan't be doing it before you've broken your fast, milady. You know how you can get."

Amelia grinned again. Her maid was usually the one who bore the brunt of her ill temper whenever she got so caught up in something that she missed meals. Amelia appreciated Sarah's persistence in keeping her fed, even if it was just toast and chocolate. Or perhaps especially when it was just toast and chocolate. Amelia sighed as she took a bite of the crispy bread, toasted to the exact hue she preferred. It was nearly dripping from the generous portion of butter that had been slathered upon it. After her exertions on the ballroom floor the night before, she certainly needed some sustenance that morning. She probably ought to even descend to the breakfast room and have something a touch more substantive, but she really needed to send off a message to her brother before she got distracted.

"Could you please bring me a pencil and a scrap of paper? I must make a list before I forget."

Sarah did as she was bidden, but she also pinned her mistress with an examining stare. "What are you up to now, milady? I thought you'd left all your studies behind."

"Well, I've found new things to study now, I have to admit," Amelia shared with her friend. "I wish to learn all I can about the running of this great nation."

Sarah stared at her as though she had lost her mind, making Amelia laugh lightly.

"I know you are probably questioning my sanity even more than usual right at this moment, aren't you?"

Sarah grinned unrepentantly and didn't bother denying it.

"Well, I don't really blame you. But I'm not so foolish as to think that I could actually be in the government, so do not trouble yourself. But I think I could be a support in some way. Really, it doesn't do any good to complain about something if you aren't willing to try to make changes, does it?"

Sarah's expression grew dubious. "I haven't really heard you complain about anything except the Season, milady, and I doubt the government is going to be able to do anything about gossips or fashion."

Amelia's laughter rang out again.

"No, Sarah, you're probably right there. But that wasn't what I meant. It has been pointed out to me that the Season is tied in to the sitting of Parliament, not the other way around. Parliament isn't for the Season; the Season is for Parliament. Do you see what I mean?"

The maid's nod was hesitant, but Amelia carried on. "Anyhow, I'm still learning, and perhaps I'll change my mind about trying to be involved in any way, but it does completely alter my view of my time here in Town and has changed my thoughts about what I hope my future might contain. I need to think about it a little more, and you know that writing it out always helps me." She paused for a moment before adding, "But there was something else, too, that I need to look into. I think Adelaide might be in some sort of trouble, and I need to find Jeffrey and enlist his help."

Sarah's sharp gaze settled on her mistress. "What are you getting yourself into now, milady? You aren't going to be walking into danger, are you?"

Amelia shrugged. "Unlikely." But she didn't seem at all disturbed by the prospect as she tapped her chin with her pencil and stared off toward the window. Sarah didn't bother to offer any further recriminations. She had the good sense to know her mistress would not be gainsaid by her if she had her mind set on a certain course. Amelia stifled a smile. No doubt the servant was trusting that the baron could influence his sister if the need arose.

Chapter Thirteen

"So, what have you gotten yourself into this time?"

"I beg your pardon?" Lucian stood up from behind his desk with a grin, moving around it in order to clap an arm around his best friend's shoulders, surprised to see that he was accompanied by Foster, Lucian's brother. "To what do I owe the pleasure of a visitation from the two of you?"

"Amelia." Jeffrey offered the one word answer as though it would explain everything. In some ways, it did, but Lucian still puzzled over it.

"You might need to elaborate slightly," he drawled wryly.

"She sent servants out looking for me with an urgent message that you were in some sort of dire predicament. She was short on details but generous with the dramatics as she seemed to be trying to convey some sort of message without actually revealing anything. It was almost as though she was trying to be subtle," Jeffrey added with a chuckle. "As you are well aware, that is not her strong suit. But it was enough to have me hotfooting it to Town. As Foster happened to be with me when I received the message, I shared its contents with him, and he agreed to join me."

"And what do you two think you're going to be able to do?"

Jeffrey shrugged. "We don't even know what she was on about. But what we were doing wasn't terribly urgent, and it seemed my sister was wrought up about something, so we couldn't not come."

"Couldn't leave a lady in distress," Lucian's brother added with a grin.

Lucian laughed. "If you think the lady is in distress then why are you in my library instead of in Lady Hanley's drawing room?"

Jeffrey grinned but offered another shrug. "Amelia's cryptic message implied the trouble was with you. That you were in some sort of grave danger. It was all highly diverting, and we thought you'd enjoy the joke. Or if there was truth to any of it, you could use a hand. Either way, it seemed sensible to get the information from you rather than her."

Lucian frowned. "Did you think she couldn't explain herself?"

"Amelia is quite capable of explaining herself in a great amount of detail. But since her concern seemed to be with you, here we are. I want to know what you've been doing with my sister."

Lucian's eyebrows headed toward his hairline at his best friend's tone before a low chuckle finally chased away his threatening anger. "Are you here to warn me away from paying my addresses to your sister, my lord?" he asked with a haughty tilt to his head.

"That all depends on whether or not you're toying with the girl's affections."

Lucian sighed, allowing the jesting to fall aside. "Tell me exactly what she said."

"It was a trifle roundabout, so I cannot tell you exactly, as she was clearly trying to be cryptic. But from what we could understand, there was some sort of incident at the Park and at a ball that involved you and some stranger. And this led her to believe you are in danger. I cannot fathom where she would have come up with the idea nor how she felt it involved her, but I was surprised enough to hear you had been squiring her around and curious to know how she came by her conclusions."

Lucian stared at his friend and his brother and wondered if he ought to brazen it out and refuse their help. Very little thought was required to realize he couldn't afford to reject assistance. It would be foolishness on his part to allow his pride to lead to further danger or damage.

With a sigh, Lucian nodded. "I don't actually believe I'm in any danger, as I am well able to look after myself, but I can't be sorry that you're here, as there is the slightest possibility Amelia might be in danger."

"I beg your pardon?" Now all joviality had left Jeffrey, and he was staring at his friend with a little less affection. "How could you have allowed her to get wrapped up in one of your starts?"

"It was certainly not intentional," Lucian scoffed. "And for your information, this is not just some whim of mine. Terrance is a very real danger to the nation. We aren't yet certain if it's France or one of the dukes backing him, but he's certainly trouble. And he knows about me. So, he's trouble for me, as well."

"Amelia didn't think he looked threatening."

"Looks can be deceiving; surely you ought to realize that," Lucian answered quietly. He had no wish to alarm his friend, but it was very well possible that Amelia could be in danger. It had been Lucian's greatest fear. That fear had been interfering with his concentration. While he was annoyed that his friend and his brother were both there trying to meddle in his affairs, if they could be counted on to protect Amelia, that would free Lucian to truly focus on stopping whatever Terrance might be plotting this time. Because this wasn't Lucian's first encounter with the man. Lucian couldn't understand it nor explain it, but the bounder had a profound determination to oppose any advancement. It seemed to Lucian that Terrance would be happy if the nation reverted back to the feudal system where they all lived in huts and served the few landowners who controlled everything. It was an odd wish considering Terrance wasn't a landowner. It would make far more sense for Lucian to wish for that, since his family was comfortably ensconced on a very large piece of England. But Lucian was determined to assist his fellow countrymen to embrace development. One of those developments was for people to become educated and enabled to control their own futures. Technology, he was certain, was going to assist with that. One of those technologies was the steam engine. But Terrance and his cohorts were doing their best to interfere with anything involving the engine, from the small factories producing them to the trains that were using them. And the king's brother was helping them in their endeavors.

Lucian thought they had arrested most of Terrance's companions and had the man himself under tight watch. With Terrance's powerful connections, his own arrest had been prevented. But now he was in London, and Lucian didn't know what he was after next. There were any number of possibilities. Lucian wanted to confront him directly and immediately. His worry for Amelia had prevented that at the ball, but now he was free to do so. He grinned, and it felt much more comfortable on his face this time as he realized some of his care had been lifted.

"Thank you for coming, Hastings. You, too, Frost. I hadn't thought to ask you, Jeffrey, but I'm glad the chit thought of it. And, Foster, I had meant to write to you myself, so this is quite providential."

Jeffrey grunted, seemingly unsure how to respond to his friend. Likely torn between his duties as big brother and best friend, he finally settled on, "That chit's my sister, so speak well of her."

Lucian's grin widened. "Have you been fed and looked after upon your arrival in Town or ought I to ring for some provisions?"

"I suppose I ought to drop in on my mother and let her know I'm finally in Town. She has been hounding me for weeks that I ought to be squiring my sister about, but I hadn't wanted to respond before now."

Lucian's smile dimmed. "You should have attended to her from the beginning. Do you know Amelia fancied herself a wallflower? You could have stopped such foolishness instead of my having to do it, and now she's embroiled in my activities."

Jeffrey's gaze narrowed. "What are you on about? I thought you said she wasn't embroiled."

Lucian sighed. "Amelia was struggling. The Season isn't quite right for her temperament. We discussed it at length, and I believe it helped her gain a different perspective, but it was because we spent time together on two occasions. The fact that she was observed in my company and the fact that she has such a keen sense of curiosity combined to get her involved. You know how she can be. There was nothing I could have done to prevent it since I didn't know the bounder was in Town."

Jeffrey looked nearly as confused by the end of Lucian's speech as he had at the beginning of it, but the anger had cleared from his face. "You're right, I do know how she can be. You're also right, considering that I should have been here from the beginning. So, while I cannot allow you to involve her in any way, I do appreciate that it has brought me to this realization."

Lucian stared at his friend. A part of him wanted to whither the other man for his daftness, but he knew how it could be as the oldest sibling, so he tried not to judge Jeffrey too harshly. As a man without sisters, Lucian couldn't judge his friend even though he himself thought he would have been glued to the side of a little sister making her debut.

He gave his head a shake. He was starting to suspect that he wasn't the least bit rational when it came to Lady Amelia. That shouldn't be. He needed his head straight and his mind focused if he was to get to the bottom of whatever Terrance had going on.

"Very well, gentlemen, if you will excuse me then, I have many matters to deal with."

Foster grinned, but there was an edge to it. "Did you think to exclude us, then, Adelaide?"

Lucian frowned. "What are you on about now?"

"We didn't come just to say hello. Even if her ladyship is daft, she is concerned about you and nothing I've yet seen has led me to believe there wasn't some truth behind her worries. You aren't in a position to dismiss us. We're going to help you."

Denial rose in Lucian's throat at his brother's words, but he managed to keep the words behind his teeth. He was man enough to admit that it was his pride that wanted to speak, not his reason.

"What do you think you can contribute, little brother?"

Foster flushed but refused to back down. "You can get all up on your high horse all you want, Adelaide. You're still my brother even if you think I'm a useless cub. I aim to assist you however I can. You might be a viscount and our father's heir, but you're still a Northcott."

Lucian was impressed by the younger man's tenacity and finally admitted both to himself and his companions that he needed help.

"The problem is that I don't know what to do. I've not found myself in quite this position before. It is far from comfortable."

"Well, I have plenty of experience being in that position, so I will guide you in how to navigate it," Foster replied with a chuckle.

"You two figure out a plan while I go check in with my family and make sure Amelia is staying put. I'll return shortly."

Lucian watched his friend leave the room before turning to his brother. "How did you two end up being together when he received a note from his sister?"

Frost shrugged. "We were looking at one of our investments."

Lucian blinked. "You have investments?"

Foster chuckled, seemingly not offended by his brother's surprise. "I do," he admitted. "We cannot all have it handed to us on a platter," he continued before laughing again as Lucian's face filled with fury. "You are far too easy to goad today, Adelaide. Have you a fever?"

Lucian shook his head and dismissed his brother's words. "Never mind about my foolishness. I'll want to hear all about your investments when this matter is behind us. I'm intrigued to say the least. But this matter must take precedence for a time."

"Of course. If it's a national matter, that would be far more important than the few quid I might be involved in."

Lucian smiled his gratitude and accepted that his brother might be able to lend some assistance. He never worked with others, so it was an odd sensation that he was surprised to identify as relief to be able to share the burden.

"Tell me, what have you done so far?"

Lucian slipped into an explanation of that morning's activities. "I'm due back at Whitehall now. It's good that you're here, as my men might return with news. I had thought to have my assistant deal with it, but he is likely to be of more use elsewhere. You can stay here to receive any intelligence there might be and save it for my return."

His brother didn't argue although his eyes lit up at hearing his brother's destination.

"I'll take you with me another time if that is your interest."

Foster bobbed a bow and sent him off with a grin. No further words were needed.

Chapter Fourteen

"Jeffrey," Amelia squealed before the butler could announce him. "What are you doing here? I've been pining for you, and there was no word of your arrival."

"Did you not summon me, Button?"

Amelia's delight in her brother's appearance dimmed with his use of the wretched pet name, but she rallied and threw her arms around his neck despite her irritation.

"Your note did sound urgent. But I offer you my apologies, my lady. I ought to have been here for the beginning of your Season just as Mother asked. But why didn't you ask me yourself?"

Amelia flushed a little under her brother's question. "For one thing, I thought I would make a delightfully successful debut without anyone's help. For another, I didn't want to bother you with my little issues. If you didn't want to come to Town, I didn't want to try to make you."

"So then why summon me now?"

Amelia frowned at her brother. "Was my message too cryptic, Jeffrey? I thought I had been reasonably clear. I asked you here, not for me, but for Lucian. I mean Viscount Adelaide," she added at the end,

116

remembering Lucian's admonition that she ought to be less informal.

Jeffrey mirrored her frown. "So, it isn't true what Adelaide implied? You haven't been having a rough time with your Season?"

Amelia laughed. "Oh that? No, Lucian fixed that for me," she answered lightly with a wave of her hand as though it were a matter of no consequence. She laughed again when she saw her brother's eyebrows draw together in a frown. She quickly elaborated. "Truly, Jeff, there's naught to be concerned about. I didn't take right at first, but Lord Adelaide helped me considerably. I asked you to come to help him, not me."

"So, tell me, in your own words, what makes you think he needs help? While I understood your note, it was scant on details besides the fact that you were obviously trying hard not to reveal anything."

Amelia grinned. "I was quite pleased with myself, to admit the truth."

Finally, Jeffrey laughed. "I can see that, Button. But get to the point. If there truly is some sort of trouble afoot, I wish to be apprised of it immediately."

"Very well, do take a seat. Shall I ring for refreshments?"

Jeffrey cleared his throat and cast his sister a significant look. "Are you dithering for a reason, Ames?"

Amelia laughed again, but this time it sounded nervous. "Perhaps a little. To be frank, I'm not sure if I allowed my imagination to run away with me or not. It was a feeling. A gut feeling, as you would say. There was this man. He just looked out of place. I saw him twice. Both times, I was in Lord Adelaide's company by coincidence. Or perhaps not coincidence at all. How would I truly know? Perhaps he was always about and it just so happened that I noticed him both times while in Lucian's company because my senses were heightened. I cannot say for certain on that score, which makes me hesitate to admit any of it despite having summoned you here. But it was really his lordship's reaction that caused me to think there was more to it. He tried to play it off that he hadn't even noticed the man when you and I both know that Luce never misses any details. It had seemed like a fun trick when we were children, but I think it's a remarkable skill. You know he never misses anything. So, the fact that he denied it made me suspicious. And that, combined with my own instinctive reaction to the stranger, made me reach out to you."

Amelia sighed and cast a beseeching look at her brother.

"Don't be angry with me if I've sent for you needlessly, Jeffrey. It couldn't be helped. I do apologize if I've wasted your time, but I didn't think it ought to be left to chance. What if I'm really right?"

"No, don't apologize. You did the right thing sending for me, and I thank you for it. Really, as I said, I ought to have been here already, so never mind your reasons, I'm glad I'm here. And I can see why you were suspicious from what you've said."

"Have you seen him already?"

Jeffrey started at her words, and Amelia delighted to see a slight pink tinge her brother's cheeks. His face was sheepish as he nodded and could barely meet her gaze. "I went there first."

"As well you should, since I told you he might be in danger."

"Did you really believe Adelaide might be in danger?" Jeffrey demanded.

Amelia shrugged and sighed, casting her glance out the window onto the busy street. "It was a feeling, Jeffrey. And yes, it felt like danger. I cannot explain it. I'm sure Adelaide is skilled in all manner of ways to protect himself. And that other man appeared to be smaller than him and no doubt far less of a sportsman. But it was Adelaide's reaction that made me suspicious more than anything."

Jeffrey nodded. "If it makes you feel any better, I don't think your suspicions were wrong. I don't know exactly what is going on, but there is obviously something afoot. So, thank you for the summons. Will you be fine if I leave you here and return to Adelaide to see what I can do?"

"Of course." Amelia scoffed lightly. "I'm not involved in this, really. I just thought to involve others," she added with a grin. That grin slowly faded under her brother's heavy stare. "What is it, Jeffrey? You look odd all of a sudden."

"I am afraid that you might be involved more than you would think."

"How could that be? I don't know who that man is. I don't have yours or Lucian's power of taking everything in at a glance. I have to study things for lengthy periods to make it stick in my mind. I couldn't even properly describe him to you, except perhaps for the strange way he had been dressed at the ball."

"That isn't the problem, my dear. Adelaide is concerned that because you have been seen in his company twice in close succession, you might be involved no matter your good intention."

Amelia narrowed her eyes at her brother even as a tingle of excitement tried to shiver its way up her shoulder blades. She really ought not be thrilled by this turn of events, but somehow, she couldn't help it. Her boring existence was being turned on its head.

"What are you trying to tell me, Jeffrey? Or rather, what are you leaving out?"

"I don't think you ought to leave the house unescorted until this has been straightened out."

"I never leave the house unescorted. I'm a debutante," Amelia countered with a roll of her eyes.

"I mean to say that you need more of an escort than your country bred maid. Do not leave this house without at least one footman in tow."

"Is that not excessive, Jeffrey? Surely there's nothing that could befall me."

Jeffrey shook his head at his sister's naïveté. "There is plenty that could befall you, Button. Don't be daft. Be glad that I haven't said you aren't to leave the house at all. Now, promise me."

Amelia sighed as dramatically as she could even while rolling her eyes just like she would have as a twelve-year-old, thus producing the desired effect in her brother. When he was smiling at her with amusement rather than staring at her with worry, she nodded her acceptance. "Very well, brother dear, I shan't leave the doors without a footman or someone even burlier. Like you. Surely you don't expect me to send my regrets for the evening's entertainments."

"No, our mother would most definitely have my head for that. I need to be off. I'll return as quickly as I can. I shall escort you myself this evening. And then hopefully, Adelaide will have his matters sorted quickly."

Amelia watched her brother hurry from the room as she tapped her chin and frowned. She hadn't wanted to ask Jeffrey how she could help, as he would surely tell her that she needed to just stay home safe and sound. *But how would that help?* No, Amelia had to do something. She'd never been one to sit idly by no matter the situation. With a nod, she quit the room, hurrying to her bedchamber for a change of clothing.

Within minutes, she had her maid buttoning her into a walking dress. Amelia was relieved that her personal servant was as glad for some activity as she was.

"We shall both need to bundle up, as there seemed to be a bit of a bite to the air when last I checked." Sarah chattered eagerly even as she plunged a few more pins into her mistress's hair to hold it in place for their exertions.

"We also need to summon a footman to accompany us," Amelia tossed out as Sarah was about to leave the room to gather her own outerwear. The maid cast her an inquisitive glance. Amelia shrugged. "Jeffrey's orders. Apparently, debutantes are to be cosseted and protected." She hadn't yet told her maid all the details about her suspicions. She didn't actually have any details to tell. Amelia had found it challenging enough to explain to Jeffrey what had prompted her summons. She didn't know how she would be able to explain it to Sarah.

But the young servant was too eager to leave the house to question her mistress beyond the curious expression. Within moments, there were three of them traipsing down the front steps of the Earl of Hanley's London townhouse. All three had varying expressions of delight covering their faces. Amelia was determined to find something useful at the Park, and her two servants were pleased to leave their usual responsibilities behind for the chance at some fresh air outside the house.

A sense of purpose filled her as she marched toward the Park, but her steps started to lag as she realized just how far it was. Even though she was country bred and traipsed all over the countryside at home, Amelia started to realize her mother might think it inappropriate for her to walk this far. She rolled her eyes at her dithering. It mattered very little if she walked or rode. It would take the same amount of time with the amount of traffic there was at this time of the day, and she was quite convinced that a walk wouldn't fatigue her for her evening's activities, which she knew would be her mother's concern. Besides, she had slept quite late. And she would only be a mess of nervous tension if she stayed at home.

With a decisive nod, she reassured herself this was the best use of her time, and she quickened her footsteps with renewed zeal as she saw the gates to the Park come into view ahead of her. While it would look quite different on foot than it had perched high on Lord Adelaide's tall carriage, Amelia was certain she would be able to find the spot where she had seen the strange man standing.

"What are we looking for, milady?"

Amelia's lips twisted in frustration. She was almost certain they had found the spot, and it hadn't been very long that she had been scouring the area, but the maid and footman clearly thought she had lost her mind. And how was she to explain it to them?

"I'm not completely certain what we're looking for, to be honest with you. I just think I'll know it when we find it."

Both servants cast her nearly equally quizzical expressions, but they dutifully resumed staring at the ground. Amelia had tried to think of a plausible explanation in case any of her or her mother's friends were to come upon them. She had determined she would claim to have lost an earring. It would explain why they were searching the ground. Or so she hoped. But she really hoped they would find something and not have to explain themselves to anyone.

Thus far, they had found a button with a tuft of fabric still attached, which made Amelia think it had been wrenched off rather than fallen off. But the colour didn't match what the man had been wearing the day he had been watching Lucian. She kept it but was dismayed to think it was of no relevance. The footman had also found a small torn off scrap of paper with what appeared to be an address on it. Amelia was far more hopeful about that, as it would lead to somewhere else they could search for clues. Sarah had spent more time fussing over Amelia than actually searching the ground, but Amelia couldn't fault her. She was probably being unforgivably daft. But she needed to feel occupied in the matter.

"What are you up to, my lady?"

The politely worded question in the rough voice made Amelia nearly start out of her skin as she whirled to see who had so spoken to her. She had been staring so intently at what appeared to be a burned spot on the trunk of a tree that she hadn't notice the man's approach. But it was him. The man she had been hoping to find clues of. Her heart lodged itself in her throat as, for a moment, fear threatened to overwhelm her. But she swallowed it down and lifted her chin, reminding herself that she was a fearless young woman and a Courtenay besides; there was nothing this man could do to her.

"I lost my earring while in the Park the other day. I have quite sentimental reasons for wishing to have it back. You haven't by any chance noticed an earring lying about have you?"

She was quite proud of her composure even as the man sneered at her.

"You think to find an earring that you lost in all this large park? Do you really think I'm going to believe that?"

Fear again rose in her throat, but Amelia intended to brazen it out. She forced a shrug that she hoped seemed unconcerned.

"I don't know you, sir, so I don't really much care what you believe. I thought you were offering your assistance. If you are not, you may be on your way."

The man stared at her for a moment as a grin spread across his face. "I can see why he likes you."

Now Amelia was really becoming nervous. The man's presence wasn't overtly threatening, so even though her servants had both noticed she was talking to him, they had continued on with their activities. Amelia couldn't decide if she were relieved or disappointed. She hoped to rid herself of the man without the need for a scene, so she supposed it was best if it appeared to be a simple exchange. On the other hand, though, because she did feel threatened by this simple looking man, she wished her footman had thought to approach her. Did he not realize he was there to protect her? She couldn't allow herself to be distracted by her own thoughts.

"If you think I'm daft for searching, you needn't concern yourself with me. I'll thank you for your interest but wish you a good day."

"You are a bold one, my lady, but I won't be dismissed so readily. I think it best if you come with me."

"I'll do no such thing," she countered firmly, raising her voice just enough that both Sarah and the footman looked up and were watching intently.

"It was wise of you to bring servants, but it doesn't seem you've brought enough for this foolish errand, girl. I'll easily be able to overpower the three of you."

Amelia almost mistook the meaning of his words, as they were offered in such a pleasant tone of voice, as though he were merely discussing the weather. When his threat sank in, her stomach clenched with nerves, but she kept her chin raised as she stared at him as haughtily as she could manage.

"What are you on about, sir? I begin to suspect you have confused me with someone else."

"I'm not confused in the least, my lady. Now, come along. It's best you don't make a scene. If you make it out of this situation, you wouldn't want your reputation soiled in any way, I'm sure."

"As I said, I shan't be going anywhere with you. We have not even been introduced. Now please, pass on. I am expected elsewhere." After a beat of time, she added, "After I find my earring, of course." She turned away from the man to address her servants. "Have either of you found any trace of my earring?"

Both of her servants started coming closer, but then she heard a sharp sound beside her. A quick glance toward the man showed he had pulled out a small gun.

"Tell them to keep searching or I'll shoot you."

Amelia's breath caught in her throat, and she felt the press of illness threatening to erupt as her stomach clenched in fear at the sight before her. Once more, she swallowed it all down and addressed the man.

"Have you run quite mad? What is the meaning of this?"

"You have insinuated yourself into my business, my lady, and I cannot allow that."

"How in heaven's name have I done that?" she demanded, her temper overtaking her fear for a moment. "I am quite clearly minding my own business, not yours. I don't even know you."

"Ah yes, the lost earring. It was a fairly good story, my lady. It would have worked for anyone else but me. I know you saw me in this very spot. And I know you weren't doing anything that could have possibly dislodged an earring."

Amelia blinked and cast about in her mind to think of some other stratagem.

"I've found it, my lady," her footman called out to her as he held up something that seemed to sparkle in the sunlight.

"Oh, thank you ever so much, Thomas," she shouted back as she wrenched herself out of the man's hand and hurried toward the strong servant, ignoring her fear about the gun in the stranger's hand. She was taking a chance that he wouldn't actually wish to draw the attention of a gunshot in the crowded park.

Catching hold of Sarah's arm as she scurried past her toward the footman, Amelia put as much distance between herself and the strange man as possible. The footman caught Amelia's arm and took off with a swift stride.

"My apologies, my lady, for manhandling you, but I couldn't think of another way to get you out of there short of throwing myself upon his gun and screaming at you to run."

Amelia grinned despite her fear. "No, Thomas, this was much better. I am impressed with your quick thinking. I didn't even realize you would have noticed his gun, to be honest, and was cudgelling my brain trying to think of a plan when you solved the problem all right and tight."

"Not completely right and tight. Home is still much too far off," Thomas muttered. "And in answer to your question, I would recognize the sound of a gun cocking anywhere. It is not a sound I wish to hear in connection with my mistress, nor in a public park like that ever again."

Amelia offered him a smile of thanks even as the air was giving out in her lungs. "A hackney. Let us hail a hackney," she blurted out between gasps, even as the footman acted on her words. Within a moment, he had both his mistress and her maid bundled into a cab and hurrying away from the Park toward her family's home.

"I thank you, sincerely, again, Thomas. I don't know what would have become of me without your quick thinking," Amelia stammered out, even as her maid was exclaiming over the sudden turn of events.

"But what could have ever prompted you to act so, Thomas?" Sarah demanded. "Surely, Lady Hanley won't appreciate that you put your hands upon her daughter."

"He saved our lives, Sarah," Amelia answered baldly but with as calm a tone as she could muster.

"What are you on about now, milady?"

"I beg that you don't tell anyone else in the household, but that man who was speaking with me had threatened me with a gun."

"No!" Sarah gasped. "But why?" She had clearly been too preoccupied with trying to keep up with them to have paid attention to Thomas and Amelia's words previously.

"I don't rightly know. But we will soon find out." She turned to the footman. "Thomas, I know you want to see us safely home, but I think it's best if we find my brother and Viscount Adelaide and tell them exactly what we just witnessed."

"It would be best if you returned home, my lady. You'll be safest there."

"That may be true, but I think we ought to first tell them, so they can act as quickly as possible."

"I could see you home and then find them, my lady."

"They would probably agree with your determination, but if any of you think I'm going to be left out of this, then you don't know me very well after all."

The footman grinned at his mistress even as he bowed to her and then turned to alter their destination with the hackney driver. Within minutes, they were being put down in front of Everleigh House.

"Thank you, Thomas. Do you think you ought to see Sarah home and I could just go in and explain what has happened?"

"Don't be daft, milady. It doesn't matter if I'm nearly in hysterics. I shan't be leaving you to so scandalous an action. It's bad enough you being here with the two of us to lend you countenance. You're just lucky his lordship hasn't taken his own lodgings. It's barely respectable, you coming to his family's home knowing as he's the only one likely to be in residence, and there's nary a female in the family besides."

Despite her own jangling nerves, Amelia had to laugh over her maid's jumbled statement. She didn't argue further and preceded her two servants up the steps to knock briskly upon the door.

Being a large, well-staffed house, they weren't left standing long, despite the surprise that was clearly evident on the butler's face. Amelia supposed it wasn't often a gently bred young woman presented herself on their front step. The thought made her smile despite the dire nature of her call.

"I'd like to speak with Viscount Adelaide, if you please. And Baron Hastings, if he happens to be about," she added, thus surprising the butler further.

"Are you Lady Amelia?" he asked with some surprise.

"I am," she answered simply, surprised that he would sound almost as though he expected her.

"Very well, if you'll follow me," he began. "Your servants can await you here or in the kitchen," he added.

"If it's all the same to you, I'd prefer if they accompany me. We have some things we need to tell their lordships."

"All of you?" the butler demanded, clearly unused to this sort of activity in his home.

"Yes," Amelia answered simply, not prepared to brook any argument.

She thought she heard him sigh, but he led the trio forward anyway, possibly against his best judgment. Amelia was pleased that she didn't need to insist any further.

Lucian was standing by one of the tall windows that allowed light to stream into the receiving room that he seemed to have commandeered for his own use. The glance he sent them as they filed into his presence was one only fit for the future Earl of Everleigh. Amelia's stomach dipped as his eyebrows rose to reveal his haughty surprise. She could almost read his thoughts. She was fairly certain he was thinking something along the lines of how dare she intrude upon his time. Her lips twisted in wry amusement. Even in his prideful disdain, he was a beautiful sight to behold. But she refused to allow her heart to follow her stomach. Even if he was involved in politics, he wasn't for her, she insisted to herself, perhaps futilely. Except, she wanted someone who would allow her at least a modicum of control. And she doubted Lucian would ever do that.

"Lady Amelia, we were just talking about you." His statement caused Amelia to realize they weren't alone in the room. When she glanced around, she wasn't very surprised to see her brother lounging back against the shelf of books.

"Oh, I'm glad to see you're both here. We have something to tell you."

Lucian looked at the trio before him. "All of you have things to say?"

"Well, maybe not Sarah, but Thomas and I have things to tell you. Thomas saved me," she added as she turned to Jeffrey. "He ought to be rewarded, in fact."

Lucian stood abruptly. "What are you on about, Button? Save you from what?" His frown was fierce.

"The man in the Park. The one we saw when we were together, and again at the ball. The one in the ill-fitting suit."

"What about him?"

Amelia swallowed at the deadly calm she could hear in his voice. It was as though he restrained a fierce anger that he didn't want to unleash upon her. Amelia appreciated the restraint, but it sent shivers through her anyway. It shouldn't be so thrilling when she was even still filled with fear.

"He had a gun this time. Mayhap he had it the last time, too, who is to say, but I didn't see it previously. It was most disconcerting."

Almost before she could blink, Lucian was urging her into a chair as Jeffrey rang for the housekeeper.

"You need a drink to steady your nerves, Button," Jeffrey said as he hovered behind his friend, who seemed determined to care for the young woman.

"Are you quite certain you saw a gun? Where were you, and why were you not safely at home?"

"I didn't go without protection. Jeffrey said I needn't stay home."

"I meant that you could keep your evening invitations when Father and I could accompany you, and well you know it," Jeffrey interjected with a touch of temper.

Amelia shrugged. "Did you truly believe I would be able to stay home and do nothing?"

Lucian soothed her with a squeeze of her hand, even as he shot a quelling glare at Jeffrey.

"Never mind about that. As we can see, you left the house. So, tell us what happened after that."

"We went to the Park. I wanted to search where I had seen the man standing. I thought perhaps he might have left something behind that could help us to identify him."

"Why did you think to do that?" His voice almost sounded merely curious, but Amelia could still here the faint note of restraint in his tone, as though he were trying very hard not to pour out his anger upon her.

"I wanted to help. You had said you hadn't noticed him at the ball, but I knew you were lying as I saw you speaking with him later. It didn't occur to me until I was falling asleep that night that it was the same man. I thought it was possible that you hadn't noticed him at the Park, so you might not realize that it was the same man both times. I thought if I could find some sort of clue, then we'd be further ahead."

Lucian's grip on her hand had grown steadily tighter as she had continued speaking. It filled Amelia with equal parts joy and dread. She was well aware that he was growing angrier by the moment. The pit in her stomach deepened at the thought of having disappointed him.

"So, did you find any clues?"

Amelia shrugged. "We found a few things, but we aren't sure if they are of any consequence. But then he found us searching."

"Did you speak?"

"Yes. He approached to ask us what we were doing. I had thought of a story to tell anyone who might ask. We were to tell them that I had lost a cherished earring and that we were searching for it."

When she paused for a moment, Lucian's eyes blazed, and Amelia almost quailed under the seeming heat of his glare.

"Why are you stopping? You must tell us all."

Despite the fear she had been suffering under, for some reason, she found his words amusing, and a giggle escaped her.

"I meant to tell all, but I'm not certain how to tell you, as I feel as though I don't actually have any information. I didn't get his name or direction or anything at all useful. The only thing is that I have confirmed for certain that the man was watching us."

To her surprise, Lucian seemed to pale in front of her as he shifted his gaze to her brother. There was an unspoken communication between the two men before the viscount turned back to her and urged her to continue.

"How do you know that, Amelia?"

"As I said, he approached us as we were searching. I probably should have been more attentive to my surroundings and thus noticed his approach. As it was, I nearly jumped out of my skin when he spoke to me. And there was no way to hide the fact that I was, in fact, searching for something. He didn't accept my tale that it was an earring I was searching for. Anyhow, he wanted me to accompany him. When I refused, he pulled out a gun and tried to frighten me with it. But Thomas acted quickly, distracting him, and we were able to run away."

Amelia watched in fascination as Lucian's pulse pounded in his temple, his jaw clenched tightly. She was reasonably sure he wasn't angry with her, but she lifted her chin in defiance anyway.

"I know you will both think I ought to have stayed at home, cowering under the bed, no doubt, but how was I to know he would be there waiting for me?"

Despite his obvious anger over the scenario, Lucian grinned at her words. "You did the right thing in coming to me with this information. And now, I will need to extract your solemn promise that you will return home. I don't expect you to hide under the bed, but I do need you to go home and stay there. We cannot proceed if we cannot be absolutely certain that you are safe."

"How can I be certain that *you* are safe, my lord?"

Lucian blinked at her, and Amelia couldn't help admiring his handsome eyes with their surprisingly long eyelashes. Perhaps she had lost her mind if she was going to be so distracted at a time like this.

"Are you concerned for my safety?" His voice held a note of wonder as he asked the question.

"Of course, I am. Why do you think I was in the Park?"

His hand came up as though to cup her cheek, but then he seemed to collect himself before he touched her, and suddenly he stood up and away from where he had been crouched by her seat.

"Hastings, could you see that your sister gets home safely and then meet me at Whitehall?"

"Of course." Amelia had almost forgotten that Jeffrey was there, but then she turned and grinned into her brother's disapproving frown.

"Don't look so pleased with yourself, little sister. I am most displeased with you."

"Why ever so? I brought Thomas with me, and you were quite right. He *did* save me."

"You ought to have stayed at home, safe and sound."

"Would you have then known for certain that this strange man was indeed involved in some sort of nefariousness? Seems to me, you ought to be thanking me rather than berating me for what I did. I went looking for evidence. The man threatening me seems to be evidence enough."

"But we don't actually know what he is after, do we? And now he knows that someone is looking into him." Jeffrey's anger roughened his tone, making Amelia stare at him in disbelief.

"Are you saying that I have interfered rather than helped?" Even to her own ears, she could hear the dismay in her tone. Both gentlemen grew visibly uncomfortable as tears gathered in her eyes. Amelia lifted her chin and blinked back the threat of crying. She would not give in to the emotions threatening her, at least not while in either man's presence.

"Milady," Thomas spoke up from behind her, just as she was being ushered from the room. "You didn't tell them about the paper we found."

Chapter Fifteen

L ucian had just bowed over Amelia's hand when he heard the footman's words. The feelings he refused to acknowledge having were already a jumble of confusion before that. Watching Amelia fight back the well of tears had caused a strange sensation in his belly and ignited an urge to pull her into his arms. He had, of course, ignored both the sensation and the urge. Now, though, his head whipped around, almost dislocating his neck in his effort to search both the footman's features and those of Lady Amelia.

"What paper?" he demanded, even as he watched in fascination while a becoming pink filled Amelia's face.

She gasped in a fine semblance of shock. Lucian chastised himself. Surely, she hadn't kept something important from him on purpose.

"I am so, so sorry, Lucian. I swear to you, it completely left my mind after that man was pointing his gun at me. But Thomas is right. We did find a piece of paper with an address written on it. Or we think it's an address. It isn't one I'm familiar with. There's no way to know for certain if it is of any significance, but it was after we found it that the wretched man approached us."

"Never mind the apologies or explanations, Amelia, just show me what you found."

"I don't have it," Amelia replied softly, a hint of fear and regret in her tone.

"You lost it again?" He tried not to allow his anger to get away from him, but the matter was of some importance.

"I have it, my lord," the footman said, holding out a ragged scrap of paper.

"Thank you," Lucian said, as he grabbed it from the man's hand. "Thomas, was it? Before you leave, present yourself to the butler. He will have a little something for you for your troubles."

The young servant flushed with pleasure even as he dutifully demurred. "Oh, no, my lord, I was just doing my duty."

"That may well be, but I'm most appreciative."

"Yes, Thomas, you must accept," Amelia said, nodding in approval. It made Lucian feel like a school boy to be so pleased by a little bit of appreciation from someone. He shook his head. This scrap of a girl shouldn't be affecting him so.

Lucian looked over the paper.

"Do you think it might be a clue as to why this man is following you?" Amelia asked.

He frowned. "I don't think so; it's just, as you said, a scrap of paper. It's nothing for you to concern yourself with. I will make sure the proper authorities know about this man who accosted you, and they will take it from there."

Before Amelia could object, Jeffrey grabbed her arm and interrupted their conversation.

"I'll see the women home."

Lucian was relieved when Jeffrey spoke from the doorway. "Come along, Amelia. You, too, Sarah. It's time you were returning. We've taken up quite enough of Lord Adelaide's time." He paused for a moment, and Lucian had to bite back his grin as his friend added for his sister's benefit. "I have a few words for our mother as to her idea of keeping an eye on you."

Amelia's gasp filled the air. "Don't be such a ninnyhammer, Jeffrey. You know this cannot possibly be Mama's fault. How was she to know any of this was going to happen? And I had a footman with me. Surely, you cannot expect me to turn into a recluse just as I am beginning to get comfortable in all this Season nonsense."

"I expect you to not go haring off on some foolish idea that you are going to investigate on your own."

"So, you'll allow me to investigate with you then?"

They were almost out of earshot, but Lucian couldn't help grinning as he heard his friend's groan of dismay. "Of course not, Ames. Why can't you ever be a normal female?"

Lucian could tell the young woman had stopped dead in her tracks over that question. "Would you rather I be having a fit of the vapours right about now, then?"

"If you were a normal female, you would have no need for the vapours, as you would have remained home where you ought to have been, and none of this would have happened."

"Would you have thought to go and search in the Park?"

"Amelia Courtenay. You are being unforgivably foolish. Hurry along. I'm taking you home."

Lucian actually laughed out loud at that and could only hope they had moved far enough away that they hadn't heard him. He was never so grateful that he didn't have a sister of his own. A sense of disloyalty swept over him at that thought. He was quite fond of Lady Amelia. While he understood Jeffrey's irritation with the girl for putting herself at risk, and a part of him wanted to shake her for doing so, he couldn't really fault her either. He was grateful for the information she had been able to provide. And while he truly hated the confirmation that she was in danger, he was relieved to know that he wasn't worrying for nothing. He would need to ensure that Whitehall was informed.

That thought spurred him to action, and he yelled for his horse to be saddled. It would be far faster if he rode over than tried to walk or catch a hackney.

Not much later, he was shaking his head with frustration. "How can you refuse sending agents to watch over Lady Amelia? Isn't it obvious to you that she is embroiled in this mess?"

"That is really your affair, Adelaide. It is you who involved her in it." Lord Chamberlain stated it calmly and in brief terms, as though he thought Lucian were being simple-minded

"While engaged in my duties for this office," Lucian retorted, appalled that the man he had so looked up to could be so blasé about a young noblewoman's safety. Lord Chamberlain oversaw all the agents of the entire Home Office, including Amelia's brother. Lucian had expected more.

"How can you expect us to accept that?"

"You expect me to be active amongst the *ton* in order to keep my eyes and ears open for any threats against the Crown. Part of that is squiring ladies about and dancing with them. The fact that I happened to be with this particular woman while being observed by Terrance is the very reason why Lady Amelia is now threatened."

"You should have been more careful, Adelaide. If you think she is in so much danger then why don't you or her family arrange for her protection? We have to have all of our agents involved in searching out the villains, not wasting their time playing nursemaid to a debutante."

"Can you not see that Terrance might turn up in her vicinity once more? He threatened her once; surely there's a good chance he'll do it again."

"Then you do it, Adelaide, if you think it so likely."

"If I do it, I'm likely to end up leg-shackled to the chit."

"There are worse fates, surely."

Lucian huffed in frustration. It was becoming evident that he wasn't going to win this argument. It was also becoming clear to him that his opinions were not of the utmost importance to the Home Office. He had thought he was doing his duty by involving himself with the work there, but perhaps he had been foolish to set so much store by it. Mayhap it was time he turned his attention to other ventures. But not until the threat posed by Terrance was neutralized. Even if it was only for Amelia's sake, he couldn't quit just yet.

He stormed out of the office without another word. They were no further ahead. All he had was the address on the paper Amelia had provided him. It shamed him to think that slip of a girl had been the one to gain the most advantage in his investigation. Lucian returned to his family's home to see what his clerks and assistant had managed to find out.

"There's no sign of him?" Lucian was incredulous. He had just interviewed all of his contacts at length, and none that had returned had anything of import to share. It was as though the cretin had vanished. He glanced down at the scrap of paper on his desk once again. It was unlikely to be of any use as surely Terrance would have ensured to be elsewhere, since he knew full well that Amelia had been searching for any evidence. But then again, perhaps the man hadn't any idea that he had lost the scrap of paper. Or it might be completely unrelated, he reminded himself with a disconsolate sigh. But it was the only thing he currently had to go on, and he couldn't sit around doing nothing. He snatched it up and set out from his house once more.

Chapter Sixteen

"**Y**ou're just a foolish little girl for going to the Park on your own. I shouldn't have had to tell you, Amelia. You should have known you couldn't conduct an investigation. This is nothing that concerns you."

Amelia had been furious with her brother when he had spoken to her in such anger. How dare he speak to her in such a way? But she had been beyond foolish to counteract his foolishness with some of her own. She never should have thought to do further investigations. Especially not on her own. And even more especially not in a neighbourhood such as this.

When she had asked Jeffrey about the address on the paper, he had led her to believe it was of no importance, that he had other leads to investigate. But Amelia was certain that Lucian would check it out. What if he went alone? Or what if none of them went at all? At the very least, Amelia needed to rule it out as a clue.

But standing at the corner, wondering which way she ought to turn, Amelia had to admit, at least to herself, that it had been her pride that had made her do it. She truly had never suspected she would find herself in such a rough neighbourhood. Lucian had been right — she was a fool who knew nothing about the realities of life. And now she had put her servants in danger for her own pride and arrogance.

She would like to think it had been fear for Lucian that had prompted her foolishness, but whatever the reason, it was certainly foolish of her to be there.

The stench emanating from the region of the river was enough to make her glad she hadn't had time for a meal before setting out, as she would have surely cast up her accounts by now. As it was, Sarah and Thomas were clutching her with fear as they lurked around each corner they came to. Amelia was certain they would be unable to find out anything of use with the spectacle the three of them presented. They practically screamed wealth and privilege. If they were not kidnapped for ransom or worse, she would consider herself to be the most fortunate young woman in all the realm.

How she wished Lucian was there, even though she had come in an effort to protect him. It was a foolish thought, but she couldn't seem to help herself. Even though he could sometimes appear almost foppish in his very particular dress and exceedingly nice manners, she knew he excelled at all manner of sports and would be quite capable of keeping her safe in such an environment. Not to cast aspersions upon Thomas's ability to keep her safe. The strapping young footman was surely well able to do so physically, provided none of them were shot at. But Amelia was certain that Lucian wouldn't be afraid, unlike the three of them. And each of their fears was only making the others' worse.

Swallowing down the lump that had lodged itself in her throat, Amelia lifted her chin and stepped forward. "This appears to be the place we've been looking for. Shall we get this over with?"

She wasn't really expecting a response from her two servants, but Sarah offered one anyway. "Milady, I think we ought to reconsider."

"I don't disagree with you," Amelia began, "but we're already here. We should just get it done, don't you think?"

Thomas and Sarah exchanged a dubious look before they hurried after Amelia, who wasn't really waiting for their company. Amelia knew they had no desire to be left behind. And they were well aware that they would no longer have employment if they were to allow something to happen to their mistress, whether it was her own foolish idea or not.

Their destination was a hovel. It purported to be an inn and taproom. But really, it was just a hovel. Amelia knew there were equal measures of fascination and disgust stamped upon her expressive features despite her best efforts to keep her thoughts to herself. In her defence, the patrons of said hovel were looking at her quite similarly. A quick glance around showed Amelia that she had not been able to escape notice in the small, dark, crowded establishment.

Amelia knew instantly that it had been a mistake to come here. What she had hoped to accomplish was really anyone's guess. She didn't even have a name to ask after. She sighed heavily. She was going to pay dearly for her prideful foolishness, she was sure. Her mother was going to banish her to the country. Or marry her off to the first gentleman who offered. If anyone would offer for her after her latest escapade.

She really needed to keep her mind upon the task at hand, Amelia reminded herself. She pasted a practiced Society smile upon her face as the individual who was no doubt the innkeeper approached her.

"You seem a might lost, my lady," the man began in an obsequious tone that set Amelia's teeth on edge.

"Not at all, my good man. I am to meet my brother here. He should be along at any minute, in fact." She didn't care if she was lying even though in the usual run of things she didn't like to tell falsehoods. If ever there was an occasion that called for it, this was one. "Since it doesn't appear that he has yet arrived, could I possibly trouble you for a pot of tea?"

Amelia knew she would never be able to pass for someone she was not. She hadn't thought this quest through sufficiently to have provided herself with a disguise. Dressed as she was, she could never pass for a servant or someone who really ought to be frequenting such a place. So, she didn't even try. She was a noblewoman. There was no hiding that fact.

"You want a pot of tea?" the innkeeper replied, his tone indicating he was torn between derision and the urge to earn her coins. "I suppose you'll be wanting a private retiring room, too, while we're at it."

"If you could be so good, I would appreciate that."

The innkeeper laughed in her face, causing a veritable cloud of bad odours to surround her. Amelia's eyes watered slightly, but her good breeding bolstered her nerves, and she barely batted an eyelash.

"If you be wanting tea, you'll have to take it in the taproom like everyone else."

"Very well," she replied with aplomb. "When my brother arrives, do send him in my direction. Thank you." She didn't bother awaiting a reply but stepped into the now nearly silent room as everyone sat and watched her. There was an empty table that she claimed, and she directed her servants to sit with her. Amelia was uncertain that she'd be able to brazen her way out of the situation she had gotten the three of them in, but she was going to do her very best.

Keeping her smile slight and her eyes as polite as possible, Amelia glanced around the room. Her gaze snagged on one man in particular. He seemed to blend right in with the rest of the crowd, so she couldn't have explained why he caught her attention, but she would have sworn he struck her as familiar. Was it the stranger she was looking for? No, she rather thought his shoulders were far too broad to be he for whom she was searching. With a sigh, she turned her attention to her servants, who were doing their best to disappear into the surroundings. They had a far better chance of it than she did.

"Well, this is an adventure, is it not?" she asked them in as cheerful a tone as she could muster.

"You're going to get your throat slit if you aren't careful, my lady," Thomas muttered to her.

"Not if we keep our wits about us."

"But is his lordship going to find us here?" Sarah asked with a shiver of fear. Amelia rolled her eyes and grinned at her maid without bothering to reply. She had never thought the other girl was quite that literal, but Amelia supposed that fear had clogged the poor dear's mind.

Turning her attention to Thomas, Amelia tried to catch his eye even as she saw that the innkeeper was walking toward them with a shabby looking tray. She supposed she was going to have to partake of what she had ordered if she hoped not to cause a riot. It was their best chance of getting out of there. She had been ridiculous to come to this place without even telling anyone where they were going. It would be a while before her mother realized she wasn't lying down as she had said she would be. Sarah wouldn't be missed, as she would be expected to be waiting upon Amelia. Thomas might be missed around the next mealtime. Of course, if they had told anyone where they were going, she would have been stopped. But she was beginning to think that would have been a good thing. She stifled her sigh even as the dirty tray was being placed before her.

Amelia wondered if she ought to object to the state of the offering. If she were being true to character of an aristocratic young lady, she would never allow such filth to approach her let alone sip from it. But she didn't suppose this establishment had many debutantes stopping by, and voicing her objections was sure to cause offence. If she offended the man, it was even less likely that he would be of any assistance to her if things got out of hand. No, she resolved, if she was going to get the three of them out of the bind she had walked them into, she was going to have to politely appreciate what had been placed before her.

"Thank you, sir. There's nothing like a good hot cup of tea to set everything to rights."

The innkeeper didn't offer her any reply, merely leering at her dubiously. Amelia gulped back her natural response and reached forward to pour a cup for her two companions as well as herself. She then found that she could use the unsavoury prop as a means to look about the room without actually having to touch it to her lips.

Her eyes were again drawn toward the man hunched over the bar at the end of the room. Amelia had noticed that Thomas was also looking in that direction, but she wasn't sure if it was because he too thought the man looked familiar or if it was because he was wishing he had been served ale rather than tea. Despite the direness of her situation, Amelia had to bite back her amusement. It wouldn't do to be grinning too widely at a time like this. Of course, if the other patrons thought she had run completely mad, they might be less inclined to accost her, she thought hopefully.

It felt to her as though all the eyes in the room were trained upon her but as she allowed her gaze to roam around the room, Amelia realized that her arrival hadn't created as big of a stir as she had first thought. It stood to reason, she realized. It was likely that a place like this catered to secrets. Everyone present had their own things to hide. They wouldn't want to draw attention to themselves by becoming involved in her drama. These thoughts helped bring her stiff shoulders down from where they had positioned themselves near her ears. She even managed to sip the weak tea and nibble on a biscuit that tasted more like cotton wool than anything that might have emerged from a bakery. But her rumbling stomach didn't object too vociferously, and Amelia started to think they just might get out of the mess intact.

As she relaxed slightly, she allowed herself to look around a little more carefully. Maybe she would be able to find something out after all. It would be the happiest happenstance if she were able to gain some useful information from her escapade. And that would go a long way to preventing her brother from killing her for it. She grinned at the thought, for surely Jeffrey was going to flay her with his very worst tongue lashing when he found out what she had been up to. If they managed to get home alive, that was.

Just as she was feeling confident that she would survive her adventure, there was a dark voice sounding from just behind her.

"It was a big mistake for you to come here. One you'll have to pay quite steeply for." As she was about to turn toward the speaker, a vicelike grip tightened on the nape of her neck. "Don't turn around. I have my gun at your back, and I won't be afraid to use it this time."

Fear nearly blinded her even as a well of hysterical laughter threatened to choke her. She managed to swallow down the inappropriate response and blink away the fear, at least for a moment. When she looked across at Thomas, she could see that he understood what was happening and wanted quite desperately to do something about it, but Amelia shook her head at him ever so slightly despite the tight grip the villain had on her. She rather suspected that if any of them made any sudden moves, her life would be considerably shortened. She could feel the cold cylinder of what she assumed was the stranger's gun pressing sharply into her side.

"What do you want?" she finally asked quietly.

"I want to conquer England," he said with a sneer sounding in his voice. She couldn't see his face, but she imagined it was twisted with maniacal intensity. "But I will settle for chaos."

"I meant, what do you want with *me*," she inserted, causing him to laugh roughly.

"Why, you're going to help me, my lady. You sticking your nose where it does not belong was just the advantage I was hoping to gain."

"But I'm quite unimportant. I don't see how I could be of any help to you on any sort of grand scale."

"That's where you're wrong. You seem to be quite important to the one man who has been causing me the most trouble. I can see that you are well matched, as you are causing me a great deal of trouble yourself. It is much too bad that you shan't live to be united."

Amelia blinked at the threat. It would seem the man had no intention of letting her live whether she helped him or not. Fear threatened to swamp her completely, but she forced her mind away from the unhelpful thoughts and concentrated on trying to find a way out of her dilemma.

"Perhaps you ought to ask my brother for a ransom for me instead," she offered, appreciating the irony of her suggestion.

"I don't need money," he said with a scoff, even as he pulled her up from her seat. A quick glance around the room showed Amelia that while there were a few individuals glancing at their byplay from the corners of their eyes, no one seemed the least inclined to interfere. So, she was on her own. Or at least it was her and her servants against this wicked stranger.

Sarah seemed to be on the verge of a screaming fit, but Thomas reached over and clasped her hand even as he kept his watchful gaze on his mistress, seemingly looking for any opportunity to intervene. He got to his feet as the wicked stranger pulled Amelia to hers and backed away from the table.

"Tell your man to stay here or I'll shoot you right in front of him."

Amelia had to swallow before she could issue the instruction. "Thomas, stay here," she said out loud even as she hoped the two servants could somehow find help for her before it was too late. "In fact, why don't you two go home?"

"We cannot leave you, my lady," Thomas insisted.

"Do as I say," Amelia insisted. "It's better this way."

The rough man pulled her backward out of the taproom and through a door she hadn't previously noticed. Before she knew it, they were outside, and she was blinking from the brightness of the late afternoon sun. Despite her insistence that he stay behind, Thomas had kept his distance but followed them as they left the dilapidated inn. She had her eyes so focused on Thomas's face that she didn't notice the commotion behind her until she was engulfed in someone's arms.

"You foolish girl, how could you have run such a risk?" Despite the fury in his voice, Amelia recognized Lucian's voice and melted into his embrace.

"I knew you'd find a way to save me," she said breathlessly.

He thrust her away from himself enough that they could examine each other carefully. "I ought to skin you alive for coming here," he said, even as his head lowered toward her.

Amelia's breath caught in her throat. He was going to kiss her. Lucian Northcott, Viscount Adelaide, was going to kiss her. Every last one of her childhood dreams was about to come true.

Chapter Seventeen

F ury like he'd never before experienced nearly overwhelmed Lucian when he saw Terrance with a gun trained on Lady Amelia. His heart nearly froze in his chest even as his anger made it near impossible to think of a strategy.

He had sensed her arrival even before he'd seen her. He had doubted the sensation at first. Surely the chit wouldn't be quite that foolish. He should have known better. He should have known to tell her not to pursue the address when she had handed him the small scrap of paper. He should have known she wouldn't be able to help herself and that her brother, as good a friend as he was, didn't have the sense to recognize how brilliant his sister was nor would he have thought to confine her to her room to prevent such an expedition.

But while he wanted to wring her neck for it, Lucian couldn't fault Amelia for her desire to figure things out for herself. He had always been the same. But he also had the strength and resources to ensure he made it out of the adventure alive. Unlike the small slip of a woman who was now being tugged at gunpoint out of the low taproom she had ventured into.

He would tear a strip off her hide for being such a fool later. If he could get her out of this situation alive.

A part of him, the only part that could be even remotely objective at the moment, was actually relieved that this had happened. Even if they had no evidence against Terrance with regard to his treachery, they would be able to throw him in Newgate for his attempted abduction of the noblewoman. And he would hang if he actually hurt Amelia. But as much as Lucian wanted the bounder out of commission, he couldn't allow anything to happen to Amelia. In that moment, when he had seen Terrance holding a gun to Amelia's side, Lucian had felt as though his life would be over if Amelia was even hurt, let alone killed or maimed.

So, he was well aware that he wasn't thinking as clearly as he ought to when he signaled for his men to circle around the back of the building after he had ascertained that Terrance was alone as far as they could tell. It was an unusual situation. The sneaky bounder usually had at least one other henchman with him at all times. It was entirely possible that he did this time, and Lucian just couldn't tell because he was too caught up in what was happening to Amelia. But it mattered very little. Lucian had come prepared and had several well-trained operatives with him besides Amelia's own footman, who Lucian was pleased to see was remaining calm and alert to his surroundings. Unlike Amelia's maid, who was on the verge of hysterics. Perhaps even beyond the verge. Lucian was just relieved that she was being quiet about it rather than shrieking the house down. Not that it would do any good if the servant did scream. In a place like this, Lucian rather thought that screams were commonplace and there would be very little interference. He was actually surprised that there had been so little attention paid to Amelia when she had walked into the shady establishment. He suspected there were too many underhanded transactions taking place for anyone to be bothered with a wellborn debutante turning up, despite how curious she might have made them. At least that had worked to Lucian's benefit.

But he couldn't be grateful to the chit for being there even if it made apprehending Terrance that much easier. Even as he enfolded her into his arms, he wanted to rail and shake her to within an inch of her life. And then he was going to continue holding onto her for the rest of his. He knew it was a ridiculous thought borne of the fear that had lodged itself in his veins, but it was real nonetheless. The only thing that prevented him from kissing her senseless despite their shady surroundings was the fact that her brother was even now clearing his throat quite significantly.

"Do unhand my sister, Adelaide. Surely you wouldn't want to compromise her in any way."

Lucian rolled his eyes and laughed even as he loosened his grip on the young woman. "I'm reasonably sure she has quite compromised herself with this latest escapade, aren't you?"

"No one needs to ever find out about this. But if you go turning her head with your reaction, that might not be so easy to recover from."

Jeffrey pulled Amelia out of Lucian's arms and shielded her from the commotion as several agents wrestled Terrance to the ground, bound him, and then hustled him away. Lucian was relieved to have that portion of the task taken care of.

"You arrived just in the nick of time," he commented drily to Jeffrey, just as Amelia pulled herself from her brother and stood glaring at the both of them. They would still have to get her home quietly if they wanted to preserve her reputation.

Thinking of that was helping to restore Lucian's equilibrium. He had lost his head for a moment when he had thought her life was in danger, but the sensation was passing. He reminded himself that he wasn't ready to get leg-shackled, especially not to such a troublesome wench as Lady Amelia. As he pondered that thought, his fury returned.

"What in the name of all that's holy were you thinking in coming here? On your own? Did you not see that it was the furthest thing from suitable that you could possibly imagine?" he demanded.

"Don't take that tone with me, Lucian Northcott. I'm not one of your lackeys you can order about at will."

Lucian's anger ratcheted up a notch at her obstinate refusal to recognize that she had been in the wrong.

"You fool," he seethed to her. "You could have jeopardized our entire mission with this little adventure of yours. And perhaps worse than that, you could have gotten yourself and others killed. Even worse than being killed, in all reality. It was only the luckiest happenstance that we were here when you needed us and it didn't ruin our plans."

Her eyes had grown in her white face but despite her obvious discomfort, Lucian watched in near fascination as she mustered up a smile. "I knew it was you at the tap," she declared with aplomb, and no degree of truth. "All is well that ends well, then, isn't it?"

Lucian looked past her toward her brother. "Please, get her out of my sight before I say or do something that I shall regret further." He turned his back and didn't watch as Jeffrey pulled her away, despite Amelia's protests.

He almost felt sorry for her; he certainly felt sorry for Jeffrey having to deal with her in that moment.

Lucian tried to hold onto his anger but knew it was a losing cause as he left the low inn behind and made his way to Whitehall. His meeting with his superiors was more awkward than usual, but it went better than expected.

"You'd best marry the girl, Adelaide."

Lucian laughed out loud, thinking the older gentleman was joking.

"I beg your pardon," Lucian choked out when the other man didn't even crack a smile. "Did you not hear what I just told you about her?"

"She is clearly an asset," the older man explained. "I know you had a bad moment when it seemed she had gotten herself into a spot of trouble, but the fact is, she was brave enough to investigate on her own and had actually figured all that out. She helped your investigation considerably, I'm sure you realize."

Lucian tried to keep his reaction contained out of respect for Lord Chamberlain and his vast experience, but he couldn't quite keep the bite out of his tone as he replied, "It wasn't brave, sir, it was the height of foolishness for her to go there by herself."

"Didn't you say she had a maid and footman with her?"

"A fat lot of good they did when she was dressed as a debutante about to make morning calls. She could have been kidnapped or worse. Terrance himself had a gun pointed at the base of her skull."

"But she got out of it all in one piece, and you wouldn't have known of that place without her interference." When Lucian made to protest further, the man waved his hand imperiously for him to maintain his silence. "As I said, you ought to marry her. Perhaps then you can control her movements as you wish. But she would certainly be an asset to our teams."

"Do you honestly think I would allow a wife of mine to be involved in espionage?" Lucian croaked the question, so great was his effort not to shout at the man he normally so respected.

The other man drew himself to his full height as he stood from the desk he had been sitting behind. "I think you ought to take yourself off before you cause offence, my lord. You did good work today. I hope you will be able to see that when you calm down from the ferocity of your anger."

Lucian didn't bother to reply. With a slight bow of his head, he quit the room at a brisk pace. Anger filled him all the way to his fingertips. He wasn't sure how he was going to dissipate it. He wished he had been able to perform an act of violence on Terrance but with Amelia there, he had been far more concerned with her safety. He couldn't find it in him to care that he was being ridiculous.

He was hot and sweaty by the time he got home. He had never walked that distance in such a short time. But it had helped him to work off some of his spleen. Could Lord Chamberlain be right? Should he marry Amelia? Not that she would have him after how he'd treated her. He scolded himself for even considering it then called for a bath.

Lucian was promised to several events that evening. He couldn't leave off his role as social agent just yet.

Chapter Eighteen

Amelia huddled in the corner of the hackney her brother had hustled her into moments before. She couldn't make eye contact with the other occupants of the carriage. Her maid's sniffles were putting her teeth on edge. Amelia knew she ought to be offering Sarah some sort of comfort, but she was too consumed with her own misery. Well aware that Jeffrey was furious with her, Amelia was trying to swallow down her own anger before she could have a reasonable conversation with anyone on the subject.

How dare Lucian upbraid her like that?

Amelia wanted to curl up into a ball and sob her misery. It had been quite an adventure until it all had fallen apart. Even the scary bits had been thrilling, now that it turned out she wasn't going to die. But now her triumph was lying in tatters around her feet. And Jeffrey was likely to send her home to Hastings without a by-your-leave from her. It was unlikely their mother would argue when she found out where Amelia had been. Perhaps Jeffrey wouldn't even have to insist. Their mother was likely to bundle her out of the city even without his urgings. And she hadn't even gotten to visit Parliament yet. Now she'd have to wait another year to get on with her life.

It was most unfair. All she'd been doing was trying to help. And why couldn't anyone see that she had actually contributed greatly to their investigation? If they had only told her there was an investigation rather than trying to keep it all from her, this might never have happened. Really, they ought to be thanking her rather than treating her as the lowest form of upstarts.

She could never see Lucian Northcott again, that much was certain. Amelia wasn't sure how she would attain that goal, but she knew she could never bear the humiliation of facing him. She would have to marry the sheep farmer from the North as she had originally planned. If she never returned to Town, she would never have to worry about avoiding Lucian.

Her heart broke apart, and she had to bite her finger to prevent the sob that wanted to erupt from her throat when she remembered Lucian's parting words. She wouldn't have to work at not seeing him. He never wished to set eyes on her, either. She couldn't subject her brother to her hysterics after what they had all been through. Although perhaps it would prevent the scene that was sure to unfold as soon as they reached their townhouse. But no, while Amelia felt fully justified in her actions, especially when one considered the good it had done, she knew it could be considered foolhardy that she had gone into that shady neighbourhood with little protection. And her brother had the right to vent his feelings. Whether she agreed with them or not, she was going to have to hear them, and she would try not to overreact to whatever he might say.

Amelia tried to remember that both gentlemen had probably been afraid for her safety. She had been afraid for her own safety, so she could only imagine how the overprotective men felt when they'd seen her in danger. But that didn't justify what Lord Adelaide had said to her. She could no longer even think of him as Lucian. He wasn't her friend. He had probably never really been her friend. She had only deluded herself into thinking he was. And all those little moments this past week when she had felt shivers and thrills in his company were only in her imagination and weren't to be thought of.

Perhaps if she told herself that enough times she would believe it.

With a sigh, she realized they had arrived at their house. A servant was opening the door, and Jeffrey was staring at her as though she ought to be doing or saying something. She offered him the brightest smile she could muster. There was no sense in going to her doom with a gloomy visage. And if it confused her brother, she wasn't going to mind that happenstance in the least.

"You are the strangest chit in all of London, Ames. I don't know how we're ever going to get you married off," her brother complained as he followed at her heels. "It's a moot point anyhow, as I'm sure you ought to be confined to the country house until you can be convinced to behave as a normal young lady."

Amelia swallowed the hysterical laughter that was threatening to evade her control.

"I had been quite convinced to behave normally, Jeffrey. And I don't actually think it was that out of the ordinary what I did. You were there. Did you consider that so very extraordinary?"

"I'm a man, Ames. Surely you must realize there is a difference." His sarcasm threatened her fragile equilibrium, but she was saved from a response by the appearance of her mother.

"What is happening?" she asked in a calm tone belying the frown that had gathered on her forehead.

"Your daughter nearly got herself killed. She needs to be packed off to Hastings before she can cause any more trouble. I have to go. Don't let her out of your sight unless you've confined her to her room under lock and key."

"Surely you are being a trifle dramatic, Jeffrey. You cannot make these edicts and then leave with no further explanation."

"I'll explain everything when I return. But I can assure you, she is not to be trusted out of your sight," he announced even as he was running out of the room, leaving mother and daughter to stare at one another.

"Shall I ring for tea?"

Amelia laughed at her mother's prosaic question and was relieved to hear it didn't sound too hysterical. She appreciated her mother's calm acceptance of the situation she had been thrust into and smiled her thanks as she sank into a chair. She opened her mouth to begin her explanation and self-defence, but Lady Hanley held up her hand to stem Amelia's words.

"I believe I need a cup in my hand before I start listening to what you have to say, my dear. I am sure it will help keep me steady."

Amelia's laughter felt much lighter this time, and she settled further into her seat to await the tea tray, not bothering to make idle chatter with her mother while they waited. There were far too many things pressing on her mind to be able to tolerate gossip at the moment.

They had just sat back into their seats with their cups in hand when there was another commotion at the front of the house, and Amelia's father rushed into the room. He stopped abruptly in the doorway, taking in the sight of his wife and daughter calmly sipping tea.

"I just came from the House. Amelia, my dearest, are you well? You look perfectly fine, so I can hardly credit what I've been told."

Amelia grinned over the rim of her teacup at her father.

"She was just about to explain herself to me, as I haven't yet heard the account. Do you wish to have a cup with us while she does so?" Again, Amelia couldn't help admiring her mother's calm. If she had ever thought to imagine herself in this scenario, she didn't think she would have been able to envision her mother remaining so very relaxed in the face of what could have taken place. It amused her to see her father's surprise over his wife's reaction as he accepted the cup she held out to him and sank into a chair.

Clearing her throat after taking another fortifying sip of her tea, Amelia was slightly distracted by the thought that her mother was correct; there was just something about the hot beverage that restored one's equilibrium. The silly thought brought a smile to her face as she launched into her explanation.

"I still don't know what was behind it all, sadly, but I encountered a terrible man while out with Lord Adelaide a few days ago."

Both her parents reacted instantly to her words, but Amelia held up her hand to stem their words.

"It wasn't his fault and please let me finish or I'll never tell the tale." With a bit of grumbling, her father settled back in his chair and her mother continued to sip her tea with a slight gleam in her eye that Amelia couldn't interpret.

"Anyhow, I saw the same man last night at the ball while I was dancing with Lord Adelaide, but Lucian claimed not to know anything about him. I thought he was lying, so this morning I took Sarah and Thomas to the Park where I had seen the man, and we found a scrap of paper with an address on it. While we were in the Park, that same man accosted us, so we went to Everleigh House to tell Lucian and Jeffrey about it. They bundled me back home and told me to forget about it, that it was nothing for me to worry myself about, but that was a foolish edict. So Sarah and Thomas and I went to the address we had seen on the paper."

Again, Lord Hanley appeared as though he were about to protest, rising slightly to his feet, but Amelia carried on and he again resumed his seat.

"It was a low place, but I didn't let that stop me, despite the servants' protests to the contrary. You really mustn't blame either of them, as they did try to stop me. Anyhow, it turned out I was correct, it was a clue related to the search for this man, whoever he might be. I still don't even know what he is up to or why he would take such exception to my searching for him as he did not allow me to ask him anything. When he threatened me with a gun and tried to drag me from the place, somehow, suddenly, Lucian and Jeffrey were there and prevented it. Lord Adelaide expressed his disdain for my investigative skills, and Jeffrey brought me home and told Mama to lock me up before he stormed out of the house once more."

By the end of her speech, her father had placed his teacup on the side table and had begun pacing about the room while Lady Hanley's eyes had grown large and her face had paled slightly, but she had continued to sip at her tea.

"Well, my dear, you have had an adventurous day, have you not? But I think it is well past time that you ought to be dressing for the evening. We shall be quite late, but that cannot be helped, I suppose."

Amelia blinked at her mother while her father protested. "You cannot think to allow the girl out of the house, can you?"

"Did the gentlemen not apprehend the fellow? So, our daughter is in no danger that I can see."

"She is a menace to her own safety, it would seem," Lord Hanley protested.

"That is a result of you having encouraged her to learn more than is considered genteel, so you only have yourself to blame, my lord," Amelia's mother replied tartly. "If any whisper of her adventure were to get out, her staying home would only add credence to the scandal that might attach itself to her. The best thing is for the lot of us to carry on as though none of this has happened."

Amelia was grinning as she headed for the door. "Don't think this means I will allow you out of my sight this evening, Amelia," her mother called after her. "And you are not in the clear. I will have to think of a suitable punishment for such blatant foolishness."

Amelia gasped. "Mama, the man was some sort of criminal, and I helped to apprehend him."

"At much greater risk to yourself than was necessary," Lady Hanley countered. "I cannot argue that going to the Park with two servants in tow was not any great risk, but once you had passed the information on to the gentlemen, and they had expressly told you to stay home, you ought to have done so."

Since she couldn't really argue with her mother on the topic, she didn't offer a reply, leaving the room without another word and hurrying up to her bedchamber to get ready for the rout they were to attend. It felt like at least a month had passed since she had last been to an entertainment of any sort, but it had only been the night before she had danced a hole in her shoes.

Unsure how she would feel facing anyone from Society after the day she'd had, Amelia presented herself to her maid to get outfitted for the event. They would have to hurry if they weren't to be unforgivably late. While it could be considered fashionable to arrive a certain amount after one was expected, there was a fine line between that and rudeness.

Sarah's eyes were still puffy from her earlier weeping, but Amelia was relieved to see that she had been restored to her usual steady humour. She must have been apprised of the intention for the family to carry on as normal since she already had Amelia's favorite gown spread out ready for her to don.

Chapter Nineteen

L *ady Amelia is here?*
     Lucian could hardly credit it. For one thing, the woman ought to be in hysterics after the day she'd had. For another, he would have thought Jeffrey would have ensured she was under lock and key, if not packed off to their country estate. But she appeared to be perfectly fit and free from all encumbrances except for her mother's more watchful than usual gaze. When Lady Hanley's gaze ensnared his own, Lucian couldn't help but bow to the older woman. Her gaze turned shrewd, and the viscount was surprised when she turned her shoulder slightly. *Was the woman about to give him the cut direct?* The thought would be amusing if it weren't so poorly thought out. If Amelia's presence at the rout that evening was an effort to prevent any scandal, Lady Hanley could not be seen to be shunning him. He stepped forward to intercept Amelia as she passed near him.

"Dance with me, my dear?"

Her eyes flew to his. "There's no dance forming, my lord."

"Not yet," he agreed amiably as he tucked her hand into his elbow. "Then walk with me a spell."

"What are you about, my lord?"

Lucian couldn't decipher her tone as it seemed to be somewhere between anger and longing. His stomach clenched. He gave voice to his thoughts.

"I spoke thoughtlessly this afternoon, Amelia. Don't stop calling me by name."

"You are the one who has been harping at me about how inappropriate it is for me to call you by name, saying I ought to be much more formal."

"What is formality between ones such as us?"

"It is what is expected, my lord."

Lucian knew her heart wasn't in her argument, so he let it go for the time being.

"Have you quite recovered from your ordeal?" His hand tightened over hers where it rested on his arm. "You look lovely, as always."

She frowned up at him from under her long, sweeping eyelashes. "Did you get struck on the head in the altercation this afternoon, Lucian? You don't sound in the least like yourself."

His heart warmed at her playful tone. He was relieved to note that she didn't seem to display any lasting harm caused by her adventures. Once again, his heart felt as though it skipped a beat at the thought of her in danger. His superiors at the Home Office were right; he needed to bind her to himself for life so that he could ensure her safety. No one else seemed up to the task. But how to convince her to join her life to his after what she had been through, besides what he had said to her earlier that very day?

He ought to wait until he could call on her and declare himself properly, but he couldn't seem to stop the impulse that had him directing her into a small alcove that would afford them a modicum of privacy while not compromising her reputation.

Her eyes were wide and watchful and she seemed hesitant to follow along as he took her out of the crush of the crowds, but she didn't dig in her heels as he had thought she might.

Even though he knew he was being foolish beyond all belief, he just couldn't stop himself as he pulled her further into the alcove and into his arms.

"What are you doing?" She repeated the unanswerable question, but this time her voice was much more breathy, as though she were struggling to control her tone and it wasn't working. She didn't sound afraid, though, which Lucian found reassuring.

"I need to tell you something."

"Here? You want to tell me something here? In the middle of an overcrowded rout? Are you quite certain you are well? Because this seems to be the recipe for a scandal. Surely that wouldn't be to your taste, my lord."

"If it meant that you would have to marry me, then it would very much be to my taste," Lucian assured her. To his surprise, she threw back her head and laughed. Despite the discomfort that filled him at her amusement over his declaration, he was relieved to note that she kept the volume of her laughter low enough not to draw attention to their location.

"Now I know that you have lost your mind. You don't want to be married to me. You think I'm too much trouble and headstrong, besides. And you don't even want to be wed in the first place. Everyone knows that."

Lucian's hand tightened where it was resting over hers. He longed to pull her properly into his arms. Or rather improperly, he thought, fighting a grin. The poor darling was obviously near the end of her tether from all that she had been through. She was right; he ought to have waited. But it was too late now. He was going to declare himself.

"Can a gentleman not change his mind?"

She affixed him with the analyzing stare that he so enjoyed even when it made him squirm, looking as though she were trying to read his thoughts.

"Are you saying that you are seeking a bride?" she asked cautiously, a frown forming between her brows. It seemed to him as though her expression was torn between hopeful and skeptical. Again, he had to remind himself that she had been through an eventful day and he ought to leave her be. But he just couldn't bring himself to do so. He recalled her question.

"Yes, I am. Or rather, one bride in particular. If she'll have me."

Her lips parted on a gasp, but no sound emerged.

~~~~

Amelia could barely credit what she was hearing. How could he make such a complete about-face? Not only had he seemed to hate her that afternoon, but it was a well-known *on dit* amongst the *ton* how very resistant to marriage the Viscount Adelaide was. But if her ears were to be believed, he was here declaring himself in front of her. Of course, she could be being foolish beyond all bounds. Perhaps he merely wanted her assistance to convince the lady of his choice.

With her heart sinking into the tight confines of her shoes, Amelia tried to smile up at him as she asked for clarification.

"Who is the fortunate lady? And how can I help?"

His eyebrows rose, and a low chuckle escaped him that did curious things to her midsection. His head lowered toward her, and his whisper started a tingle progressing all over her.

"You are, my dear," he answered, as his head lowered even closer. When his lips were barely a hair's breadth from her own, Lucian added, "And you can help by saying yes, as I have discovered I cannot possibly live without you."

Amelia was hard-pressed not to shout with joy and was just about to throw her arms around his neck and close that final distance between them when she was stopped cold by her mother's voice.

"Just the two people I was looking for. What fortuitous timing." Her voice was very collected and a little cold when she added, "Were you planning to announce your engagement at the rout this evening, Adelaide?"

To Amelia's surprise and immense delight, even though he lifted his head a little, he did not step away or release her. Her heart had found its way back into its rightful position within her chest and was pounding madly as joy and delight coursed through her.

"I had hoped to discuss matters over with Amelia as well as her father before making a public announcement," Lucian answered Lady Hanley while still keeping Amelia snuggled close. "But if you'd like to announce it now, I would be delighted. The young lady hasn't accepted me yet, so if you would force her hand, I would be forever grateful," he concluded with a wide smile in Amelia's direction.

"The library is currently free of other guests. I could allow you five minutes for this discussion." Amelia's mother winked at them both before stepping back. "But no more than five minutes."

Before Amelia could even fully grasp what had happened, she found herself tucked into a corner of the library, well hidden from any prying eyes, with Lucian warm and towering before her.

"Amelia, my darling, put me out of my misery and give me an answer. I know I was beastly to you earlier, but I promise to make it up to you."

Despite her joy, Amelia was always ready for knowledge.

"Are you truly miserable, Luce?"

Rather than offering a verbal answer, he finally closed the distance between them and settled his lips over hers. But he barely allowed time for their breaths to mingle or for her to even grow accustomed to the sensations coursing through her before he lifted his head once more.

"Despite how much I want to wed you, I won't compromise you into it. You must give me the words, Amelia. Will you have me?"

Amelia's laughter was filled with joy even though she tried to keep the volume contained. She drew up to the tips of her toes and threw her arms around his neck.

"Of course, I'll have you. I've been waiting for you since I was ten years old. It took you long enough to come to your senses."

"Oh, Amelia, I do love you quite desperately."

He cut off any recriminations she could add by squeezing her tightly in his arms and settling his lips over hers in a less sedate kiss than the first one, only coming up for air when Lady Hanley cleared her throat from the doorway and said, "Welcome to the family, Lucian."

Epilogue

"**Y**ou have one of those creases forming between your eyebrows again, Luce. What seems to be the trouble?"

He had been reading a letter from Everleigh moments before, but now he was staring out the window of the carriage they were riding in. The scenery beyond was rather monotonous as they had been looking at similar vistas for hours, so Amelia knew he was deep in thought.

"Gilbert seems to be having a bit of trouble."

"Trouble on the estate? Is your father all right?"

"Not on the estate or in the family. It seems there's a girl chasing after him. Or rather, her father," he interjected as he looked back to the paper in his hand before turning toward her with a smile. "I know you were hoping to get to London right away to begin your life as a political wife, but would you mind terribly if we stopped off at Everleigh on the way?"

Amelia would never grow tired of seeing love shining in Lucian's eyes when he looked at her. And when he looked just like he did in that moment, she could deny him nothing.

"I had actually thought that was where we were heading. It only makes sense to stop off there and check on things for a spell before we go back to Town. And if we don't get back to Town this Season, there's always the next."

Lucian's eyes dropped to her midsection with a wink. "The next Season might be a bit of a problem for you if we work things right."

Amelia laughed as she allowed her hand to follow his gaze. With a shrug she replied, "If we work things right, it won't be a problem at all. I've heard babies can travel just fine."

Lucian's laughter joined hers even as he pulled her over to sit beside him rather than across. Amelia snuggled close but allowed her mind to return to her husband's words.

"Why are you concerned about Gilbert? What does he say?"

"It's not so much what he said as how he said it that has me worried. I cannot explain it, in all actuality. I've caught one of your feelings," he added with a chuckle.

"We'll find out soon enough, in that case. I think it would be delightful for your brothers to be caught by some wives."

"Like I was, you mean?" Lucian asked, his eyes twinkling, as he lowered his head down to meet his wife's smiling lips.

The End

- - - - - - - - - - - - -

Want to find out what happens with Gilbert?
Read the next book in the *Northcott Kinship* series:

Convincing Mr. Northcott

Her reputation is on the line. So is his heart...

The *Northcott Kinship* series is connected to the *Sherton Sisters*. Have you read those yet?
Start with Book 1

A Duke to Elude

She's waiting for true love. He's tasked with uncovering the truth. When nefarious schemes threaten her reputation, he finds his heart on the line with it.

About the Author

I learned to read when I was four or five, listening to my mother read to me when I was lonely after my brother started school. Ever since, I've had my head buried in books. I love words – historical plaques, signs, the cereal box – but my first love has always been novels.

A little over ten years ago my husband dared me to write a book instead of always reading them. I didn't think I'd be able to do it, but to my surprise I love writing. Those early efforts eventually became my first published book – Tempting the Earl (published by Avalon Books in 2010). It has been a thrilling adventure as I learned to navigate the world of publishing.

I believe firmly that everyone deserves a happily ever after. I want my readers to be able to escape from the everyday for a little while and feel upbeat and refreshed when they get to the end of my books.

When not reading or writing, I can be found traipsing around my neighbourhood or travelling the world with my favourite companion.

Stay in touch:

Website Facebook Instagram Twitter

Stay in touch with Wendy May Andrews
and forthcoming publishing news.

Sign up for her biweekly newsletter

Other books by Wendy May Andrews:

Ladies of Mayfair

The Governess' Debut

The Reluctant Debutante

The Debutante Bride

A Dangerous Debut

Sweet Surrender

Mayfair Mayhem

The Duke Conspiracy

The Viscount Deception

The Countess Intrigue

The Bequest

Inheriting Trouble

Inviting Misfortune

Courting Intrigue

Sherton Sisters

A Duke to Elude

A Lady to Reveal

A Viscount to Conspire

A Sister to Beguile

A Gentleman to Avoid

Orphan Train

Sophie

Katie

Cassie

Melanie

Proxy Brides

A Bride for Carter

A Bride for Ransom

A Bride for Alastair

A Bride for Hamilton

Dear Aunt Judy

Torn in Toronto

Singed in Saint John

All titles available on Amazon

Another breathtaking series you don't want to miss:
The Ladies of Mayfair - Book 1:

The Governess' Debut

The governess must charm both the spoiled child and the haughty earl.

Orphaned and destitute, gently born Felicia Scott must find a way to keep a roof over her head. No longer able to enter the Marriage Mart, but also not of the servant class, the only option is to find a position as governess.

After his spoiled, seven year old daughter has sent off three governesses in the 18 months since her mother died, the Earl of Standish doubts the young, inexperienced Miss Scott could possible manage the position. Since he's desperate and she comes so highly recommended, the earl agrees to give her a chance. Much to everyone's amazement, the beautiful, young governess succeeds where the others had failed. The entire household benefits from the calm, including the jaded earl.

How does he overcome his arrogance to see his governess' true value?

Available now on Amazon

If you like Regencies with a touch of adventure, you will love **the Mayfair Mayhem series. Book 1 is:**

The Duke Conspiracy

Anything is possible with a spying debutante, a duke, and a conspiracy.

Growing up, Rose and Alex were the best of friends until their families became embroiled in a feud. Now, the Season is throwing them into each other's company. Despite the spark of attraction they might feel for one another, they each want very different things in life, besides needing to support their own family's side in the dispute.

Miss Rosamund Smythe is finding the Season to be a dead bore after spying with her father, a baron diplomat, in Vienna. She wants more out of life than just being some nobleman's wife. When she overhears a plot to entrap Alex into a marriage of convenience, her intrigue and some last vestige of loyalty causes them to overcome the feud.

His Grace, Alexander Milton, the Duke of Wrentham, wants a quiet life with a "proper" wife after his tumultuous childhood. His parents had fought viciously, lied often, and Alex had hated it all.

Rose's meddling puts her in danger. Alex will have to leave the simple peace he craves to claim a love he never could have imagined. Can they claim their happily ever after despite the turmoil?

Available now on Amazon

If you like Regency Romance, read

Inheriting Trouble

Book 1 in the Bequest Series

The inheritance was meant to better her life, not muddle it.

Georgia Holton, wellborn but nearly penniless, is best friends with one of the Earl of Sherton's five daughters. When she is invited to accompany her friend for two weeks of the Season, Georgia jumps at the opportunity to have a little adventure away from her small village.

The Earl of Crossley is handsome, wealthy, widowed, and jaded. He has no intention of courting any of this Season's debutantes. After all, every woman he's ever known has been dishonest, including his late wife. But when a chance encounter throws him into contact with the Sherton ladies and their lovely friend, he can't help being drawn to Georgia's beauty and endearing personality.

When confusion about Georgia's small inheritance becomes known, a sense of obligation to right a wrong, forces the earl and Georgia into close association.

But is she really different from any of the other women, or does she have an ulterior motive?

And can Georgia even consider getting close to a man from High Society, when all she wants is to return to her simple village life?

Sparks fly between these two, but it will take forgiveness and understanding on both their parts to reach a happily ever after.

Available now on Amazon

Made in the USA
Coppell, TX
13 February 2022

Ana María Machado

Siempre con mis amigos

Traducido por Rafael Chacón

Dirección editorial: María Jesús Gil Iglesias
Colección coordinada por M.ª Carmen Díaz-Villarejo

Diseño de cubierta: Estudio SM

Título original: *Amigo é comigo*
Traducción del portugués: Rafael Chacón

© Ana María Machado, 1999
© Ediciones SM, 2001
    Joaquín Turina, 39 - 28044 Madrid

Comercializa: CESMA, SA - Aguacate, 43 - 28044 Madrid

ISBN: 84-348-8040-7
Depósito legal: M-31707-2001
Preimpresión: Grafilia, SL
Impreso en España / *Printed in Spain*
Imprenta SM - Joaquín Turina, 39 - 28044 Madrid

1 Mi mejor amiga

—¿**V**AS a salir *así*?

No sé muy bien cómo reflejar la entonación de este *así*. Tal vez deba añadirle signos de interrogación al principio y al final de la frase. O escribirlo todo inclinadito, para recordar la boca torcida con que él pronuncia esta palabra. O ir variando el tamaño de las letras, e incluso repetir esa *i* final para mostrar cómo su voz va subiendo y se prolonga en un espanto total. Sus cejas arqueadas acompañan a la pregunta con un aire de crítica, de reprobación, del más profundo desprecio.

—¿Vas a salir *asíííí*?

Puede parecer estúpido escribir una palabra de esta forma. Pero eso no es nada, comparado con la cara de estúpida ambulante que se me pone cuando veo que estoy a punto de salir, ya casi despidiéndome, y oigo el comentario asesino.

Porque es un comentario, por más que parezca ser solamente una pregunta. Pero es también una forma de asesinato, ya que mata toda mi alegría, por bueno que sea el plan que me espera. Un plan por el que llevo muchos días esperando, para el que yo me he venido preparando con la mayor dedicación.

Y solo con mirar el montón de ropa que queda encima de mi cama después de vestirme, ya da una idea de cómo he experimentado con blusas y pantalones, de cómo me he probado faldas y vestidos, de cómo he intentado comprobar si me quedaba bien esta o aquella pieza, o si un color combinaba con otro. No, si me pongo este pantalón, no puedo vestirme con una blusa holgada. Este *top* no me pega nada, voy a sentir frío, y ninguna chaqueta va con su color. Este otro me aprieta un poco el pecho y hace que la barriga parezca mayor de lo que es. ¿Y si me cambiase de pantalones? Estos de aquí, no; hacen que la poca celulitis que tengo en los muslos se vea más, a pesar de que todo el mundo dice que estoy delgada y que una chica de mi edad casi nunca tiene celulitis. Sin embargo, el espejo me dice algo distinto. Quiero decir que yo lo veo así. A fin de cuentas, tengo la obligación de observar cómo mi propio cuerpo cambia antes de que lo perciban los demás. Con suerte, incluso antes de que el espejo me lo muestre.

Y siempre es así. Yo pienso en esas cosas, converso conmigo misma, a veces incluso hablo entre dientes o refunfuño en voz alta. Y voy sacando perchas del armario, vaciando cajones, escogiendo o rechazando cosas, y lo echo todo encima de la cama. Veo cómo crece aquel montón de ropa y me entra pereza. Sé que debería ordenarlo todo antes de salir, para no tener que enfrentarme con aquella montaña de tela cuando vuelva de la fiesta con sueño y ganas de dormir.

Pero pensarlo no me vale de nada, porque siempre que me pasa esto, es ya la hora de salir y sé que no me va a dar tiempo. Y al volver, por culpa del asunto este de dejar las cosas tal cual, de cerrar la puerta de mi habitación con llave y salir con disimulo para que nadie me vea, más de una vez tuve que tirarlo todo al suelo, porque vengo muy cansada y quiero irme derechita a la cama. Y, además, tengo otras preocupaciones. Miro el reloj a cada instante, compungida porque todavía no he comenzado a maquillarme. Ni siquiera veo la manera de cómo arreglarme este pelo, en el que, para variar, se me ha formado una onda tan grande, que debe servir incluso para que alguien practique el *surf* en ella. Necesito encontrar unos zapatos adecuados en el armario de mi madre, especialmente si voy a llevar falda, porque si la llevo, no quiero ir en zapatillas deportivas, aunque, a fin de cuentas, siempre acabo usando las mismas sandalias.

En resumen: me lleva siglos escoger la ropa, años conseguir un peinado más o menos satisfactorio, horas maquillarme para parecer de lo más natural y casi sin maquillaje, como todas las revistas aconsejan. Y, al final de toda esta tarea, cuando me miro en el espejo antes de apagar al luz y salir de la habitación, cuando tengo suerte o un día feliz, pienso que no me ha quedado todo tan mal, que puede ser que por una vez no me sienta la más desastre y horrorosa de la pandilla.

En ese momento paso por la sala para despedirme de mis padres y oigo:

—¿Vas a salir asííí?

El que me conozca, sabrá ya quién ha hablado. Y siempre es él, Rodolfo. Mi hermano Rodolfo, en verdad Luis Rodolfo, dos años mayor que yo. Especialista en chafarme todo y hacerme sentir una basura.

Mi madre intenta salvarme la noche:

—¿Así, cómo? Tienes una gracia...

Y es justo en ese momento cuando Rodolfo comienza a argumentar que mi blusa está demasiado escotada, que la falda me va demasiado justa, que el vestido está demasiado apretado, o demasiado transparente. Qué sé yo, todo es demasiado, pero nunca de aquella maravillosa e incomparable forma, que evidentemente es un elogio, de quien suspira y dice: *¡Vaya, ella sí que es demasiado!*

No, con Rodolfo no pasa nada de eso. Es siempre señal de que me he pasado del límite y que llevo una ropa *demasiado* absurda. Tan absurda que la gente —no sé quién, pero él siempre dice «la gente»— va a creer que yo soy lo que no soy.

Pero esta vez él no tiene ningún motivo para decirlo. No llevo nada *demasiado*. En todo caso será de menos. Voy a salir vestida con ropa supermoderada. Me he puesto una camisa a cuadros de mi padre por encima de la blusa y de los pantalones largos, como si fuese una chaqueta.

—Estás ridícula. Menos mal que no vienes conmigo, iban a tomarme por la última mona. Pareces uno de esos tipos que van a un baile *funk*. Solo te falta un pantalón bien ancho y un gorro con el ala vuelta hacia atrás —fulmina Rodolfo—. Vas a acabar creando todo tipo de confusiones.

Echa una risita para aprovechar la pausa, y añade como si estuviese explicándose:

—Si vas así, Tatiana, corres el peligro de que los *funkies* te confundan con alguien de una banda rival.

¡Ya está bien! ¡No aguanto más! Me siento una basura, fea, como si tuviese formas de hombre. Así ningún chico va a fijarse en mí.

Ahora ya no me da tiempo a cambiarme de ropa. El padre de Adriana ha llegado para recogerme y ya ha dado tres bocinazos abajo, y él es de los que se enfadan si alguien se retrasa.

Entro en el coche casi asfixiada.

—¡Vaya, Tatiana, estás *demasiado!* ¡Ese vestido es superguay!

Debo de estar hecha un horror. Apuesto a que Adriana ha comprendido desde el principio que yo necesitaba unas palabras de aliento y dice estas cosas solo para consolarme. Y continúa:

—Tendría que haberme puesto de acuerdo contigo para que me ayudases a vestirme en casa y darme al-

9

gunos toques. Incluso te he llamado para saber qué ropa ibas a llevar, pero el teléfono estaba ocupado.

—Era mi hermano con una de sus novias —expliqué.

—Ya me lo imaginaba —dijo Adriana—. Aunque he insistido porque quería pedirte tu opinión.

—¿A mí? ¿Cómo voy a dar ninguna opinión sobre la ropa de los demás? Además, yo, con esta pinta...

—¡Claro que puedes, Tatiana, qué tontería! Todo el mundo se viste de la misma manera, parece que van uniformados. Tú, no. Incluso puedes repetir la misma camisa o el mismo pantalón, pero siempre consigues inventarte un toque diferente para combinarlos. Leí algo de eso el otro día en la revista *Ternura*. Hay gente que es así, que crea moda, inventa cosas que al poco tiempo usa todo el mundo. Es un don especial, un talento exclusivo. Tú eres así, Tatiana. Y eso tiene un nombre, niña: estilo.

¡Qué grande es Adriana! Adriana, mi mejor amiga. No sé cómo sobreviviría sin ella. Quiero decir hoy por hoy, porque la verdad es que viví mucho tiempo sin saber que ella existía. A fin de cuentas, hace menos de dos años que somos amigas.

Para decirlo todo, antes ni siquiera nos conocíamos. Ella no vivía aquí en Palmeiral. Cuando conocí a Adriana, empecé a comprender lo que puede ser una amiga de verdad.

Desde la primera vez que hablamos, un día frío de

10

invierno, con mucho viento y cielo nublado, supimos que nos entenderíamos.

Fue en las vacaciones de verano. Yo había ido al paseo que bordea la playa, que está muy cerca de mi calle, para ver si Rodolfo estaba jugando al fútbol, porque mi madre quería hablar con él. Hacía tanto viento que no había nadie; solo aquella niña que yo nunca había visto, sentada en la arena. Con una camisa de lana, chaqueta y gorro. En un primer momento pensé que era una extravagante. Pero ella me sonrió e incluso me pareció simpática cuando me preguntó si quería jugar con ella.

—¿A qué?

—¡Qué sé yo! A cualquier cosa, a lo que quieras. Yo no tengo nada que hacer.

—No puedo, tengo que volver a casa. Solo he venido aquí porque mi madre me ha pedido que buscase a mi hermano. Tengo que ir a decirle que no lo he encontrado.

Realmente, yo pensaba que allí no se me había perdido nada, con aquella chicha tan rara y extraña que quería que jugase con ella.

Se levantó y me dijo:

—Entonces voy contigo. Después de que hables con tu madre, jugaremos.

Y fue exactamente eso lo que sucedió. Vino conmigo a casa y acabó quedándose a comer; luego jugamos todo el día. En esa época, yo ya no acostumbraba a jugar, ya no era propio de mi edad tales niñerías.

11

Prefería oír música, ver un vídeo, leer... Aunque, además de algunos ositos de peluche, yo aún conservaba algunos juguetes en mi habitación. En compañía de mi nueva amiga, me fui animando. Comenzamos a jugar al teatro, a maquillarnos y a vestirnos de cosas diferentes.

Fue muy divertido. Ni siquiera sentimos que el tiempo pasaba. Adriana se fue a su casa después de anochecer.

Mi madre me comentó:

—Un poco lanzada esa chica... Si no le hubiese dicho que telefonease a su casa a la hora de comer, ella ni se enteraba... Así, sin pedir permiso ni nada. Y ahora se ha ido porque le he dicho que era ya muy tarde, que si no...

Era lo mismo que yo pensaba. Recordé que ella se había venido conmigo sin avisar a ningún adulto. Es más, no había ningún adulto con ella en la playa. Tal vez mi madre tuviese razón, y fuese una lanzada y no le importase mucho lo que hacía o no. Pero también pudiese ser que solamente fuese más independiente que los demás. Si continuásemos viéndonos, lo sabría.

Pero ¿cómo volveríamos a encontrarnos? Yo no sabía dónde vivía Adriana. No había quedado en nada con ella para vernos otro día. Ni siquiera me había dado su número de teléfono. Bueno, siempre podría ir a la playa otra vez y...

12

Pero nada de eso fue necesario.

Al día siguiente, muy temprano, yo estaba aún medio dormida cuando mi madre abrió la puerta de mi habitación y me dijo:

—Tatiana, esa niña está aquí...

—¿Qué niña?

—La de ayer, Adriana. ¿Quieres que le diga que vuelva más tarde o te levantas ya?

Di un salto en la cama y dije:

—Dile que ya voy. O mejor, mamá, dile que venga aquí.

—No. Si quieres jugar con ella, debes levantarte.

Cuando fui al salón, mi madre ya se había ido al trabajo y Adriana estaba sola frente a la televisión, viendo cómo un gato corría detrás de un ratón en unos dibujos animados. Se reía abiertamente, aunque un poco entrecortadamente. La escena era divertida y me puse a reír con ella. Momentos después estábamos las dos riendo a carcajadas, untando la mantequilla en el pan y sirviéndonos chocolate y leche fría. Y otra vez, pasamos juntas el día entero.

Fuimos ya inseparables el resto de las vacaciones. Supe que aquella semana ella se había mudado de casa a otra en mi misma calle, al edificio enfrente del nuestro. Venía de otro barrio y no conocía a nadie de aquí. Sus padres también se iban muy temprano a trabajar y ella se quedaba sola el día entero, con la chica de servicio, que no se enfadaba si ella salía. Por eso, prácticamente terminó por venirse a vivir conmigo. Solo

13

faltó que mi madre la adoptase, porque tenía la manía de pensar que Adriana llevaba una vida un tanto desordenada.

—Pobrecita, nadie se preocupa de lo que hace, de dónde está, con quién anda... ¡Absurdo! Esta niña necesita atención, cariño..., pobrecita. Carece de muchas cosas...

Mi madre también trabaja —siempre ha trabajado fuera de casa—, y se pasa el día en un despacho lleno de ordenadores, pero casi siempre viene a comer a casa. Y, si no viene, llama por teléfono para controlar la comida. Nunca me ha dejado ir a casa de gente que no conociese. Si yo quiero ir a algún sitio, tengo que pedirle permiso a ella o a mi padre, decirles dónde voy, con quién voy, a qué hora vuelvo y dejar el número de teléfono de donde estoy. En fin, no me da tanta libertad como la madre de Adriana le da a ella, que a mí me parece lo máximo.

Cuando comenzó el segundo trimestre, tuvimos un motivo más para estar más cerca la una de la otra: Adriana se matriculó en mi colegio. No somos del mismo curso, nunca lo hemos sido. Yo ahora estoy en 4.º A y ella en 3.º C. Pero desde aquel momento, nos vemos en el recreo, vamos y volvemos juntas del colegio, y muchas veces acabamos comiendo una en casa de la otra. Y, como yo me apunté a clase de danza a la misma academia que ella, y ella se vino a inglés a la mía, con el mismo horario y en el mismo nivel, tuvimos mucho más tiempo para estar juntas. Fue en esa época cuando ella comenzó a ser mi mejor amiga.

Yo nunca había tenido una amiga así, de verdad. Tenía un montón de compañeras en el colegio, con las que a veces salía el fin de semana, o estudiábamos juntas para algún examen. Además de eso, en vacaciones, cuando íbamos a casa de mi abuela, yo me reencontraba con mis primas y era siempre superdivertido. Pero una gran amiga, que me pusiese en primer lugar en su vida, y con quien yo sabía que podía contar para todo... ah, eso era una novedad. Una novedad maravillosa, además.

Adriana tenía mucha más experiencia de la amistad que yo. En el barrio en el que ella vivía antes, y en el otro colegio, había tenido una gran amiga, Rafaela. Me contó que ellas habían estado muy unidas, casi como nosotras lo estamos ahora, aunque tal vez un poco menos, porque me parece que amistad igual a la nuestra nunca habrá y nunca pudo haber existido antes. Rafaela le hizo una cosa horrible a Adriana, y justamente en el momento en que ella más la necesitaba; por eso dejaron de ser amigas.

Incluso hoy recuerdo la cara de Adriana, llorando, cuando me contó lo que le había pasado. Unas lágrimas llenas de tristeza y de rabia. Lo que sucedió fue que Rafaela, que siempre había sido su amiga, dio un gran fiesta de cumpleaños cuando cumplió los trece. *¿Sabes, una de esas fiestas que se dan en un club, que tiene de todo, incluso sorteos de premios,* disc-joquey *y baile?*

Pues una fiesta de esas. Adriana le había ayudado a pensar en todas las cosas que debía haber en la fiesta, y con ellas habían hecho una lista. Y otra lista con los nombres de todos los chicos que debían asistir. En cuanto a las chicas, ya se sabe que las madres encuentran la forma de que todas sean invitadas, incluso las más bordes, esas que siempre queremos evitar. Pero Adriana y Rafaela trataron de organizarlo todo lo mejor que pudieron. Se habían aconsejado sobre los vestidos que cada una iba a llevar, habían escogido juntas la música que se iba a poner, el lugar de la fiesta, la fecha más apropiada, ¡todo!

Y claro, como siempre, habían tenido que cambiar algunas cosas. El padre de Rafaela se opuso a algunas ideas, porque dijo que de aquella manera la fiesta iba a costar un capitalazo, tenía que ser en un lugar más barato... Y su madre dijo que el día escogido por ellas —un sábado después del cumpleaños, como es lógico— no era la buena, porque ella debía estudiar para los exámenes de la semana siguiente. Dijo que era mejor tres sábados más tarde, cuando ya estuviesen de vacaciones. A pesar de todos los inconvenientes, la fiesta fue lo máximo. Todo el mundo salió hablando de ella, contando lo maravillosa que había sido, cómo se habían divertido, qué apetitosa había sido la comida, con tanto chico guapo, tanta música guay... Solo que, a fin de cuentas, Adriana no fue invitada. *¿Qué te parece?*

Cuando ella me lo contó, lloraba:

16

—¡Acabé quedándome fuera de la fiesta que yo misma había ayudado a organizar! Y en el momento en que yo más necesitaba...

—¿Por qué? —pregunté, afligida, sin saber lo que hacer al ver los ojos de mi amiga llenándose de lágrimas.

—Porque yo estaba mudándome de casa, me iba del colegio donde estudié toda la vida, el Santa Rita era como si fuese mi casa... Dejaba el curso, perdía a todos los colegas y amigos... Necesitaba consuelo y amistad. Y ella no contó conmigo, ¡como si ya no le sirviese para nada, como si ya no tuviese un lugar en su vida! ¡Qué idiota!

—No, no te he preguntado por eso. Te pregunto por qué ella hizo lo que hizo... —insistí.

—¿Y qué sé yo? Debió de pensar que ya no iba a necesitar nada de mí, porque me iba a mudar a otro barrio, muy lejos... Pensaría que mi padre ya no la recogería en su casa para ir al colegio, como hacíamos siempre... Yo ya no la llamaría más para ver un vídeo en mi casa, o invitarla a pasar un fin de semana en Santa Helena. Ya no le servía para nada... Demasiado interesada, eso es que ella es... Y yo que pensaba que era mi amiga... Bueno, me estoy pasando un poco...

Al tiempo que hablaba, Adriana se encogía de hombros y ponía cara de desprecio. Pero estaba claro que lo estaba pasando mal, sí. ¡Y tanto! Las lágrimas caían por su rostro y a cada instante sollozaba. Intenté consolarla, le pasé el brazo por los hombros, le acaricié el pelo, le hablé con dulzura:

—¡Olvídate de todo eso! Soy tu amiga, Adriana, de verdad... Tú no necesitas a Rafaela. Deja de pensar en ella.

Furiosa y resentida me respondió:

—¡Qué imbécil! Pero nunca más hablé con ella. Se cansó de llamarme por teléfono, pero nunca me puse.

—¿Aún tiene valor para llamarte por teléfono? —pregunté, extrañada.

—Un montón de veces. Pero incluso, cuando mi madre me obligó a atenderla, desconecté con el dedo y fingí que le estaba hablando.

—Pero, ¿qué fue lo que ella te dijo? —insistí, curiosa.

—No lo sé ni quiero saberlo, ni ganas de que me lo cuenten. Debía de querer pedir perdón, o inventarse una disculpa cualquiera. Pero no tiene perdón. Una cosa de esas no tiene disculpa. Nunca. Y nunca más quiero ver su cara delante de mí.

—¡Claro que no tiene perdón! —asentí—. ¡No llamar a la mejor amiga en su cumpleaños!

Mi tono de voz quería decir más de lo que dije. Era una especie de promesa de que yo nunca haría nada semejante, jamás. Un juramento de amistad fiel y eterna. Como yo sabía que sería la nuestra.

2 Una amiga está para estas cosas

La fiesta no fue nada del otro mundo, pero nos divertimos, a pesar de la presencia de unas estúpidas del colegio. Especialmente Débora, que piensa que ella es lo máximo y que anda siempre mariposeando alrededor de los chicos de manera que ellos acaban inevitablemente fijándose en ella. Es de esas que a la hora de saludar siempre da besitos, habla muy despacio, suelta risitas a cada instante, como si lo que el chico de turno le está diciendo fuese de lo más divertido del mundo y ella el súmmum de la inteligencia. Solo falta que se le caiga la baba delante de ellos. De vez en cuando, simula un tremendo cansancio, afectadísima, y apoya la cabeza en el hombro o en el pecho del chico que está a su lado. Y a la hora de despedirse, mucho peor... Tarda horas en despedirse, va uno a uno, susurrándoles cositas al oído, secretitos... ¡Detesto a Débora! Es una idiota, una ignorante que no tiene idea de nada, ya ha repetido curso dos veces y fue expulsada del colegio del que vino. Y, además, se ríe de todo aquel que estudia.

Fue ella la que empezó a decir que yo hablo de «forma complicada», solo porque usé una palabra que había leído —no me acuerdo de cuál, tal vez algo como el súmmum que he dicho antes— y ella no sabía qué quería decir. Cuando ella está cerca, sé que en cualquier momento alguien puede reírse de mí. O se forman grupitos y se ponen a cuchichear, a mirarme, y se alejan. ¡Me entra una rabia! He llorado mucho por su culpa.

Antes de ser amiga de Adriana era mucho peor. En una fiesta de esas, si yo no estuviese con Adriana, podría haber sido un desastre. Estaba medio perdida, totalmente sola. Pero con mi amiga, todo es diferente. Tengo compañía y refugio en ella, como si me desentendiese de lo que pasa a mi alrededor. Una amiga está para estas cosas.

Fue lo que hicimos en la fiesta. Fuimos las dos a nuestra bola, y dejamos de lado a los chicos que conocíamos del colegio. Todos revoloteaban alrededor de Débora, como si fuesen moscas en un panal de rica miel.

Al final, encontramos a un chico interesante, que estaba solo en la terraza. Me gustó, aunque no era exactamente lo que se dice guapo. Tenía unos ojos bonitos. En un momento en que Adriana se fue detrás de un camarero que llevaba una bandeja de refrescos, él se puso a hablar conmigo.

—Hace mucho calor ahí dentro...

—Sí... —asentí.

—Por eso me he venido para aquí...

—Sí..., hace más fresco.

—¿Tú eres amiga de Carla?

—Sí. Estudiamos en el mismo colegio. ¿Y tú?

Yo sabía que él no estudiaba en nuestro colegio. Si lo hiciese, ya lo habría visto. No iba a dejar de fijarme en un chico con aquella mirada. Y, por lo menos de vista, conozco a todo el mundo en el Anita. A fin de cuentas, no es un colegio tan grande y hace tiempo que estudio allí.

—No. Soy su primo.

—¿Dónde estudias?

—En el Cruzeiro.

Me entró la mayor de la dudas. ¿Hablo? ¿No hablo? Hablaré: siempre es motivo para continuar la conversación.

—¡Qué coincidencia! Mi hermano también estudia allí.

—¿Quién es tu hermano?

—Luis Rodolfo, no sé si lo conoces...

No, no lo conocía. Si fuese un amiguete de los suyos, sería un desastre.

Cuando Adriana volvió con dos vasos de refresco, solo había podido descubrir que él era dos años mayor que yo y que se llamaba Diego. Los presenté, y aproveché para decirle mi nombre pero la conversación no siguió adelante. No sé si a él Adriana le pareció una enana —ella es muy joven y, como es bajita, parece todavía más niña, o si ya se había cansado de hablar o si no encontró forma de hacerlo con dos chicas a la vez. Se despidió educadamente y entró. Desapareció de nuestra vista.

Carla vive en un dúplex. Pienso que Diego debe de haberse metido en algún lugar del piso de arriba, probablemente con Víctor, que es el hermano de Carla, muy guapo y un poco mayor, pero que no se dignó a aparecer por la fiesta ni un minuto. Si Diego era su primo debía de ser íntimo de la casa.

Pero en la fiesta había mucha más gente. Y nosotras dos bailamos, y anduvimos todo el tiempo de un lado a otro hablando con la gente. Apenas había nadie interesante. Quiero decir chicos, que es lo que interesa. Estaban divididos en dos grupos, salvo Diego, completamente aislado, y que luego desapareció, como ya he dicho. Los mayores formaban una nube de moscas alrededor de Débora. Los otros —unos niñatos— habían comenzado por una batalla de palomitas de maíz, luego se tiraron patatas fritas unos a otros, más tarde jugaron a las prendas con los bocadillos, y finalmente acabaron dándole toques con el pie a un palito de chupa-chups como si fuese una balón de fútbol. Y así, en medio de un griterío total, contaban a ver quién conseguía darle más veces sin dejarlo caer; y el palito aquel se llenaba de porquería a cada golpe. No consigo ver qué gracia encuentran los chicos en esas porquerías.

¡Un asco!

Está claro que una fiesta siempre es el mejor tema para una charla. Al día siguiente, cuando estaba desayunando, Adriana me telefoneó. Teníamos muchísimas cosas que comentar del día anterior, pero era domingo, y mis padres estaban en casa en medio de un montón de periódicos esparcidos por el salón. Muy pronto mi madre me reprochó:

—Te pasas la vida entera colgada del teléfono.

Apenas había hablado un rato, cuando mi padre pasó muy cerca de mí enseñándome el reloj en su muñeca izquierda y golpeando la esfera con un dedo de la mano derecha, señal para que acabase rápido. Ya lo sabía, no podría hablar mucho tiempo más.

Poco después, volvió a la carga:

—Tatiana, lleváis más de quince minutos colgadas del teléfono.

Tuve que desconectar. Será que nadie entiende que Adriana es mi mejor amiga y que tenemos millones de cosas que decirnos. En su casa es diferente, sus padres no están pendientes del tiempo que su hija habla por teléfono.

Esa es otra cosa que envidio de mi amiga:

—¡Mis padres son de piñón fijo! Para todo hay que tener un horario. Si quiero levantarme a las once un domingo, no puedo. No me vale decirles que es domingo, que no tengo clase, que puedo hacer lo que quiera. Y, a decir verdad, ellos me dejan estar en cama el tiempo que quiera, pero cuando me levanto ya no hay desayuno, ni nada, y tengo que arreglármelas sola...

—Tú podías dormir aquí el sábado —me propuso ella—. Aquí, en mi casa no pasa eso que me cuentas. Está siempre la asistenta que también viene los domingos. Nadie se preocupa de la hora a la que te levantas.

Y acepté su ofrecimiento. La primera vez fue muy divertido. Pero la segunda vez me desperté yo sola a las ocho. Estaba en casa ajena, no podía levantarme y empezar a revolver en cosas que no eran mías. Ni encender la luz, o coger un libro, o ir al salón y poner la tele... Fui al cuarto de baño, me cepillé los dientes, intenté arreglarme el pelo y ensayé un montón de peinados, lo recogí, me hice unas trenzas, lo solté de nuevo... Después miré el reloj y ni siquiera eran las nueve... Me metí en la cama y allí me quedé esperando, observando la habitación y pensando en la vida. Siglos más tarde, volví a mirar el reloj otra vez: no habían pasado ni quince minutos.

Si estuviese en mi casa, ya me habría levantado, estaría en la cocina ayudando a mi madre a preparar el café o en la mesa desayunando con todo el mundo —seguramente Rodolfo estaría metiéndose conmigo, y ahora no me parecía mal, era divertido...— Y si nadie se hubiese levantado, yo ya habría cogido leche de la nevera, ya me habría hecho una tostada con mantequilla o mermelada, y luego seguramente me tumbaría en el sofá del salón y me pondría a leer mi libro, viviendo cosas que la familia March vive, ¡ay, qué maravilla! No sé si habéis leído *Mujercitas*... Si lo habéis

24

leído, no me contéis el final. Si no lo habéis leído, buscadlo, es buenísimo. Es la historia de cuatro hermanas —incluso hicieron una película, *Mujercitas*—. Pues aquella vez que dormí en casa de Adriana, me quedé en una cama plegable de su habitación, esperando a que alguien se despertase, e imaginando lo que Jo March haría en el próximo capítulo de aquel libro que me había dejado en casa.

Si estoy metida en una buena lectura, siempre me pasa esto, que me cuesta salir de la historia cuando cierro el libro. Y siento que deseo comentarlo con todo el mundo. Es una pena que a Adriana no le guste leer. Si le gustase, sería la desesperación de mi padre, porque tendríamos materia para pasar horas y horas colgadas del teléfono.

De cualquier manera, no me parece mal. Somos amigas, pero ella no está obligada a que le guste lo que a mí me gusta.

Por ejemplo, ella flipa con las películas de terror, y yo no las soporto. Cada vez que vamos a ver un vídeo a su casa, ya sé que voy a asistir a cosas del tipo *Pesadilla, Viernes 13,* o *La noche de los muertos vivientes*. Para mí son una pérdida de tiempo. Son todas tan idiotas que hasta tiene su gracia y algunas pueden ser divertidas por eso. De todas formas, con una película de terror de vez en cuando, ya basta. Si veo más de una, me parecen todas iguales. Los mismos sustos, las mismas caras horrorosas. Y después no se me queda nada bien el cuerpo, no tengo ningún buen recuerdo de ellas, ¿entendéis? Al contrario. De vez en cuando, a medianoche, cuando me despierto para ir a beber agua o ir al cuarto de baño, recuerdo aquellas imágenes idiotas, no consigo dormir y me quedo un buen rato sin poder apagar la luz. No es exactamente miedo, sino una cosa muy desagradable, como si mi piel estuviese a punto de sufrir un estremecimiento y yo esperase la aparición de un monstruo de esos para dar un grito.

Sé que es ridículo que me sienta así, pero no consigo controlarme. De día, comprendo que pueda ser divertido. De noche, y yo sola, me da una cosa...

Intenté explicarle eso a Adriana, pero a ella le parece graciosísimo. No tiene ni la menor idea de lo que siento. Yo tampoco consigo imaginar cómo ella puede decir que los libros son tonterías, que le producen sueño, que no ve la menor gracia en esa gran cantidad de letras negras que manchan el papel, que encuentra un montón de palabras que no entiende, o que se distrae, que se olvida de lo que ha leído antes, qué sé yo... ¡Es que somos diferentes y ya está!

Y en otras cosas también lo somos. Cuando nos conocimos y ella se vino al Anita —el nombre de mi colegio es Anita Garibaldi—, no comprendía que yo quisiera quedarme a jugar al voleibol después de salir de clase.

—No sé qué gracia le encuentras, francamente, Tatiana... Estar toda sudada en un campo de cemento esperando a que alguien te haga un bloqueo de balón... ¡Hay cosas mucho más interesantes en la vida!

—No es eso, Adriana, es un juego que mola cantidad.

—¡A mí no me mola nada! Tener que tirarse al suelo par darle al balón, y, cuando fallas, todo el mundo te lo echa en cara... Si aciertas, va luego otra jugadora y estropea todo tu esfuerzo... Te matas para nada. Una idiotez.

¡Pero yo adoraba el voleibol! No iba a dejar de jugar por causa de ella.

Poco después descubrí que ella no sentía lo que decía. Adriana protestaba porque no sabía jugar. El equipo del Santa Rita, su antiguo colegio, era tan bueno que ella nunca tuvo una oportunidad de jugar. Con el tiempo, y las clases de Educación Física de Alcides, fue aprendiendo y hoy en día ya le gusta. De vez en cuando me dice:

—Si no fuese por ti, Tatiana, yo no jugaría al voleibol...

Creo que es verdad. Y también tengo que reconocer que si no fuese por ella, yo no bailaría.

Siempre tuve ganas de saber bailar, me parecía lo máximo. Pero no sabía bailar y prefería decir que no me gustaba. Nadie me había enseñado. Cuando lo intentaba, me encontraba torpe, estúpida, una cosa muy diferente de esas jóvenes tan ágiles y tan guapas que se ven bailando en la tele, y que son una hermosura.

Y tengo que reconocer que también me sentía muy diferente de las chicas de éxito, como Débora.

Y mira que lo había intentado veces. Aunque tengo que decir que solo lo hacía cuando había mucha gente bailando al mismo tiempo y yo creía que nadie se iba a fijar en un desastre como yo en medio de la multitud, allí con todo el mundo sacudiéndose al son de la música. Pero incluso Cris, que era mi mejor amiga antes de llegar Adriana, no conseguía disimular la risa:

—¡Ay, Tatiana, qué haces! No das pie con bola...

Y llamaba a las otras chicas y les decía:

—Mirad, mirad cómo baila Tatiana...

Me ponía furiosa, pero fingía que no me importaba. Ellas reían y querían enseñarme:

—Es así, mira...

—Suelta el cuerpo, mueve las caderas...

—Haz así con el pie.

—Balancéate de esta forma... Mírame.

Lo intentaba, pero me obsesionaba no saber cómo iba a echar el pie y cómo iba a mover los brazos al mismo tiempo... y no lo conseguía. Ellas se reían. Y yo me quedaba toda chafada, loca por ser como ellas. Tenía que reconocer que Cris tenía razón: yo debía parecerles un elefante en una cacharrería, como ella me dijo una vez.

Cris siempre tuvo esa gran cualidad: la franqueza. Siempre me habló con toda sinceridad de mis defectos.

Incluso la admiraba por eso. Me dolía lo que me decía, pero la admiraba. Tenía que reconocer que era honrada, por más furiosa que me pusiese. Y creo que mi rabia aumentaba al reconocer esa franqueza y ni siquiera poder odiarla. Es una gran cualidad, y además muy rara. No tenía otra salida más que admirarla. ¿Complicado, no? Pero eso es lo que yo sentía.

Más tarde, después de conocer a Adriana, un día ella me dijo:

—Me parece una tontería esa forma que tienes de vestirte de forma diferente a todos...

Y, de repente, ese comentario me pareció un arco iris en el cielo, con muchas campanitas sonando. Porque, al momento, como un rayo que cae, como una luz que se enciende en la oscuridad comprendí que la franqueza de Cris era siempre del mismo tipo: me señalaba mis defectos y me derrumbaba. En tantos años de amistad —a fin de cuentas éramos compañeras desde la guardería infantil— ella nunca había usado su franqueza para decirme algo bueno de mí. ¡Nunca! ¿Sabéis lo que es eso? ¡No era posible que yo no tuviese algo que mereciese ser elogiado! O, si yo tenía alguna cualidad y Cris no conseguía descubrirla, sería porque no era una amiga de verdad...

Claro, yo no sabía bailar. Eso ni siquiera Adriana podía negarlo; y no lo negó. Pero la primera vez que me vio bailar, no dijo nada en aquel momento, ni lo comentó con nadie.

Esperó a una tarde en que estábamos solas en su casa y me propuso:

—¿Qué tal si bailamos un poco?

—No me gusta bailar —me disculpé.

—¡No es posible, Tatiana! ¡Es superguay! Es lo mismo que si alguien dice que no le gusta la música, o que no le mola la playa.

—A mí no me gusta.

—No lo creo, Tatiana. Le gusta a todo el mundo. ¡Es una de las mejores cosas del mundo! ¿Has visto a algún bebé cuando oye música? ¿Acaso no se pone a mover los bracitos y a balancearse? ¡Pues eso! Bailar es algo natural, como andar o correr. No se puede decir que no nos gusta, que no nos mola...

—Es que yo no tengo mucha facilidad para bailar, ¿sabes?

—Entonces es que te falta práctica. Tienes que entrenarte. Vamos, yo te enseño...

Escogió un CD, lo puso y empezó a enseñarme cómo se hacía...

Al principio, me moría de vergüenza. Pero después lo repetimos un montón de veces y me fui animando. Descubrí que muchos de aquellos ritmos que la gente baila en las fiestas tenían una coreografía que solo se podía aprender si se ensayaba antes, unas chicas con otras. Los chicos no lo hacen; por eso ellos bailan menos en la fiestas y sienten vergüenza por no saber. A la madre de Adriana le gustaba mucho salir de noche a bailar. Aprendía todos los pasos, ensayaba en casa y se los enseñaba a su hija. Luego también me enseñó a mí.

Hoy por hoy me las voy arreglando. Puedo no ser Madonna, pero no me corto un pelo. Incluso me apunté a una academia de jazz y danza moderna con Adriana.

3   Parloteos y patabalón

¡INTERMINAAAABLE!

Mi padre cuenta que antiguamente pasaban por la tele un anuncio de una hoja de afeitar y en él decían que duraba más que todas las demás porque era así: ¡Interminaaaable!

—Creo que las conversaciones de estas dos deben de ser del tipo de esa hoja de afeitar. ¡Un parloteo interminaaaable! —comentó él hablando no se sabe con quién o tal vez consigo mismo, después de atender el teléfono—. Ahora va a comenzar de nuevo.

No se dio cuenta que yo estaba a punto de entrar en el salón, porque gritó hacia el fondo del pasillo:

—¡Tatiana, el teléfono!

Y en voz más baja, me dijo:

—Es Adriana, claro.

Solo la mala fe de un padre puede llamar parloteo a un intercambio de ideas entre dos personas que comparten determinados intereses. ¡Caray, qué bien me ha salido esto! ¡Qué lástima que no se me haya ocurrido hace un momento, cuando me dio el teléfono! ¡Se lo soltaría en su cara! Pero ahora él está a punto de salir. Martes y viernes, llega un poco más temprano, se cambia de ropa y sale corriendo para jugar al fútbol —al que yo tengo el respeto de no llamar *patabalón*— con los amigos en un campo de arena que hacen en la playa, muy cerca de nuestra calle. Va un montón de gente a verlos desde el paseo marítimo.

Pero todo va bien, porque mi madre ha llegado a la hora de siempre y Adriana y yo podemos charlar a nuestras anchas. Comentamos las cosas del colegio, el nuevo corte de pelo de Luana, el examen sorpresa de Matemáticas en su clase, el trabajo de grupo que el profesor de Historia nos mandó hacer, y un montón de cosas más.

Y sé muy bien que, si mi padre estuviese cerca, se pondría a protestar: «¿Por qué en vez de ese chismorreo no os vais a jugar?» me pregunta él a veces. «Moveos, tomad el aire libre, practicad algún deporte, en vez de estar siempre con ese bla, bla, bla...».

O tal vez me preguntaría si no hemos tenido tiempo suficiente en el colegio para charlar de esas cosas. Pues no lo hemos tenido. Primero, porque son muchas cosas; segundo, porque no estamos juntas todo el tiempo, no estamos en el mismo curso... No podemos decírnoslo todo entre clase y clase; tercero, y más importante, porque algunas cosas son muy delicadas y no se puede poner una a hablar de ellas con todo el mundo alrededor, interrumpiéndonos a cada momento o poniendo la oreja para enterarse. Siempre puede haber alguien que nos oiga. Y, aunque no lo parezca, esa falta de intimidad puede causar problemas serios.

34

Además hoy, queríamos comentar unas cosas de Cris, y no podía ser en el colegio.

Ya sabéis quién es. Ya he dicho que Cris era mi mejor amiga antes de que llegase Adriana. Después me di cuenta de que solo es franca a la contra, nunca a favor. Y me aparté un poco de ella. También porque ya hablaba más con Adriana. Pero me gusta Cris y continúo siendo su amiga. Solo que últimamente le dio por meterse un poco con Adriana.

No sé si meterse es la palabra exacta. Tengo la certeza de que no lo hace a mala idea. Cris suelta sin pensarlo dos veces todas las cosas que le pasan por la cabeza, aunque la mayoría de ellas son tonterías, cosas inofensivas. Ella no quiere perjudicar a nadie. Es una persona legal, que sería incapaz de hacer eso a propósito, puedo garantizarlo pero es tan irresponsable que hace daño. Y de vez en cuando provoca situaciones un tanto extrañas.

El otro día, por ejemplo, hubo una reunión en el colegio en la que nos juntamos varios cursos para discutir un proyecto de intercambio que desarrollamos con la Escuela Pública Ana Neri, de la Favela de Teimosía, que está muy lejos de nuestro colegio. Es algo que llevamos años haciendo.

Ellos tienen un profesor de *capoeira*, o lucha brasileña, que viene a darnos clases a nuestro colegio. Una vez al mes, los alumnos del Ana Negri nos visitan y hacemos una mesa redonda conjunta. ¡Es lo máximo! Además nosotros nos comprometimos a proporcionarles libros para su biblioteca. Durante todo el año hacemos campañas para recaudar dinero, vamos a las librerías, escogemos libros, los compramos, y se los damos. Tenemos también unos equipos que van allí una vez por semana a contar cuentos e historias a los pequeños. Luego organizamos debates con los mayores sobre los libros. Es estupendo y hemos conocido gente increíble.

Pues el caso es que en esa reunión surgió una idea para ampliar nuestro trabajo e incluir en él a los niños abandonados en la calle. Al momento, todo el mundo comenzó a hablar al mismo tiempo y se formó un gran debate. Estos son algunos de los puntos que se discutieron:

1. Si esto no iba a comprometer nuestra meta actual, que era la de desarrollar muy pronto un proyecto de colaboración en tareas de informática con el Ana Neri, aprovechando que el Gobierno le había concedido unos ordenadores.

2. Si valía la pena correr el riesgo de trabajar en varios frentes y dispersar nuestro esfuerzo.

3. Si nuestra colaboración con el Ana Neri, después de tanto tiempo, no se había transformado en un asunto entre amigos y que estamos tan animados porque disfrutamos mucho con esto, y ya no vemos más allá.

4. Si, de verdad, transformar solidaridad en amistad no es exactamente la mejor consecuencia de ese

proyecto; mientras el objetivo es ir cada vez más al fondo del problema.

5. Si de esta forma no estaríamos dejando de lado a quien más nos necesita.

6. Si, para intentar incluir a los niños de la calle, no íbamos a precisar una ayuda más especializada por parte de los adultos, además de los profesores —es decir, asistentes sociales, y todo eso—, porque por mucho que queramos, no tenemos preparación para salir por toda la ciudad a buscar niños abandonados... ¿para hacer qué? Y si ellos no fuesen niños abandonados y fuesen solamente pobres que están jugando en la calle o yendo a cualquier parte? ¿Cómo hacemos para saberlo sin ofenderlos? ¿Los vigilamos para saber dónde duermen por la noche? ¿Qué les preguntamos? Ya me lo imagino: «Oye, disculpa, soy Mariana, del Colegio Anita Garibaldi, y quería saber si tú eres un verdadero niño de la calle?» ¿No es ridículo?

En fin, ya podéis imaginar que la tal reunión estaba a punto de convertirse en un volcán. Los profesores intentaban poner orden, y la coordinadora estaba a punto de perder su nombre, porque no coordinaba nada, y todos daban su opinión a la vez.

Pues bien, en el momento en que todo parecía que se iba al garete y por todos los lados se oía a hablar de niños pobres y no sé qué más, Cris resolvió disparar:

—¿Qué es lo que piensas de todo esto, Adriana? Podía ayudarnos mucho tu opinión, porque todo este asunto de los abandonados tiene mucho que ver contigo misma, ¿no? Por experiencia propia...

Menos mal que la confusión era tanta que poca gente escuchó lo que dijo. Pero a Adriana se le llenaron los ojos de lágrimas. Se levantó de repente y salió del auditorio.

Intenté echarle una bronca a Cris, pero ella comenzó a justificarse, como si hubiese hecho el comentario más natural del mundo:

—Déjate de bobadas, Tatiana. No vengas a darme lecciones de moral solo porque he sido sincera. Su propia madre anda diciendo a todo el mundo que Adriana es una inocente a la que nadie le hace caso. Y todo el mundo sabe que es verdad. Es solo un chiste. En la vida hay que tener sentido del humor, ¿sabes?

Me pareció que era mejor no discutir. Me fui tras Adriana, que disimulaba en el pasillo, bebiendo agua y diciendo que tenía una mota en el ojo. Respeté su voluntad de no hablar del asunto, pero yo sabía que el comentario la había machacado y me enfadé mucho con Cris.

La semana pasada ella hizo otra faena, aunque muy diferente. Para explicarla, tengo que comenzar contando algunas cosas antes, si no, no se entendería. Y, además, tengo que hablar de Fabio.

Pienso que Fabio es un asco. Pero él se cree interesante y simpático, solo porque anda con una pandilla de guapitos. Y, como anda en medio de ellos, tiene siempre chicas a su alrededor. Pero él no se imagina que no van por él, sino por los otros. O, si lo imagina, sabe perfectamente que usa a los otros como anzuelo solamente para quedarse con las sobras. Hay mucha gente así. Incluso yo, que no tengo apenas experiencia de estas cosas, ya he conocido a algunos. Si os fijáis, descubriréis gente así.

De cualquier manera, Fabio es un horror. Un tipo que quiere aparentar lo máximo, y por encima, un tremendo pelota. Prácticamente vive en casa de Carla, porque es muy amigo de Víctor, su hermano. Ese sí que es un tipazo, pero a él debemos de parecerle unas crías, porque ni siquiera nos mira. Bien, Fabio dice que es muy amigo de Víctor, pero no hay nada de eso. Es amigo de ellos porque el padre de Víctor y Carla es Vic Bellini. ¡El vocalista de Razones Ocultas! ¡Él mismo! Ese rubio de pelo largo y ojos azules que aparece a todas horas en la televisión y en las revistas. Mi madre dice que él fue muy guapo y un excelente músico. No sé, para mí es un poco viejo, no me lo imagino de joven, pero puede ser. Quiero decir que, por su aspecto actual, me creo que pueda haber sido guapo. Víctor se le parece mucho y no puede ser más guapo. Es un tipo tranquilo, buen alumno, con novia de siempre, Marta, de su mismo curso...

En fin, volviendo a Fabio, tengo la certeza de que no es un amigo de verdad de Víctor. Quiere estar cerca de él para aprovecharse de la fama de su padre..., eso de vivir en su casa, fingiendo ser íntimo de los artistas que aparecen por allí, que van a ensayar, y que le piden favores, que les vaya a buscar cualquier cosa...

No quiero perder mucho tiempo hablando de Fabio, solo quiero contar algo de Cris. Por lo que ya he dicho, podéis imaginar de qué va. Algunos días después de la fiesta que dio Carla, Fabio estaba a la salida del colegio con Marcie y Claudia— no debía dar sus nombres porque ellas son de otro curso y no van a entrar en esta historia— y allí, parados en la calle, charlaban mientras esperaban a la madre de Claudia, que iba a buscar a su hija en coche. Adriana salía en ese momento y, como ese día su padre había traído a Claudia al colegio —vivían muy cerca una de la otra— fue normal que la llamase:

—Oye, Adriana, ¿quieres que te llevemos a casa? Mi madre no tardará, está a punto de llegar.

Y así fue como, en un coche atestado de gente con la que ella no tenía confianza ninguna, Adriana oyó que Fabio decía:

—Pues Carla no me invitó a su fiesta...

—Yo pensé que Víctor te avisaría —dijo Marcie.

—No, no era su fiesta. Era solo de su hermana y de toda aquella panda de críos.

—¡Ah, por eso no fuiste!

—Pero no fue por eso; habría ido si quisiera. No necesito invitación para ir, yo soy de la casa, como ellos mismos dicen. Pero no fui y le dije que se quedase a gusto con esos amiguitos que tiene. ¿Te imaginas tener que aguantar a Carla? Charlar con ella y todas esas cosas. ¡Dios me libre! Es un espantajo, parece una bruja. Si alguien se la encuentra en la oscuridad se lleva tal susto que se muere de miedo... ¿O no? Es la chica más fea que he visto en mi vida.

Adriana se quedó espantada, tenía vergüenza de estar oyendo aquello. Pero él continuó:

—¡Y todavía hay más!

Las otras se quedaron en silencio, prestando atención. Él añadió:

—No os lo podéis ni imaginar, pero es verdad. Carla huele muy mal. Cuando está muy cerca de uno, despide un olor ácido, como de mal aliento, o a no sé qué. No es un olor muy fuerte, sino vaho asqueroso que se pega y no se te va. Da asco, ganas de salir corriendo. Me parece que no se ducha mucho...

Adriana me dijo que todo el mundo sintió el mismo malestar que ella al oír aquellas cosas. Debió de haber sido así, porque desde el asiento delantero, la madre de Claudia, que era la que conducía, sacó rápidamente otro tema de conversación y nadie habló más del asunto. Pero al día siguiente, a la hora del recreo, cuando Adriana me contaba esto, toda horrorizada, Cris se acercó y quiso saber de qué estábamos hablando. Adriana se lo contó desde el principio.

La reacción de Cris fue igual a la nuestra. Se puso furiosa.

—¡Qué tipo más asqueroso es Fabio! Vive metido en casa de Carla, dice que es como si fuese de la familia y viene con una bajeza de estas, en público...

¿Que huele mal? Francamente, nunca he tenido esa sensación.

—Claro que no, Cris, porque nada de eso es verdad. Como mucho, puede ser que no use suficiente desodorante, o que use una marca que no funciona bien. Si oliese mal de verdad, todo el mundo lo sabría, no solo la delicadísima nariz del cerdo de Fabio, evidentemente. Es más, si la miras bien te darás cuenta que no es fea, de verdad. Puede parecerlo, pero no lo es. Carla es mona, lo que pasa es que es diferente. No tiene un tipo común, como todo el mundo. Tiene una cara expresiva, con rasgos definidos, así un poco... —intenté describirla.

—No importa —me cortó Adriana—. Aunque fuese horrorosa e inmunda, Fabio no debe decir esas cosas.

—Si él piensa que le huele el aliento, o que necesita darse más duchas, debía acercarse a ella y decírselo, francamente... —comenzó Cris su discurso, fiel a su línea de defensora de la franqueza—.¡Francamente, en absoluto! —la interrumpí—. No tiene que decirle nada. Ese tipo de franqueza no hace ningún bien a la gente...

—Como mucho, y si fuese verdad y él quisiera ayudarla, podía hablar con Víctor, con tacto, con la mayor diplomacia y delicadeza, para que él le diese un toque a su hermana —sugirió Adriana—. A fin de cuentas, ¿no anda él diciendo por ahí que son muy amigos?

—Bueno, eso es... —asintió Cris—. De cualquier modo, lo que yo te quería decir es que es absurdo que

Fabio se ponga a hablar de esa manera sobre Carla. ¡No tiene derecho! ¡Es un borde, un idiota!

—¡Un bocazas!

—Un...

Estábamos todos de acuerdo y le buscábamos a Fabio los adjetivos más adecuados. Las tres opinábamos lo mismo sobre él. Y todo podía haber quedado ahí.

Pero al día siguiente, cuando estábamos en la cola del comedor para recoger nuestra bandeja, apareció Fabio. Y Cris decidió tomarse la justicia por su mano.

—Francamente, Fabio, ¿cómo tuviste el coraje de hablar de Carla en la forma en que lo hiciste?

Él puso cara de santito:

—¿Yo? ¿De Carla? ¡Tú deliras, chica!

Ella se puso furiosa y empezó a hablar más alto:

—¿Te atreves a negarlo? ¿Vas a decir que no dijiste que Carla es la chica más fea...

—¿Estás hablando de mí? —interrumpió, muy sonriente, Carla. ¿Quién podía ser, si no? La cual se acercaba en aquel momento y, nada más oír su nombre, entró en la conversación.

Apenas tuve tiempo de coger a Cris y salir con ella de la cola antes de que nadie dijese ninguna palabra más. Adriana se quedó e intentó desviar la conversación. Pero en cuanto Carla se fue, se lanzó contra Adriana.

—¡Eres un loro! Repites todo lo que oyes, ¿no? Eres una niñata enredadora... Eso es lo que pasa por hablar delante de niños pequeños. Pero me las vas a pagar, esto no a quedar así. Vas a ver tú...

De nada le valió negarlo, decir que no sabía de qué hablaba, prometerle que ella no había dicho nada. El mal estaba hecho.

En una esquina del patio, yo le cantaba las cuarenta a Cris. Un poco después apareció Adriana, aún a tiempo de oír lo que me dijo:

—Parte de la culpa es vuestra. ¿Quién os ha mandado contarme esas cosas sin pedirme que las guardase en secreto? Si me hubieseis dicho que no debía contárselo a nadie, yo me lo guardaba para mí...

—¿Crees que era necesario, Cris? Hay cosas que son tan evidentes que cualquiera las comprende... —le respondí yo.

Adriana no dijo nada. No hacía más que llorar. Cris continuaba haciéndose la ofendida por la bronca que le había echado.

—Todo el mundo sabe que soy una persona muy discreta, que sé guardar un secreto. Pero hay que decirme que es un secreto, no lo voy a adivinar yo. Si no es un secreto, yo puedo comentarlo, francamente, con cualquiera. No hice nada de particular. Lo que pasa es...

—¡Cris! —la interrumpí—. ¿Cuándo vas a aprender que esa franqueza tuya, de la que tanto presumes, no siempre es una virtud? A veces se puede convertir en un arma de doble filo, ¿sabes?

—¿Qué dices? ¿Quieres que me vuelva una menti-

44

rosa? ¿Una cobarde? ¿Que alguien vea cómo atacan a Carla por la espalda, pobre, y ese alguien, que se dice amigo, no haga nada? ¿Que ni siquiera intente hacer algo en su defensa?

—No se trata de eso. Solo quiero decirte que hace solo un momento has estado a punto de hacerle mucho daño a Carla, de machacarla, de hacerla sufrir. ¿O no te das cuenta? ¿Te imaginas lo que ha podido pasar? Ella, que llega tan contenta e inocente, tiene que oír, en medio de tanta gente, que Fabio anda diciendo que es fea y que huele mal. ¿No te parece que eso duele mucho? ¿Que ibas a causarle un sufrimiento que podía durarle mucho tiempo, quizás para toda la vida. Pues eso es lo que has estado a punto de hacer. Ya sé que no lo haces a mala idea, pero eso te pasa porque no piensas antes de hablar, no mides las consecuencias de lo que dices. Las palabras pueden tener mucho peso en la vida de las personas.

—Pero Carla ni siquiera estaba allí, fue una casualidad que llegase así, de repente. Yo no lo decía para que ella lo oyese. Fue un accidente que apareciese en aquel momento. Yo solo quería demostrarle a Fabio...

Yo estaba perdiendo la paciencia. Cris no le da importancia a estas situaciones, pero esta vez no iba a dejársela pasar. Insistí:

—Pues no debías de haberte metido. Y si querías meterte, no debías haber usado las palabras que has usado, en aquel lugar, con todo el mundo alrededor poniendo la oreja. ¿Tú no has pensado que todos lo

45

que estaban en la cola podían haber salido diciendo que Carla huele mal? ¿Ni que Fabio podía coger manía a Adriana? ¿Ni que Carla podía quedar machacada, arrasada, y que pasaría toda la tarde y toda la noche llorando y suspendería el examen de mañana? ¿Ni que todo esto puede echar por tierra la amistad entre Fabio y Víctor? Qué sé yo, pueden pasar tantas cosas por culpa de un comentario de estos que ni siquiera podemos pensarlas todas. Pero tu no has pensado en nada, nunca piensas, solo te preocupas de hacer ese papel de heroína defensora de los maltratados. Pero eso que tú llamas defensa acaba muchas veces siendo el mayor ataque contra quien tú quieres defender.

Quedamos las tres en silencio. Y sin comida, porque era ya tan tarde y la cola tan grande, que, tener que volver a ponerse al final de ella, nos desanimó. Pero Adriana y yo aprendimos que hay cosas que no podemos contárselas a Cris. Cosas de las que no podemos hablar en el colegio. Es mejor que las dejemos para decírnoslas por teléfono. Por eso, nuestras charlas tienen que ser interminaaaables...

Y más ese viernes. Además de comentar todos los asuntos del día, de la víspera y de la semana pasada —siempre hay aspectos nuevos y detalles que se escapan en charlas anteriores—, teníamos otro gran tema: la final del torneo intercolegial de voleibol, mañana en la cancha del Coqueiros.

Me parece que es necesario explicar aquí que el Coqueiros es el nombre del mejor club de Palmeiral.

46

Pienso que le pusieron ese nombre porque en Sao Paulo existe el club Pinheiros, el club Palmeiras, y otros más con estos nombres. Seguramente algún directivo pensó que todos los clubes tienen que tener nombre de árbol. Aunque nadie se decidió por el de Bananeiras, que iba a ser de lo más ridículo.

En fin, mañana es la final del intercolegial de voleibol en el Coqueiros. Y hay algo que no me gusta: Adriana no fue seleccionada para formar el equipo. Está claro que teníamos mucho de qué hablar sobre eso por teléfono. Y hablamos un montonazo de tiempo. Era importante.

—Me parece la mayor de las injusticias —dije yo, para acabar—. Tú estás jugando cada vez mejor.

—Pero aún no tan bien para el equipo, Tatiana.

—Sería el mayor estímulo.

—No, no Tatiana, es mejor así.

—Deja de tener miedo, no seas tonta.

—Aún no juego tan bien como para estar entre esas fieras, como tú, Tatiana. No iba a dar pie con bola.

—¡Qué va! —la animé—. Tú necesitas confiar en ti misma.

—No es falta de confianza. Es porque no soy buena. Incluso le tengo un poco de miedo al balón... Bueno, eso es lo que pienso. Cuando me hacen un pase cruzado, me encojo toda y cierro los ojos. Aunque...

—¿Aunque qué?

—Aunque no voy a jugar...

—¿Piensas que ganaremos?

—No lo sé. No quiero desanimar a nadie, de ninguna manera, pero el equipo del Santa Rita es muy bueno.

—Ya lo sé. Por eso llegaron a la final, como nosotros. Nuestro equipo es también muy bueno. Los dos disputan la final porque son los mejores.

—Ellas son mejores.

—¿Por qué dices eso?

Me puse a pensar si Adriana también estaba empezando a tener ataques de franqueza. ¿Era buen momento para tanta sinceridad? ¿Qué es lo mejor en vísperas de un encuentro decisivo? ¿Estar con la moral muy alta, pensando que vamos a ganar o amilanarse porque el adversario es tan peligroso que parece que será imposible derrotarlo?

—Porque las conozco bien, Tatiana. ¿Te olvidas de que yo estudiaba allí? Eduardo, su profesor de Educación Física, fue técnico del Independiente. Si hay algo de lo que sabe, es entrenar a un equipo de voleibol.

—¿De qué lado estás, Adriana? Ahora me vienes con que Eduardo es el mejor. ¿Me insinúas que él es mejor que Alcides solo porque fue técnico de un equipo profesional? Alcides puede que sea un profesional mejor, sabe enseñar de forma que la gente aprenda más... y eso es muy importante —estaba comenzando a irritarme y subiendo el tono de voz—. A fin de cuentas, ¿cuál es tu equipo? ¿Eres del Santa Rita o del Anita Garibaldi?

—¡El Anita, claro! Pero tengo miedo, porque ellas

están muy metidas en el voleibol. Todos los sábados tienen partido, todos los días se quedan a jugar después de la salida de clase... En el Santa Rita es así...

—¿Me estás diciendo que piensas que no podremos ganar? ¿De ninguna de las maneras?

—Se puede ganar, claro que se puede ganar... Solo te digo que va a ser difícil.

—Por lo que parece, va a ser difícil para todo el mundo. Rodolfo me dijo que el Cruzeiro también...

—¿Quién es Rodolfo?

—Mi hermano... ¿O es que tú conoces a otro Rodolfo? ¿O te olvidas de que él está en el Cruzeiro y que en la final masculina el Anita tiene que enfrentarse con el Cruzeiro?

—Perdona, solo pensaba en nuestro equipo...

—Yo pienso en todos. Me gustaría mucho ganar por lo menos una de las finales.

—Los chicos quizá le ganen al Cruzeiro. ¿Quién sabe?

—Por lo que Rodolfo dijo, no hay la menor posibilidad. Si nosotras, en nuestra categoría, no conseguimos darle una paliza al Santa Rita, lo que va a pasar es que, una vez más, el Anita se vuelva a casa sin ni siquiera una copa. Siempre con el eterno consuelo del segundo puesto.

—Siempre es algo...

—Pero, Adriana, ¿tú sabes lo que es eso? Tenemos la mejor afición, que nos anima todo el año, y no conseguimos pasar del segundo puesto. Nunca, en toda la historia del colegio Anita Garibaldi conseguimos ganar ningún torneo. Por muchas esperanzas que la gente tenga, siempre cunde el desánimo...

—Podía ser peor, Tatiana. A fin de cuentas, hay mucho colegios que nunca han llegado a una final.

Desistí. Ella lleva poco tiempo en el Anita, no es como yo, que entré en párvulos y ya me quedé para siempre, como si fuese mi casa, mi familia. Ganar es lo que más deseo. Pero no quiero enfadarme en vísperas de la final. Y menos, con mi mejor amiga. Mejor me invento una disculpa, corto la conversación y desconecto.

Lo hice muy a tiempo. Cuando colgué el teléfono, me tumbé en el sofá y eché las piernas por encima del reposabrazos, para continuar con la lectura de *La isla del tesoro* —estoy en un momento emocionante cuando el chico oye el ruido de pisadas de una pata de palo aproximándose en medio de la niebla—. Al momento llegaron mi padre y Rodolfo. Los dos sucios y sudados, porque venían de jugar al fútbol.

—¿El teléfono estaba descolgado? —preguntó mi padre nada más abrir la puerta.

—No. ¿Por qué?

—Hemos intentado llamar y siempre daba comunicando. ¿Ha llegado tu madre?

—Aún no —respondí.

Hice una pausa y sugerí.

—Tal vez esté averiado.

Mi hermano fue a comprobarlo.

—No, da la señal de siempre.

—Entonces debió de haber algún problema de línea —concluyó mi padre, tirando la camisa sudada para entrar en la ducha.

Al mismo tiempo, oí el ruido de una llave en la puerta de entrada. Mi madre volvía del trabajo. Antes de que ella comenzase con aquel dale que te dale de que también ella había intentado llamar y el teléfono estaba ocupado, me levanté y dije:

—Voy a poner la mesa.

—Te ayudo —dijo Rodolfo.

En la cocina, cuando cogía los cubiertos en el cajón, él me miró y me dijo:

—Tatiana, ten cuidado. Ese asunto de estar todo el tiempo colgada del teléfono te va a dar un disgusto gordo.

—¿En el teléfono? ¿Quién? ¿Yo?

Él insistió con firmeza:

—Un día de estos, te vas a encontrar a papá de mal humor y se va a poner pesado. Ni te imaginas lo que ha protestado, durante todo el camino desde la playa hasta aquí. La suerte que has tenido fue que él haya marcado un gol increíble y esté feliz, como en una nube. Incluso quiere salir para celebrarlo, ir a cenar fuera con mamá. Por eso estaba deseando telefonear, para que ella se fuese arreglando. Pon mucho ojito, porque un día te van a caer todas juntas.

—No sé de lo que me estás hablando.

Con las manos llenas de cubiertos, cerró el cajón

dándole con la cadera derecha, me miró fijamente y me habló en un tono muy serio, como si se estuviese dirigiendo a una niña pequeña:

—Entérate. Cuando me puse el teléfono en la oreja para ver si estaba averiado, me di perfecta cuenta de que estaba caliente, después de estar hablando tanto tiempo. Y no dije nada, para encubrirte. No estoy aquí para chivarme de nadie, pero otra vez puede que no tengas esa suerte.

Me quedé quieta. ¿Era una amenaza? ¿O era un consejo de hermano? Y, si lo fuese, ¿qué significaba? ¿Que mi hermano no daría más la cara por mí? ¿O que estaba nervioso por causa de la final y quería mi apoyo en el momento decisivo? Negativo. Yo no iría nunca contra mi colegio.

4 *Una mano amiga*

¡Vaya, qué día!

En ese sábado de la final del torneo de voleibol pasaron tantas cosas que no sé cómo contarlas.

Primeramente pensé que debía hacer una especie de reportaje y describir cómo fueron los partidos propiamente dichos. Pero a fin de cuentas, el resultado del torneo intercolegial fue el acontecimiento del día.

El caso es que en ninguna descripción podría mostrar cómo fue ese encuentro decisivo. Si lo intentase, me saldría una retransmisión deportiva de las de la tele, pero sin imagen, que no reflejaría la emoción sentida por todo lo que sucedió en aquel campo. No iba a poder expresar ni la décima parte de lo pasó, no podría dar cuenta de las increíbles recepciones de balón de Luana cuando una grandullona de pelo pincho del Santa Rita estaba al servicio y nos lanzaba aquellos saques con efecto, o en la suerte que tuve al conseguir colocar un balón imposible justo en la esquina del campo contrario, en el momento en que asegurábamos una ventaja decisiva que, además, acabó convirtiéndose en punto y nos llevó a la consecución del segundo set. Ni siquiera sé cómo lo hice, cómo vi, de repente, que aquella zona estaba descubierta y que a la jugadora que debía cubrirla no iba a darle tiempo de llegar al rebote. Pero, sin haber estado en el campo en medio de la afición, nadie puede comprender cuál fue el decisivo papel de Cris en este partido, una gigante en la cancha, cortando con una precisión de campeona olímpica, bloqueando como si fuese la Muralla China.

¡En fin, un partido emocionantísimo! Ellas habían ganado el primer set. Pero no perdimos la calma y, cuando estábamos 14 a 13 en el segundo set, conseguimos darle la vuelta al resultado y garantizar que las cosas no iban a quedar así. En el tercero, salimos a por ellas con garra, fuimos creciendo cada vez con más fuerza...

Que nadie se engañe. No fue un paseo, nada de eso. Las del Santa Rita son unas fieras, pero después de un tiempo en que el juego estaba superequilibrado —ventaja para nosotras, ventaja para ellas—, inesperadamente fallaron un saque y enseguida las sometimos a un fuerte bloqueo. Recuperamos la pelota y Cris hizo un remate cruzado, genial, que aún hoy ellas deben de estar preguntándose por dónde les pasó. Para defendernos, era preciso ser la misma Santa Rita, que dicen que es la abogada de los imposibles. Porque, si dependiese de gente normal como nosotros, sería difícil.

No es preciso decir que todo fue una fiesta: pitido final del árbitro, el campo invadido, griterío, abrazos por todos los lados, lágrimas, cantos de la afición, tamborrada... y allí estábamos nosotras, ¡por primera vez en la historia el Anita festejaba el campeonato y conquistaba la copa! Cris fue paseada a hombros y dio una vuelta a la cancha. Una alegría sin fin.

El equipo masculino, en la otra categoría, no tuvo la misma suerte —o la misma capacidad, a fin de cuentas una victoria de estas no es solo cuestión de suerte— y se llevó la paliza tradicional y esperada: fue eliminado en el segundo set, por 15 a 8 y 15 a 5. Rapidito. El equipo del Cruzeiro tenía mucha experiencia, con jugadas muy hábiles, ensayadas; el nuestro no les daba ni para empezar. Tenían a un tal Biel que era un fenómeno, no perdía una, parecía un jugador de la selección. Por eso eran los favoritos. La derrota del equipo masculino del Anita no sorprendió a nadie, la gente no contaba ya con la victoria. Para decir toda la verdad, con ninguna victoria. La nuestra fue una sorpresa.

Por todo eso, la alegría fue todavía mayor. Y como nuestro partido lo jugamos antes que el partido de los chicos, después aún tuvimos tiempo de animarlos, pero de nada valió. Creo que ellos estaban demasiado nerviosos, no podían con la tensión por la responsabilidad que sentían después de nuestra victoria, y eso no hizo más que empeorar las cosas para ellos.

Pero, por lo que se refiere a la historia que estoy contando, en aquel momento sucedieron cosas importantes en las gradas.

Además, pienso que debo hacer una pausa para explicar un aspecto importante de todo esto que escribo, que es el problema del tiempo verbal que uso en ocasiones. Por una cuestión de honradez. A veces hablo, o mejor, escribo, «hoy», para referirme al día en que pasan las cosas que digo. Por ejemplo en el capítulo anterior, hice eso todo el tiempo. Pero eso no quiere decir que ese «hoy» sea de verdad, que he escrito lo que he escrito exactamente en el mismo día en que sucedieron las cosas. Es solo una manera de contar. Incluso hablé con Clovis, profesor de Lengua, para saber un poco más de este asunto. Él me explicó que existe un «presente histórico», que los escritores usan para narrar hechos pasados como si estuviesen sucediendo ahora mismo. De esta manera no usan el pasado, sino un presente. ¿Sabéis como es? En vez de decir: «Hoy Adriana me ha telefoneado, etc.» yo escribiría una cosa como «El teléfono suena. Voy a cogerlo. Es Adriana...» Y así todo.

No me gusta mucho lo que hago. Por los menos, no todo el tiempo. Estoy usando un artificio para aproximar el pasado al presente —eso fue lo que Clovis me explicó—. Su explicación fue totalmente teórica, sobre técnicas de la narrativa, como dice él. Porque yo no le enseñé este texto ni le dije que lo estoy escribiendo. Es cosa mía, que nadie debe conocer. Quien sabe algo es Diego, y aun así, de forma muy vaga. Como contaré más adelante, en cierto modo la idea de escribir esto surgió después de una conversación con él.

Pero eso queda para más tarde, porque ahora, hasta el momento, Diego apenas ha entrado en esta historia. Ahora va a aparecer otra vez. Justamente en las gradas del club Coqueiros, entre la gente que asistía a la final del torneo intercolegial de voleibol.

Sin embargo, antes que Diego, aún va a parecer de nuevo otra persona, que ni siquiera podíais imaginar que se cruzaría nuevamente en vuestro camino. Una chica rubia, de ojos brillantes, de gesto tímido y cara simpática. Comienzo entonces hablando de ella.

Cuando acabó el partido entre el Anita y el Santa Rita, lo celebramos como ya he contado. Incluso les arrebatamos el grito de guerra de su afición, porque ellos siempre gritan:

> *¡Es la mejor, la más bonita!*
> *¡Es la victoria del Santa Rita!*

Pero aquel día todo el mundo gritaba:

> *¡Es la mejor, la más bonita!*
> *¡La gran victoria del Anita!*

Y otras variantes:

> *¡Viva el Anita!*
> *¡Que acabó con el Santa Rita!*

Pues bien, en medio de aquella confusión que se había formado después del final del partido, con un montón de colegas empujando y dándonos abrazos, apareció una niña con la camiseta del Santa Rita, y comenzó a darnos abrazos y a felicitarnos. Nadie se daba cuenta ni le prestaba la menor atención, pero lo encontré un poco raro. Más aun cuando vi que le decía algo a Adriana, que puso cara de contrariada, y, como a punto de llorar, empujó a la chica y desapareció; ni siquiera pude ver por dónde salió. Recordé que Adriana había estudiado en el Santa Rita y que las dos debían de conocerse de allí; tal vez ella vino a meterse con mi amiga. Decidí pedirle explicaciones. Me libré como pude de todas aquellas felicitaciones y abrazos y fui a preguntarle:

—Oye, chica... ¿tú no eres del Santa Rita? ¿Qué estás haciendo aquí?

—Discúlpame —respondió, un poco sorprendida y con aire de estar disgustada—, vine a felicitaros y a hablar con una amiga que hace mucho tiempo que no veo...

—¿Con quién?

—Con Adriana. ¿La conoces?

—Sí, la conozco. Y, por lo que he visto, ella no quería hablar contigo. ¿Por qué no la dejas en paz y te preocupas de tu vida?

—Disculpa —repitió ella, bajando los ojos y tragando saliva.

No sé por qué, pero fue algo que vi en ella que me afectó. Le pregunté:

—¿Eres amiga suya?

La chica no dijo nada. Yo insistí:

—Te he hecho una pregunta. ¿No me has oído?

Ella me dijo, muy bajito, tanto que casi no la oía en medio de aquel griterío:

—Ya no lo sé. No sé lo que pasó. Antes éramos muy amigas. Ahora no lo sé, solo sé que desde entonces ya no nos hemos vuelto a ver. Y yo la echo mucho de menos...

—¿Cómo te llamas?

—Rafaela.

«Ah», pensé, «la de la fiesta de cumpleaños, la que hizo que mi amiga llorase tanto.» Comencé a entender... Le hice otra pregunta.

—¿Y por qué habéis dejado de ser amigas?

—No lo sé. Ella se cambió de casa, se fue del colegio, no fue a mi fiesta, y nunca quiso hablar más conmigo. Debe de haber sido algo serio, pero no lo sé...

Y los labios empezaron a temblarle, como quien está punto de llorar... ¡Eso no! ¿Ponerse así en medio de la mayor fiesta que el Anita nunca tuvo? La corté:

—Escucha, espera un poco que tengo una idea. Yo conozco a Adriana. ¿Vas a estar por aquí?

—Sí. Me gustaría irme pero mis padres vendrán a buscarme cuando acabe esto, no antes.

—Pues entonces, después te traigo a Adriana para que hables con ella. Ahora es mejor que te vayas con la gente de tu colegio, porque aquí la fiesta es nuestra...

—Está bien.

Anduvo unos pasos, pero cambió de idea y regresó. Yo ya me iba hacia el centro de todo aquel jaleo, cuando ella me tiró de la camiseta para que me diese la vuelta y me dijo:

—Perdona, yo no quería estropearos la fiesta, solo quería hablar con Adriana porque la aprecio mucho. Te estoy muy agradecida, has sido muy legal conmigo.

Y se marchó.

Me volví con mi gente y en aquel momento no pensé más en lo que había pasado. Lo celebramos todavía un rato y después nos fuimos al vestuario a tomar una ducha y cambiarnos de la entrega de los trofeos y medallas. Entretanto, ya había comenzado el partido de los chicos contra el Cruzeiro.

Cuando volví, limpita y perfumada, preparada para subir al podio en la ceremonia final, me senté en las gradas. Adriana me había guardado un sitio cerca de ella y entonces me acordé de aquella chica. Le hice una señal a Adriana para que me esperase, fui donde estaba la gente del Santa Rita y no necesité ni siquiera buscarla. Rafaela salió de entre ellos y vino corriendo hacia mí.

—¿Ya has hablado con ella? —fue lo primero que me preguntó.

—Aún no —le respondí—. Antes de hablarle quiero que tú me expliques qué historia es esta.

—Bien, éramos muy amigas, ¿sabes? De verdad,

Adriana es un encanto de persona, era mi mejor amiga, yo la adoro.

—Eso ya me lo has dicho. Lo que no me has dicho es lo que ocurrió.

—No puedo decírtelo. Ella es mi amiga —repitió ella—. Discúlpame pero no puedo hablar de ella así... Solo hablaré con ella. Porque, si yo hablo con otras personas, puede parecer que hizo una cosa fea, pero tengo la certeza de que debió de tener otros motivos. Y no quiero que nadie piense mal de mi amiga.

Me gustó la respuesta. Me pareció que era una actitud legal, propia de gente buena, de una verdadera amiga. Todavía insistí, para provocar:

—¿Amiga? ¿Una amiga que lleva casi dos años sin hablar contigo?

—¿Cómo es que sabes que son dos años? —reaccionó ella—. Yo no he dicho cuánto tiempo...

—Ya he oído hablar de esa historia. Y, por lo que sé, es muy diferente de lo que tú me has contado.

Su firmeza me dejó admirada:

—Entonces, cuéntamelo, porque, para mí, es exactamente tal y como te lo he contado. Yo iba a dar una fiesta, Adriana me ayudó en todo, cuidamos de los mínimos detalles. Y luego ella no asistió, no telefoneó, no dio señales de vida. Y nunca más quiso hablar conmigo.

—¿Estás segura de que tú la habías invitado? —la provoqué, siempre en defensa de Adriana.

—Tú no entiendes... ¿Cómo te llamas?

—Tatiana.

—Pues mira, Tatiana, no sé si has tenido una gran amiga, de verdad, de esas que sabes que es para siempre, que puedes contar con ella para todo, confiarle todo, como si fuese una hermana. Más aun, porque una hermana no se escoge, y a una amiga, sí.

—Sí que la tengo, sí —confirmé sin decirle que era la misma persona de la que ella estaba hablando—. Solo que no sé cómo eso justifica que des una gran fiesta y no invites a esa amiga.

—Es lo que te estoy explicando. Una amiga así es una persona muy especial. No necesita invitación. ¡Está claro que ella estaba invitada! Era nuestra fiesta, de nosotras dos, tanto de ella como mía... Dos días antes de la fiesta, cuando quería arreglar los últimos detalles, la llamaba y nunca había nadie en su casa. Pero yo tenía la certeza de que todo estaba claro, de que ella no se iba a olvidar de mi fiesta, de que iría. Solo que no fue.

—¿Y por qué no hablaste con ella después?

—¿Tú piensas que no lo intenté, Tatiana? Estuve llamándola por teléfono y nadie lo cogía. Fui a su casa, pero ya no había nadie, el portero me dijo que se habían mudado. Yo era la mejor amiga de Adriana y ella se mudó de casa y no me dijo adónde. Ni me dio su nueva dirección ni el número de teléfono. Como única explicación, pensé que podía haber sucedido algo muy serio. Estoy segura. Al oír esto no quiero que tú pienses mal de ella.

Decidí ayudarla, echarle un cable. Por lo que me decía, Rafaela lo merecía:

—No voy a pensar mal de ella. A mí también me gusta mucho Adriana. Y sé que ella te aprecia mucho. Solo que pensó que no había sido invitada a tu cumpleaños y se enfadó. Vamos ahora mismo a hablar con ella. Seguro que os entenderéis.

Teníamos que ir pronto, para aprovechar el intervalo entre los dos partidos y cambiarnos de sitio. Durante el recorrido hasta las gradas, donde estaba la afición del Anita, Rafaela todavía me contó más:

—No creo que podamos aclarar esto ahora... Esa historia estropeó mi fiesta de cumpleaños, mis vacaciones, todo. Cuando empezó el curso, yo estaba loca por hablar con Adriana y entonces descubrí que ella ya no estudiaba en mi colegio. Me quedé tan contrariada, que vivía en un continuo malhumor, comencé a tener problemas con las notas. Mi madre fue a hablar con la tutora, y volvió con el nuevo número de teléfono de Adriana. Solo que no me sirvió para nada, ella no quería hablar conmigo. Mi madre lo intentó de nuevo, habló con la madre de Adriana, y Adriana se puso al teléfono, incluso llegué a oír su voz diciéndome: «¡Diga!», pero cuando empecé a hablar, me colgó en mi propia cara. Y ahí ya no pude más. Tengo mi orgullo, no me rebajaría otra vez ni me humillaría ante quien me estaba haciendo una cosa como esa...

—Es... —dije yo sin saber qué decir.

No era capaz de decirle nada. Íbamos subiendo los

escalones y nos encaminábamos adonde estaba Adriana, que nos miraba con la boca abierta, sin entender lo que estaba pasando. Tampoco la ocasión era la adecuada para entender nada. ¡En un intermedio del partido decisivo del torneo, y en medio de toda la afición!

Apenas había sitio para una persona al lado de Adriana. Mientras estábamos allí de pie, mientras intentábamos buscar sitio, comenzó el segundo set. Todo el mundo nos pedía que nos sentásemos. De repente, alguien me tocó en el hombro por detrás, levanté la vista y vi más arriba un brazo que salía de entre la multitud y se dirigía a mí. Como una mano de alguien conocido. ¿A que no os imagináis quién era el dueño de aquel brazo? Era Diego que me hacía señas:

—¡Oye, ven aquí, que hay sitio!

No tenía tiempo para dudar ni para elegir. Subí y me senté. Él me explicó:

—No había asiento entre la afición del Cruzeiro y he acabado sentándome aquí con el Penumbra, un amigo. Ni siquiera nos hemos dado cuenta de que estábamos justamente en medio de la afición del equipo contrario. Él no aguantó la presión y se marchó.

¡Mira por dónde! Porque no puede haber dos Penumbra. Y el Penumbra que yo conozco es un moreno con la mirada caída, como de mosquita muerta. Un amigo de mi hermano, de su curso. Y para mí, por definición, todo amigo de mi hermano es un tonto.

Nos quedamos allí los dos, Diego y yo, sentados uno al lado del otro, asistiendo a la final del campeonato como si estuviésemos en la iglesia. Mirando al frente, concentrados, en silencio. No estaba a gusto, porque en aquel partido no había ni siquiera una jugada brillante de los nuestros que pudiésemos celebrar. El equipo del Anita se estaba llevando una paliza y no era capaz de sacarse de encima a su adversario. Además de eso, estaba con un ojo en la cancha y otro en las gradas, preocupada por el encuentro entre Adriana y Rafaela. Por lo que veía, ellas se entendían, hablaban sin parar, ni siquiera veían el partido. En cuanto a Diego, nuestro silencio tenía otra explicación: él debía controlarse para no saltar de alegría y ponerse a dar gritos en favor del Cruzeiro. Si se atrevía a celebrar alguno de los puntos que ellos conseguían, podría salir mal.

Casi al final del partido, me comentó:

—Bueno, parece que este partido lo vamos a ganar... ¡Vosotros no os vais a llevar todo! Todavía no te he felicitado. ¡Has jugado genial! Cuando hablé contigo en casa de Víctor, no imaginaba que estaba hablando con una campeona...

—Es que... hoy hemos tenido suerte... —dije yo, reventando de orgullo, pero intentando parecer modesta.

—¡De suerte, nada! Sois muy buenas... —insistió él.

Le miré a la cara y le sonreí. ¿Cómo no sonreír ante un comentario de esos de un chico tan interesante? Y con una sonrisa tan... ¿bonita? No, no es esa la palabra. ¡Transformadora, eso es! En sus ojos ya me había fijado antes. Pero en ese momento descubrí, así, de repente, algo sorprendente e inesperado, que me dejó alucinada. Y es que, cuando Diego sonríe, su rostro se transforma por completo. Se vuelve realmente guapo, con los ojos semicerrados y unos dientes blanquísimos que llaman la atención en su cara tan bronceada. Una se olvida de su nariz un tanto grande y de su piel así..., digamos que algo picada. La sonrisa realza aspectos positivos: su mirada, sus dientes, y, sin duda, su pelo, muy negro, liso, cayéndole un poco por la frente.

No pude sacar mucho provecho de mi descubrimiento. Ya todo el mundo se levantada y empezaba a descender los escalones de la grada. Nosotros dos también. Entonces llegó Adriana en sentido contrario, subiendo los escalones y pidiéndome a voz en grito:

—¿Tienes un boli y un papel que puedas dejarme? Necesito anotar una cosa.

Me senté de nuevo, y Diego se sentó a mi lado. Mil piernas pasaban a mi lado y me empujaban, estaba en la mayor de las confusiones. Él se giró y se enfrentó a los que me empujaban, mientras yo abría sobre mis rodillas la bolsa. Estaba a tope y, para coger un cuadernito del fondo, tenía que sacar las cosas que estaban encima. Entre ellas, el libro que estaba leyendo. Era tan emocionante que lo llevaba siempre conmigo a todos los lados, para ver si podía adelantar algo leyendo en el autobús o en los recreos... ¡*La isla del tesoro*! No sé si ya os he hablado de él, pero si no lo habéis leído, es lo máximo.

—¿Te gusta? —me preguntó Diego.

—¿El qué? ¿La derrota? ¿Los empujones? —respondí un poco enfadada.

Él sonrió de nuevo. Me olvidé de lo que tenía que hacer, o lo que es lo mismo, no sabía qué hacía allí en medio de aquella multitud, con un bolso abierto sobre mis rodillas, sacando fuera de él mi camiseta de uniforme del equipo de voleibol, toda sucia y sudada.

—El libro, claro... —me explicó.

—Venga, Tatiana... ¿tienes o no tienes? —insistió Adriana que ya estaba cerca de nosotros y extendía la mano.

—Sí que tengo, mujer, espera. Por fin encontré el cuadernito, cogí el bolígrafo del bolsillo exterior del bolso y se lo di todo. Guardé todo lo que había sacado antes y me levanté. Al momento vi la cara de Rodolfo, mi hermano, unos escalones más abajo. Estaba muy animado en medio de un montón de amigos del Cruzeiro, festejando el triunfo. Miró hacia mí y dijo:

—¡Anda, tío, vente! Vamos al vestuario a hablar con Biel...

No entendí nada. ¿Tío, yo? ¿Y meterme en el vestuario de los chicos? ¿Con mi hermano? ¿Para hablar con el seboso de Biel? Rodolfo debía de haberse vuelto loco... No me lo podía creer.

Pero esa sensación solo me duró un segundo. Porque rápidamente comprendí. No era conmigo. Los amigos de Rodolfo, a su alrededor, también gritaban:

—¡Vente ya, Didi!

Diego descendió los escalones y se despidió de mí con prisas:

—Chao, Tatiana...

—Y le gritó a Rodolfo.

—Ya voy, Frajola...

¿Didi? ¿Frajola? ¡Eso sí que no! ¿Entonces todo aquello que yo acababa de descubrir en el rostro de Diego era también de Didi? ¿El famoso Didi, el amiguete de mi hermano? ¿Uno de los de la infecta pandilla de Biel, Quico, Penumbra y no sé quién más? ¿Y este era el tal Didi, que llamaba a todas horas y que ponía a mamá de los nervios cuando decía que quería hablar con Frajola?

A mi alrededor, la confusión era enorme. Adriana y Rafaela me llamaban. La gente que todavía quedaba en las gradas comenzaba a descender con prisa los escalones para llegar a la cancha. Bajé, casi a empujones, hasta donde estaban ellas. Las dos estaban contentas, hablando casi abrazadas.

—Tatiana, ni te lo imaginas...

—No era nada de lo que yo pensaba...

—Fue solo una confusión...

—Ahora somos de nuevo amigas...

Me era imposible distinguir quién de las dos hablaba, pero no importaba mucho. En menos de un minuto, yo me había caído de las nubes y era arrastrada por la fuerza de la corriente.

Pienso que, cuando alguien escribe, debe usar unas imágenes de este tipo para que el lector pueda entender mejor lo que pasa, debe hacer comparaciones con cosas que el lector conozca. Pero, como no tengo apenas experiencia, no sé si lo que he escrito ayuda a comprender o a confundir. En fin, que estaba como atontada en medio de todo aquello, eso es lo que quiero decir. Y «todo aquello» eran dos cosas que habían sucedido muy seguidas, y que me habían trastornado.

La primera, claro, fue descubrir que Diego era un chico muy interesante, pero que no pasaba de ser uno de los amigos de Rodolfo, uno más de aquella pandilla de asquerosos. La segunda fue ver, después de este *shock*, que no podía ni siquiera contar con la ayuda de mi mejor amiga, porque ella no se daba cuenta de que yo existía y de que la necesitaba, sino que estaba toda sonriente y abrazada a una chica rubia, esa sí, su mejor amiga desde mucho antes de conocerme.

Ellas empezaron a contarme lo que había dicho, pero yo no conseguía prestarles atención. Tuve que preguntar todo más tarde y escuchar cómo Adriana me contaba toda la historia otra vez, con más calma. Por eso lo dejo, para contarlo más adelante. En aquel momento me estaba produciendo una irritación muy grande. Menos mal que pasó Luana y me llamó:

—Tatiana, estábamos buscándote. Van a hacer entrega de los trofeos y Alcides quiere ver el equipo al completo en el podio.

Fue un alivio tener ese maravilloso pretexto para salir de allí.

Seguí a Luana hacia el podio. Bueno, exagero en

eso de podio. No era nada parecido a los que la gente ve en la tele cuando retransmiten competiciones deportivas, con sus escalones de mayor a menor, en los que los campeones se suben y luego bañan con champán a todo el mundo. Tampoco había champán ni televisión. Lo que había era una gran confusión y mucha alegría, que me hizo olvidar mi enfado anterior. El público llenaba la cancha y los profesores de Educación Física llamaron a los campeones, que subieron unos escalones de la gradas y así quedaron en un lugar más alto, como si fuese un palco.

Estábamos todos muy contentos, hablando entre nosotros mientras aguardábamos a que la ceremonia comenzase, cosa que aún tardó un poco, porque hubo que esperar a que los chicos del Cruzeiro volviesen de la ducha para recibir el premio. Unos señores dijeron unas palabras, unos discursitos, en los que hablaron de la importancia de la práctica del deporte y de aquello de que *mens sana in corpore sano,* esas cosas de siempre. Después llamaron a los capitanes de los equipos vencedores para que recogiesen las copas. Y a los jugadores nos dieron una medalla con un cinta larga, para colgarla de nuestro cuello. Al final, incluso cantamos el himno nacional.

Fue emocionante.

Nunca en mi vida había sido campeona de nada. No sé si algún día lo volveré a ser. Fue una sensación muy agradable. Allí estábamos nosotras, con el corazón latiendo a toda prisa —a mi lado las lágrimas resbala-

70

ban por el rostro de Cris, nuestra figura en la cancha—, con todo el mundo serio cantando el himno nacional, y con todos aquellos rostros allá abajo pendientes de nosotros, y nuestras familias mirándonos, algunas madres se enjugaban los ojos, los padres llenos de orgullo...

Fui corriendo a mirar desde lo más alto de las gradas, y, como si me hubiese convertido en un cámara de la tele, empecé a enfocar uno por uno. Mi madre, mi padre. Los padres de Luana con sus hermanos gemelos en los brazos. La abuela de Débora —que siempre piensa que su nieta es la mejor del mundo— y el resto de la familia. Una tía de Bebel, que ya ha jugado en la selección regional de voleibol y a veces viene a animarnos. La madre de Carla y de Víctor —Vic Bellini no vino porque estaba de gira con su banda—. La familia completa de María Freitas —y haced las cuentas, porque son seis hermanos—. Padres, madres, hermanos, todos compartían con nosotros aquel día tan grande.

Cuando se acabó el himno nacional, llamaron otra vez a los capitanes de los equipos para que recogiesen la copas y las mostrasen al público. Biel, por parte del Cruzeiro, y Cris, por el Anita, subieron un escalón más, para situarse más altos que el público, y fueron ovacionados en medio del mayor griterío. Vi a los dos, allá arriba, vi que Cris hacía esfuerzos por no llorar, pero lloraba —unas lágrimas extrañas, que parecían más de tristeza que de alegría—, con el rostro tenso, recorriendo con los ojos toda la cancha de un lado a otro. El labio inferior le temblaba. Me volví y miré hacia abajo, siguiendo su mirada. Seguramente estaba buscando a sus padres. ¿Dónde estaban? Los busqué en el lugar reservado para las familias de los vencedores. No había nadie de su familia. ¿Otra vez? ¿Por qué ellos le hacían eso a Cris? Me daba una rabia... Cuando hicimos la representación teatral, ellos fueron los únicos que faltaron. En la fiesta de fin de curso, tampoco se dignaron a aparecer por allí. Pero ahora era demasiado, ¿cómo no asistir a una final de voleibol en la que su hija había brillado con luz propia?

Cuando la ceremonia acabó, Alcides nos dijo:

—Avisad a vuestros padres porque no vamos todos a comer a la pizzería Vesubio. Tiene unos salones especiales, reservados. Y estamos todos invitados, para celebrarlo.

Así que fuimos saliendo en dirección al restaurante. La pizzería quedaba un par de manzanas más abajo del club Coqueiros, y hacia allí iba aquel montón de gente andando por la acera. De repente, cuando doblamos una esquina, vi a Cris en una parada de autobús, al otro lado de la calle. Estaba sola. Hablé con mi madre, me separé del grupo y me acerqué a ella. Al llegar, vi que Cris estaba llorando. Muy pronto comprendí que no era solo por la emoción de la victoria.

No sabía qué decirle, le pasé el brazo por el hombro.

—¿Qué pasa, Cris?

—Nada.

—Vente con nosotros a la pizzería.

—No estoy de humor.

—Pero, Cris, has sido la mejor jugadora del equipo. Sin ti, la fiesta no será igual...

—Gracias, Tatiana, pero no tengo ganas de celebrar nada...

Y volvió a sollozar.

Quedé desconcertada, no sabía qué debía hacer y Cris me daba mucha pena. En aquel momento, yo quería que todo el mundo estuviese contento, y que no hubiese nada que nos hiciese sentirnos tan mal como ella estaba. Solo que, y lo sabía, no podía hacer nada. No estaba en mi mano.

Cuando el autobús llegó, ella no subió. Me pareció que era una buena señal. Quiero decir que tal vez hubiese alguna oportunidad de que viniese con nosotros a la pizzería. Le insistí y le pregunté si tenía algún problema, si le podía ayudar, si quería que hablásemos.

—Ahora, no. En otro momento, tal vez —me respondió ya más calmada, como si el llanto la hubiese ayudado a tranquilizarse un poco.

—¡Está bien! —asentí—. Pero ahora vente con nosotros a celebrarlo...

—Todo el mundo está con sus padres, menos yo...

—¡Qué tontería! Todas somos amigas, Cris... Estamos nosotras, las de tu clase, las del equipo que tú acabas de llevar a la victoria... Es un gran día... Vente, te sientas conmigo... Ven.

Vaciló un poco, pero vino.

Cuando entramos en el restaurante, mucha gente todavía estaba de pie, entre las mesas, agrupándose y buscando sitio. Había una mesa grande y otras más pequeñas alrededor. Llevé a Cris hacia donde estaban mis padres, para sentarnos juntos, pero Alcides nos llamó y nos dijo que las jugadoras tenían que sentarse en la mesa principal, en un lugar de honor, cerca de él y de la directora.

—Está bien, ya vamos —dije yo.

Y le susurré a Cris:

—Vete al cuarto de baño y lávate la cara, para que nadie sepa que has llorado.

Mientras ella fue al baño, busqué un teléfono, llamé a su madre y le dije con el mayor cinismo de que fui capaz:

—¿Es usted la madre de Cris? Soy Tatiana... Discúlpeme que la llame, pero quería decirle que hemos ganado el torneo y su hija ha estado insuperable. Estamos ahora en la pizzería Vesubio con la directora del Anita, celebrándolo, y me han pedido que la llamase.

—Muchas gracias, pero no sé si voy a poder... De cualquiera manera, mi enhorabuena —dijo ella, educada pero distante.

—Yo solamente le doy el recado. Pero si yo fuese usted, no me lo perdería... A fin de cuentas, es una fiesta muy especial para su hija, que ha sido la mejor... Es un homenaje que la directora nos hace. Todos los padres están aquí, menos usted y su marido. Puede sentar mal en el colegio, ¿no?

Fin de la charla.

Me fui a mi sitio. Cris llegó poco después. Todo el mundo comenzó a pedir refrescos. Los camareros trajeron pan, mantequilla y aceitunas. Fue una reunión muy animada, todo el mundo comentaba algunas jugadas. Es muy divertido descubrir que, una vez acabado el partido, cada jugadora veía la misma jugada desde una perspectiva distinta, que sus versiones eran muy diferentes...

La pizza era tan grande como una rueda de molino. El camarero iba cortando un trozo después de otro, cada uno con un sabor distinto —a queso, a jamón, a morcilla, a tomate, y no sé a qué cosas más. Fue muy divertido. Al final, pudimos elegir el helado que queríamos en un mostrador refrigerado. Se produjo un barullo enorme. Todo el mundo estaba en pie y quería hacer su propia combinación, buscando las mezclas que más le gustaban, plátano con chocolate, fresas con nata, vainilla con granizado... Después, de vuelta a la mesa, cada una quería probar de la mezcla de la otra, todo era pasarse el helado de aquí para allá y otra vez de vuelta... Nos reímos mucho, fue superdivertido.

Casi al final, Alcides dio unos golpecitos en un botella con un tenedor, muy leves, como si estuviese tocando una campanilla, y todo el mundo quedó en silencio. Después se levantó y dijo unas cosas muy bonitas, que pienso que nunca olvidaremos. Dijo que el Anita nos estaba muy agradecido, que éramos su chicas del voley, que habíamos probado que un equipo sin tradición de ganador puede triunfar cuando tiene disciplina, perseverancia, ganas de vencer; que a eso se le llama garra y que es una conquista mucho más importante que la misma victoria en el campeonato de voley; que el deporte nos forma para la vida y nos enseña a trabajar en equipo, a no dejarse abatir, a dedicar mucho esfuerzo a aquello que se quiere hacer... Y así, un montón de cosas más. Todo el mundo aplaudió.

Luego se sentó. Entonces se levantó Débora, y, como no pierde ocasión para exhibirse, toda afectada y con aquellos ojillos chispeantes, hizo un discurso de agradecimiento al Anita —o de pura pelotería, como queráis—. Habló del privilegio de estudiar en un colegio así, con el apoyo de la dirección, con la dedicación que nos ofrecen nuestros profesores... Fue poco aplaudida, ya sabéis, con unas palmaditas flojas y sin fuerza, que apenas hacen ruido y acaban pronto; totalmente fingidas.

Inmediatamente después, vi que Cris se levantaba. Antes de empezar a hablar, ya todo el mundo la aplaudía, silbaba y gritaba su nombre. En aquel día, ella era nuestra «ídola»; no importa que ídolo no tenga femenino.

Habló muy poco:

—Solo quería decir una cosa. Y es que estoy contenta de estar aquí con vosotros, porque el voley es un deporte de equipo. Son seis personas en la cancha, y en el banquillo, el resto, con las que se puede contar en cualquier momento. Todo el mundo anda diciendo que yo he jugado muy bien, pero no es verdad. No es cosa de una persona sola. Siempre hay alguien que antes preparó una jugada, o alguien que acaba lo que otros empezaron, alguien que nunca nos traiciona ni nos deja de lado, que es capaz de superarse para que nuestro esfuerzo no se pierda... El voley funciona porque es así. Por eso, en este momento, me gustaría pensar que eso también pasa en la vida normal. Que siempre podamos confiar en la eficiencia de las compañeras. Y que en los momentos más difíciles siempre aparezca una mano amiga. Como me ha pasado a mí hoy.

Acabó con una sonrisa y me miró antes de sentarse, en medio de una gran ovación. Me pareció que aquello de la mano amiga iba conmigo, que ella había hablado de muchas otras cosas además de voley. Y, cuando me iba a levantar para darle un abrazo, apareció por detrás de nosotras una mujer que comenzó a darle besos. Era su madre. Al acercarme, oí que ella le decía:

—No he podido venir antes, pero me parece que llego a tiempo... ¡Ay, hija, qué orgullosa estoy de ti!

La cara de felicidad de Cris, abrazada a su madre,

decía mucho más de lo que soy capaz de describir. Era evidente que, para ella, aquellos besos y abrazos valían más que el trofeo.

Y hay que añadir: una mano amiga, a veces, tiene que ser ayudada por palabras amigas. Incluso las dichas por teléfono a una madre que yo apenas conocía.

5 *Los amigos hay que conservarlos*

En los días que siguieron a aquel agitadísimo sábado de nuestra victoria, muchas cosas fueron modificándose y cambiando de lugar. Principalmente, cosas del corazón, de esas que se guardan en el lado izquierdo del pecho.

La primera de ellas fue la relación entre Adriana y Rafaela. Fue muy emocionante saber que yo las había ayudado a hacer las paces. Salimos las tres juntas el domingo por la tarde, fuimos al cine y, después, a merendar. Sentadas alrededor de la mesa, entre hamburguesas y perritos calientes, metiéndonos en la boca una patata frita tras otra, sorbiendo por una pajita de un bote de refresco, las dos recapitularon la historia que, muy resumida, pasó como sigue.

El caso fue que en la preparación de la fiesta de cumpleaños de Rafaela, dos años antes, ellas estaban tan entusiasmadas que a Adriana solo le faltó irse a vivir a casa de su amiga, estaba allí todo el tiempo. La madre de Adriana se lo permitió —aunque no venga mucho a cuento, desconfío de que le diera permiso para no tener a la hija cerca todo el día, como dijo mi madre— e incluso le pareció bien, porque estaba organizando la mudanza, ya que muy pronto se vendrían a vivir a nuestro barrio. Y Adriana, despreocupada como siempre, solo pensaba en la fiesta de su amiga y ni siquiera se acordó de dar a Rafaela más datos sobre el traslado, aunque en su casa los preparativos continuaban, pero ella ni se daba cuenta. Hicieron la mudanza la víspera o pocos días antes de la fiesta y la tonta de la Adriana se quedó esperando una invitación de Rafaela o una llamada de teléfono que nunca se hizo. Ni siquiera se le pasó por la cabeza alguna de las siguientes hipótesis:

a) Ella no necesitaba ser invitada; tan solo debía decirle a su madre que tenía una fiesta en tal día y en tal lugar y pedirle que la llevase.

b) No le había dado la nueva dirección ni el número de teléfono a su amiga, solo le había dicho de pasada que se iba a mudar, pero no le dijo cuándo ni adónde.

c) Era ella la que tenía el número de su amiga y, por eso, debió telefonearla y contarle cómo era la nueva casa y el nuevo barrio. Y, luego, cómo era el nuevo colegio.

En vez de eso, no se percató de la nueva situación y se enfadó porque Rafaela no la llamó para ir a su fiesta. Aún más, estaba tan furiosa que ni siquiera quiso hablar con su amiga cuando ella, finalmente, encontró su teléfono y la llamó.

Yo oía aquello y me parecía tan increíble que, si quisiera inventar uno de esos libros de historias raras, no iba a tener el valor de inventarme un caso como este. Porque cualquier lector lo encontraría absurdo y nadie se lo creería. Pero como es verdad y sucedió en realidad, no tengo más remedio que contarlo. Aunque claro, hay un atenuante, como dice mi padre en estos casos —algo que disminuye la gravedad o la culpa de una acción—, y es que ellas eran, por aquel entonces, muy pequeñas, muy crías, y no tenían mucha iniciativa propia ni estaban en condiciones de juzgar con imparcialidad la situación. Pero, de cualquier manera, ya que he citado a mi padre, también vale la pena citar a mi madre. Porque ella, de vez en cuando, al referirse a Adriana, dice:

—Esa chica es tan buena persona..., ¡qué pena que le afecten tanto las cosas! Así va a sufrir mucho...

La primera vez que lo dijo, yo no sabía qué significaba «afectar», y tuve que preguntárselo. Ella me explicó que, en cierto modo, es sentirse dolida por cualquier cosa, por una tontería cualquiera.

No estuve de acuerdo con mi madre, me pareció que ella no tenía razón porque aquello no había sido ninguna tontería.

Muy pronto iba a comprender que no era así.

El caso fue que de un dúo inseparable pasamos a un trío. Quiero decir, en cuanto a su número, porque no éramos un trío inseparable. Inseparables éramos Adriana y yo. Y a nosotras se sumó una nueva amiga. Rafaela no estudiaba en el Anita ni vivía cerca. Pero era un encanto como persona y me agradó mucho, aunque no me entregué totalmente a esa amistad, solo en parte. Otra parte de mí sentía temor de que entre Adriana y yo las cosas no fuesen como antes, ahora que se había reencontrado con su mejor amiga y además, más antigua que yo. Por eso mismo valía la pena esforzarse un poco y procurar hacerse amiga de Rafaela.

El caso es que nos pasábamos todo el día hablando por teléfono de multitud de cosas. En el puente que tenemos a comienzo del mes que viene, iremos las tres a Santa Helena, donde vive la abuela de Adriana, de la que habla a todas horas y que yo aún no conozco.

Antes de eso, pasaremos el próximo fin de semana juntas. Rafaela vendrá a dormir a casa de Adriana el viernes, y mi madre nos llevará a todas en coche al centro comercial el sábado, para pasar allí la tarde entera. Tenemos que depender siempre de alguien que nos traiga y nos lleve en coche, aunque mi madre está dispuesta a colaborar.

Mientras la semana pasa y nos hablamos por teléfono, ya es hora de hablar de la segunda cosa que fue aumentando en importancia en esos días: Diego. Aunque no debería decir «cosa», porque es una persona y de las más increíbles.

Aunque yo no hubiese contado nada, apuesto a que ya os habréis dado cuenta de que pensé mucho en él después del partido de voleibol. Por una parte, me agradó mucho haber descubierto el efecto «transformador» de su sonrisa. En él mismo y en mí. Por otra

parte, estaba furiosa con otro descubrimiento: la reve-
lación de que él me había mentido en la fiesta de Víctor cuando me dijo que no conocía a Rodolfo, a pesar
de que era realmente íntimo amigo suyo. Por eso, el
domingo por la mañana, me quedé sin saber qué hacer
cuando sonó el teléfono y mi madre me llamó:

—¡Tatiana, es para ti!

—¿Es Adriana?

—No, es un chico...

—¿Quién es?

—No lo sé. Solo me dijo que es un amigo tuyo. Y
tiene la voz igual que la de todos esos, como la de los
colegas de Rodolfo...

O sea, ella reconoció la voz pero no pudo identifi-
carla. Eso fue lo que se me ocurrió de inmediato. ¿Sería
él? Cogí el aparato con el corazón latiéndome a toda
prisa en el pecho.

—¿Sí?

—¡Hola, Tatiana! Soy Diego.

—Sí...

Estuve a punto de rectificar y decirle: «Didi, tú
quieres decirme que...», pero mi madre rondaba muy
cerca y no quise que se mezclara en la conversación.

—Ayer tuve que salir a toda prisa y no te hablé
nada claro...

—Sí..

—¿Tienes a tu hermano por ahí cerca?

—No. ¿Por qué? ¿Quieres hablar con él?

—No, yo ya sabía que iba a ir a la playa. Solo quiero hablar contigo.

—Pues ya ves, ya lo estás haciendo.

—¿Por qué te pones así? ¿Estás enfadada? ¿Es porque ayer yo me largué casi sin despedirme?

—No. Pero estoy un poco disgustada, porque tú me has mentido. No me gusta la gente que miente.

—¿Que te he mentido? ¿Cuándo?

Él soltó una risita. Me imaginé la sonrisa «transformadora» que debía estar poniendo en aquel momento, y que acompañaba a las palabras que me llegaban por el teléfono.

—¡Ah, es eso, Tatiana...! No me imaginaba que Frajola era tu hermano... Tu me dijiste un nombre tan diferente...

—Luis Rodolfo. Es su nombre. ¿Me vas a decir que no lo sabías?

—¿Cómo lo iba a saber? Los dos somos del Cruzeiro, pero yo no voy a su mismo curso... Y todo el mundo en el colegio le llama Frajola.

—¿Por qué?

—Qué sé yo... Esos motes nunca se sabe cuándo ni cómo se ponen. Me parece que es porque las chicas dicen que él es como un gato...

Echó otra risita y añadió:

—Pero es tan desastre y tan desmañado que nunca caza un pajarito. Se le escapan siempre y lo dejan con las ganas.

Esta vez fui yo la que estuvo a punto de echarse a reír. Pero me contuve, y le pregunté:

—¿Y tú?

—En absoluto. Ni soy un gato ni vivo con la preocupación de querer cazar todo pajarito que pasa a mi lado...

¡Vaya! A nada de eso me refería yo con mi pregunta. Le corregí:

—No, yo quería saber por qué tú te presentaste como Diego y no me dijiste que eras Didi.

—Por la misma razón que tu hermano no se presenta diciendo que es Frajola. La gente siempre usa su nombre propio.

—Sí..., tiene sentido.

—Por eso mismo se le llama nombre propio...

Era un chiste sin gracia, pero los dos nos reímos. El hielo estaba roto. De esto pasamos a hablar de otras cosas. Incluso un poco del partido..., y, enseguida, él sacó el tema del libro.

—Te llamo porque me entraron muchas ganas de hablar contigo cuando vi el libro que llevabas en tu bolsa, pero en aquel momento no me dio tiempo. Tú estás leyendo *La isla del tesoro*. ¿No es así?

—Sí.

—¿Y te gusta?

—Mucho —respondí, en un tono un tanto provocativo, porque ya me estaba preparando contra el recochineo que siempre surge cuando la gente descubre que a mí me gusta leer.

—A mí también me gustó mucho. Fue uno de los mejores libros que leído en mi vida. Fue demasiado... Hace tiempo que tenía ganas de comentarlo con alguien, pero no tenía con quién. A mis amigos no les gusta mucho leer, ¿sabes?

—Sí que lo sé. A mis amigas tampoco...

¡Ya estaba! Eso fue como un toque mágico. Al poco, estábamos conversando animadísimos, como si fuésemos viejos amigos.

Fui descubriendo que Diego —nunca le llamaré Didi. Diego es un nombre bonito— es un chico bastante inteligente. Habló del libro de una forma increíble, que no consigo explicarme. Solo puedo decir que su interpretación era «transformadora», pero me parece que es abusar de este adjetivo para referirme a él. Pero el hecho es que, en palabras de Diego, *La isla del tesoro* dejaba de ser una emocionantísima historia de piratas y se transformaba en otra cosa, en un libro sobre el alma humana, como él dice, sin miedo ninguno de que alguien se burlase o dijese que hablaba muy raro. Esa es una de las ventajas de no tener cerca a alguien como Débora siempre dispuesta a reírse de la gente...

—Long John Silver es uno de los personajes más fascinantes que jamás he visto —dijo él.

¿Que «ha visto»? ¿Cómo? ¿Es que lo conoce? Eso pensaba decirle, tan solo para echarle algo de humor a la charla. Pero no quise hacer tal cosa; en vez de eso, asentí:

—Sí... No se sabe nunca si se va a portar como un

bandido terrible o como un tipo capaz de proporcionarle una ayuda inesperada a Jim.

—¡Eso mismo! Es un peligroso villano, pero que gusta a la gente, a pesar de su crueldad. Un tipo astuto, que se adapta a las circunstancias...

Mientras Diego me comentaba todas estas cosas, yo me di cuenta de que su voz era agradable, que se expresaba bien, que escogía las palabras adecuadas. Continuó hablando de los escenarios de la obra:

—... es uno de los puntos fuertes de Stevenson... en todos sus libros. Yo leí una historia que ocurre en Escocia y parece que vamos con los protagonistas hasta las montañas. ¿Y *El Dr. Jekyll y Mr. Hyde*? ¿Lo has leído?

—Aún no.

—También es suyo. Es lo mismo. Parece que estamos en Londres, en aquellas calles oscuras, llenas de bruma, oyendo solamente el ruido de los pasos que se aproximan... ¡Es demasiado! Él construye muy bien la atmósfera de cualquier lugar. En *La isla del tesoro* nos hace viajar. ¡Es increíble! Desde el comienzo, aquella pensión junto al mar, en medio de la niebla, hasta la playa tropical de la isla, llena de sol, con palmeras y el rumor de las olas.

Yo iba recordando.

—¿Y el puerto? ¿Y el buque con aquella tripulación en la que cada uno va poco a poco desconfiando de los otros? ¿Y la canción de los piratas?

Entusiasmados, comenzamos a cantar:

Quince hombres sobre el cofre del muerto.
Ron, ron, ron...
La botella de ron.

Solo que, como el libro no traía la melodía, al leer los versos cada uno de nosotros imaginó una música completamente diferente. El intento de cantar juntos por teléfono fue un desastre. Pero un desastre gracioso. Acabamos riéndonos a mandíbula batiente, un escándalo de carcajadas.

Atraído por el barullo, mi padre entró en salón. Comenzó a protestar por aquella conversación tan larga, a decir que era la segunda vez que Adriana me telefoneaba, que aquel chismorreo ya se pasaba de la raya. Antes de que él descubriese que ahora era Diego, traté de despedirme.

—Tengo que colgar. Mi padre quiere hablar por teléfono.

—Está bien. Hablaremos otro día.

—¡Adiós!

—¡Adiós!

Salí al pasillo con ganas de cantar y de bailar. Acababa de descubrir a un amigo con quien podía hablar de verdad sobre los libros que me gustaban. Un tesoro muy especial. Era algo que había que conservar y proteger; incluso esconderlo y no dejar pistas para que nadie lo encontrase.

Aquellos días trajeron todavía una cosa más, algo que tocaba al corazón: un cambio en mi relación con Cris. Ya he hablado de que, antes de conocer a Adriana, Cris era mi mejor amiga, pero esa amistad era mucho menor de la que luego Adriana y yo entablamos. Con el tiempo, nos alejamos un poco la una de otra. Pero lo que vivimos cuando nos encaminábamos a la pizzería, cuando ella lloraba y yo le ofrecí mi ayuda, nos aproximó de nuevo

Por eso, no me extrañó cuando el lunes me regaló un perrito de caucho, muy blando, y me dijo:

—Toma, es para ti.

Se lo agradecí y le dije que era una hermosura. Recordé que Cris tenía un perro estupendo, Biriba, un perro sin raza negro con una manchita amarilla alrededor del ojo izquierdo. Le pregunté por él. Así nos pusimos a hablar las dos solas; hacía mucho tiempo que no lo hacíamos. A ella le gusta mucho ese animal, igual que a mí, y eso fue algo que siempre tuvimos en común.

En un momento dado, ella me dijo una cosa que me impresionó mucho:

—Todo el mundo dice que el perro es el mejor amigo del hombre. Debe de ser cierto, porque Biriba es mi mejor amigo.

¿Un animal el mejor amigo? Me pareció muy triste. Seguimos la conversación y comprendí algo en lo que nunca había reparado: Cris es una chica que está muy sola, sin amigas de verdad. Tal vez sea culpa suya, por aquella eterna manía de su franqueza. Seguramente es eso: dice todo lo que se le pasa por la cabeza y la gente se aparta de ella, porque no se puede aguantar tanta sinceridad junta. O porque, como ya he dicho, siempre emplea su sinceridad para criticar, nunca para elogiar.

Así, nadie puede estar seguro con ella.

Lo cierto es que Cris no tiene muchos amigos. Tampoco tiene hermanos. Ni siquiera primos cerca de aquí, porque sus tíos viven lejos. Y sus padres, francamente, son de lo no que hay... La única ocasión que le prestaron alguna atención a su hija fue aquella vez en la pizzería, después de haberme metido yo por medio, cuando les telefoneé y les dije todo aquello que apenas tenía algo de verdad. Pero tuvo un efecto increíble: su madre apareció, Cris se puso muy contenta y nosotras volvimos a ser amigas.

Aunque no es un amistad igual a la de Adriana. Por lo menos, para algunas cosas debo de ser mejor que Biriba. Sin embargo, hay que reconocer que, con toda seguridad, tampoco tengo alguna de sus mejores cualidades, como es la de permanecer a su lado en silencio, moviendo el rabito sin rechistar, o la de ser fiel en todo y con dedicación exclusiva.

De cualquier manera, y por todo lo dicho, decidí incluir a Cris en mi programa para pasar la tarde del sábado en el centro comercial. La llamé, y quedó encantada con la idea, lo que no fue sorpresa alguna. A quien no le gustó nada fue a Adriana. Y eso sí que me sorprendió.

90

—¿Ahora va a ser así, no? —fue su reacción—. ¿Vas a llevar a Cris contigo a todos los lados?

—No a todos los lados, Adriana. Solo la he llamado para que venga con nosotras al centro comercial.

—Pero ella se va a entrometer en nuestras conversaciones. Tendremos que hablarnos en clave si ella está presente. No es lo mismo cuando estamos solas las dos.

—Pero esta vez no vamos a ir solas. Rafaela también va a venir. ¿Te acuerdas?

—Pero Rafaela es mi amiga, ya lo era antes. Y ahora lo vuelve a ser. Hablamos a todas horas por teléfono; ella ya sabe todo de mi vida.

Yo ya me había dado cuenta de que en los últimos días Adriana me telefoneaba menos. Y era por eso: estaba todo el día de charla con Rafaela. Una razón más para que yo hablase con Cris. Si ella podía, ¿por qué yo no? Insistí:

—Cris es amiga mía desde hace tiempo, antes de...

—¡Está bien! No hay problema... —cortó ella.

Fue así de simple. ¡Una gran amiga!

El sábado por la mañana, me vestí pronto —ya sabéis el lío que me traigo con la ropa a la hora de salir—, y después aún tuve que ponerme a arreglar mi habitación, porque mi madre estaba implacable. Mientras guardaba las últimas cosas, ella se acercó a la puerta y me dijo:

—Tatiana, tienes arroz y pollo en la nevera. Solo tienes que calentarlo... Y te he dejado una lechuga ya lavada, por si quieres hacer una ensalada. Solo tienes que aliñarla.

Me quedé sorprendida. ¿Ella iba a salir?

Después, mi padre añadió:

—Vamos a ir a una churrascada a casa de Freitas. Al caer la tarde ya estaremos de vuelta. ¿Vas a estar en casa?

—Había quedado con mis amigas para ir al centro comercial... —gemí.

—Vale, puedes ir. ¿A qué hora vuelves? ¿Con quién? —me interrogó él, muy amable.

—Mamá, me habías dicho que nos ibas a llevar... —empecé a protestar, aunque ya sabía que no iba a funcionar.

—Ya, pero no sabía que tu padre tenía otros planes —me respondió, como disculpándose.

—¿Y no podéis ni acercarnos?

Ella lo pensó, vagamente, pero no, no era posible. Mi padre estuvo de acuerdo. Éramos cuatro y no había sitio en el coche; además, ya iban con retraso. Y la casa de Freitas quedaba en la otra punta de la ciudad.

Todavía insistí, y protesté un poco:

—Pero si he quedado con mis amigas... No es justo, contábamos con que nos llevaríais.

—Pues llámalas —me cortó él—, y déjalo para otro día. El centro comercial no va cambiar de lugar.

Ya en la puerta de la calle, mi madre me sugirió:

—Mira, si la madre de una de ellas os puede llevar

es una solución. Eso sí, si por fin vas a ir, déjame una nota por favor. Adiós.

¿Así, de repente y sin avisar? ¿En un sábado? ¿La madre de Cris o la de Adriana? Jamás, estaba segura...

Corrí al teléfono y le di la pésima noticia a Adriana, pero a ella no pareció importarle mucho. Me dijo que, si no íbamos a ir al centro comercial, Rafaela y ella aprovecharían el día para arreglar unos asuntos, que iban a alquilar un par cintas de vídeo, y que si quería, podía pasarme por su casa más tarde...

Llamé a Cris. El teléfono comunicaba. Lo intenté otra vez. Comunicaba. Repetí la operación, pero siempre daba comunicando. Alguien debía de estar navegando por Internet. Decidí salir e ir a su casa. Estaba muy cerca de la mía, y en un instante volvería.

Fue una idea estupenda. Aunque, al principio, se disgustó tanto como yo por no poder ir al centro comercial, luego tuvimos la mejor de las suertes: su madre estaba apunto de salir en aquel momento y nos dijo que nos llevaría. Y que, por la tarde, podía ir a recogernos, porque ella misma tenía que comprar un regalo de boda. ¡Fue lo máximo! Solo tenía el dinero que llevaba en el bolso, pero no me dejó ir a casa, ni siquiera para dejar una nota. Tenía tanta prisa que tampoco nos dejó llamar a Adriana y a Rafaela.

—De ninguna manera —dijo—, tengo que ir al supermercado para hacer la compras del mes, y no quiero perder tiempo, porque luego está muy lleno. Si queréis venir conmigo, venga, que ya me voy. Solo tienes tiempo de llamar a tu casa y dejarles un mensaje.

Ni siquiera eso. El padre de Cris continuaba navegando por Internet. La única forma de dar el recado fue llamar después desde el centro comercial y dejar un mensaje.

Arreglado el asunto, allí nos esperaban todos aquellos pasillos llenos de gente y de tiendas. No para hacer compras, que nosotras no somos de esas que tienen la manía de llenarse de cosas inútiles. Pero vimos muchos escaparates, tomamos helados, hojeamos libros en una librería —acabé de leer un álbum de Astérix que había comenzado otro día en otra librería—, nos probamos ropa en varias tiendas diferentes, encontramos a gente del colegio, y juntas fuimos a ver las novedades que había en una tienda de música. Después compré una pinza para el pelo. Cris encontró un portaminas que llevaba tiempo buscando. Al final, aun tuvimos tiempo de ir al cine y de tomar algo. ¡Fue estupendo!

Cuando volví a casa, mis padres aún no habían llegado. Y mi mensaje estaba allí, esperando.

Todo había salido bien. Fue un día que comenzó mal y que acabó siendo un sábado perfecto.

Pero el domingo... Bastó que yo le contase a Adriana que había ido con Cris al centro comercial para que se desencadenase una tormenta. Bueno, hay que decir que los rayos no empezaron a caer de inmediato. Pero comenzó a armarse algo extraño y amenazador, como unas oscuras nubes que se van juntando lentamente en el cielo, unas ráfagas de viento de esas que soplan repentinamente, pero que al momento se calman. Primero, ella se puso furiosa, no había más que oírla, pero no se enfadó conmigo, sino que empezó con ironías:

—¿Piensas que me voy a creer esa historia?

Después insinuó que lo había hecho a propósito, que desde el principio ya me había puesto de acuerdo en todo con Cris, solo para dejarlas solas, a ella y a Rafaela. Luego fue sacando otras cosas, como que yo ya no la llamaba, que solo quería saber de Cris, que ella ya se había dado cuenta que desde la final del torneo de voley yo estaba un poco distante, que ya no la trataba como su mejor amiga, y otras cosas así. Cada vez que, para demostrarle que no tenía razón, yo usaba un argumento que se refiriese a Rafaela, Adriana se calmaba. Cuando me dijo que al final del partido yo me había ido a celebrarlo con Cris, no tuve más remedio que responderle:

—Adriana, no es posible que estés disgustada por eso, fue casi todo el colegio a la pizzería... Por lo menos, quien quiso ir. Alcides se lo dijo a todo aquel que encontró. Y tu dijiste que no ibas porque querías estar con Rafaela y esperar a su madre... ¿Te has olvidado?

—Bueno, pero ese fue un caso especial. Había pasado un montón de tiempo sin verla...

—Está bien, no te estoy reprochando nada. Has sido tú la que ha sacado el tema...

—Es cierto...

Se calmó. Pero también me dijo que el jueves pasado, cuando quise saber hasta qué página había que estudiar para el examen de Geografía, había llamado a Cris —Adriana no podía decírmelo, porque no es de mi curso, pero eso no lo tuvo en cuenta—, y que, después, a lo largo de toda la tarde no la había llamado ni siquiera una vez.

—Eso es lo que tú piensas. Lo intenté más de veinte veces y siempre estaba comunicando. Luego me dijiste que habías estado hablando con Rafaela.

—¿No será porque no has insistido?

—¿Más de lo que insistí? Solo si tuviésemos una línea directa, uno de esos teléfonos rojos que nunca se desconectan. Pero tampoco nos iría bien, porque el tuyo iba estar siempre llamando al de Rafaela.

Ella volvió a usar su viejo argumento:

—Pero, Tatiana, ¿es que no lo entiendes? Hace dos años nos enfadamos, y ahora necesitamos demostrarnos que nuestra amistad no ha cambiado.

—¿Y la nuestra, Adriana? ¿No está cambiando?

—Sí, sí que está cambiando. Tú ahora no quieres saber más que de Cris, esa falsa.

—¡Eso sí que no! Tenía que protestar.

—Discúlpame, Adriana. Cris puede tener millones de defectos, y los tiene, como todo el mundo. Pero si una cosa no es, es falsa...

—¿Lo estás viendo? Mira cómo la defiendes, pobrecita... ¿Ves lo que haces, Tatiana? Ahora discutes conmigo a causa de ella. Hasta qué punto hemos llegado...

No voy a reproducir todo, porque seguramente encontraréis esta charla de lo más tonto. Sirva de consuelo, que yo también estaba harta. Solo he reproducido unos pequeños fragmentos, para que veáis de qué iba todo aquello. Y que entendáis que, evidentemente, si enfocaba así las cosas, Adriana estaba sacando de la nada una gran escena y montándose en su cabeza una historia en que la yo estaba traicionando nuestra amistad y que las había dejado de lado, a ella y a Rafaela, porque no quería ir al centro comercial con ellas, para que no nos estorbasen. Fue muy estúpido todo, tanto que me costó mucho trabajo deshacer aquel embrollo y varias llamadas por teléfono e infinitas broncas de mi padre.

Pero de algo sirvieron, porque el lunes, en el colegio, Adriana estaba de nuevo tan normal conmigo. Estuvimos juntas en el recreo, volvimos juntas a casa, como si nada hubiese pasado, e hicimos planes para el fin de semana en Santa Helena.

El fin de semana fue estupendo. El lugar era precioso, con mil cosas que hacer para pasar el tiempo. Nosotras tres nos divertimos mucho, y, además, el domingo apareció un tío de Adriana con sus hijos: dos chicos y una chica, gente muy maja. El mayor, Gilberto, bastante guapito. Jugamos al voleibol, nos dimos un baño en el río, y montamos a caballo. Todo debidamente documentado por Adriana, que había recibido como regalo de su abuela una cámara y no paraba de sacar fotos durante todo el tiempo. Incluso de madrugada me desperté con un flash en mi cara, porque las dos, muertas de risa, querían sacarme un retrato mientras dormía. Supongo que estaba muy arrebatadora, así, despeinada y con el aparato dental.

Volvimos el domingo por la tarde, cansadas, pero satisfechas. Fue estupendo ver que nuestro mal rollo ya había pasado, y que ahora mi amistad con Adriana navegaba otra vez por aguas serenas.

Estaba feliz. Eso para mí era lo más importante. Cuando más tiempo pasa, más me parece que la amistad es una de las cosas más importantes de la vida. Un verdadero tesoro. Lleva razón aquella canción que dice:

Los amigos hay que conservarlos
en el lado izquierdo del pecho

6 *Amigo del rey*

Unas dos semanas después, el grupo de teatro del Anita se disponía a prepararse para la fiesta de fin de curso, que es ya algo tradicional. Una verdadera superproducción conjunta con la gente del Ana Neri. Quiero decir que cada colegio ensaya sus números por separado, pero los presentamos dentro de un único espectáculo, en nuestro auditorio, con las familias y los padres reunidos. Queda todo bastante bien integrado. Sobre todo, porque uno de los números que ellos traen y que se deja siempre para la gran apoteosis final es un maravilloso grupo de samba, lleno desafíos y pasos improvisados. Y, como nadie se resiste, todo termina con un montón de alumnos, profesores y padres de los dos colegios subidos al escenario para cantar e inventar versos de respuesta en los desafíos que unos y otros se lanzan.

Básicamente, nuestro espectáculo nunca se improvisa y necesita bastantes ensayos. Esto siempre produce grandes discusiones, hasta que conseguimos ponernos de acuerdo sobre la obra que vamos a montar. Es necesario que tenga muchos personajes, y variados, para que puedan participar muchos alumnos, y que puedan elegir papeles diferentes según sus preferencias. Pero no puede tener mucho texto para aprendérselo de memoria, porque nunca hay mucho tiempo para ensayar, y además, como es al final de curso, hay exámenes, y es preciso estudiar...

Resultado: siempre acabamos por escribir una obra nosotros mismos, para que en ella encajen todas nuestras necesidades. Creación colectiva, como aquel que dice... Es decir, después de horas y horas de reunión y debate, hacemos siempre lo mismo que el año anterior: decidir el tema sobre el que vamos a investigar, para luego trabajarlo y escribir la obra.

Pero esta vez, sabiendo ya que siempre pasaba eso, yo me había preocupado de pensar un poco en el asunto mucho antes de la reunión. Por eso, cuando llegó el momento, mientras surgían propuestas de un lado y de otro: un espectáculo musical, un gran número de danza, un paso de Navidad, volver a montar la obra del año pasado, y qué sé yo qué más, expuse mi sugerencia:

—Vamos a ver, yo he pensado lo siguiente. Es una fiesta conjunta del Anita Garibaldi y del Ana Neri, ¿no es así?

—Sí —asintió Clovis, que es el profesor de Lengua y coordina la sección de teatro, taller de escritura y actividades dramáticas.

—¿Y acaso no son dos colegios con nombre de mujer?

100

—Sí... —confirmó él, con cara de quien parecía no tener ni la menor idea de adónde quería llegar yo.

—Bien, yo no sé si ellas vivieron en el mismo lugar y en la misma época, pero tal vez pudiésemos escribir una pieza en la que las dos se encuentren. Me parece que así a todo el mundo podía interesarle.

Él me miró con aire pensativo, y dijo:

—¿Sabes que no es mala idea?

Me sentí muy orgullosa. Él pensó un poco más y continuó:

—Pero no sé cómo vamos a hacer para que las dos se encuentren frente a frente, porque puede resultar una obra teatral muy complicada. Tal vez podamos hacer algo diferente, a ver qué os parece. Podemos montar un espectáculo sobre mujeres importantes en la historia de Brasil, y a cada una le dedicamos una pequeña escena. Podemos hablar de Anita Garibaldi, de Ana Neri, pero también de Joana Angélica, María Quiteria... Así tendremos muchos buenos papeles femeninos, y también masculinos, porque ellas vivieron en un mundo en el que estaban rodeadas de hombres en todos los cargos importantes. Podemos comenzar haciendo una lista de otras mujeres que podrían entrar en el espectáculo.

—Ciquinha Gonzaga... —sugirió Carla, siempre tan aficionada a la música popular.

—La princesa Isabel... —recordó alguien.

—María Bonita, la mujer de Lampiao...

Y Gilda, que es profesora de Historia, y presume de ser feminista, muy pronto se animó:

—¡Es una idea genial! Hay un montón de nombres de mujeres: Bartira, que es otra india, y Ana Pimentel y Branca Duarte, al inicio de la colonización, dos esposas de colonos que tuvieron que luchar para establecerse y construir una vida en tierras hostiles. Con todo, ninguna de ellas vino a Brasil porque quiso, siempre fueron los maridos los que obtuvieron las tierras porque eran amigos del rey. Ellas no habían escogido una vida tan dura, pero tuvieron que venir y luego se quedaron aquí, criando a su familia con todos los sacrificios... Y, en muchos casos, fueron ellas las que realmente crearon y desarrollaron los núcleos de colonización.

Yo no tenía ni la menor idea de quién eran esas personas a las que ella se refería, pero, por lo que estaba viendo, tendría que dejar mis preguntas para más tarde, porque Gilda seguía hablando con Clovis:

—Y además de esas luchadoras del Sur y de Bahía que has citado, hay también otras heroínas: como María Ortiz, que resistió contra la invasión holandesa; y Luisa Grimalda, contra los corsarios ingleses, en Espírito Santo. Y varias ex esclavas que participaron en la resistencia en Quilombo dos Palmares. Confía en mí, que yo te organizo los grupos de investigación...

Todo el mundo se animó y nos distribuimos el trabajo para la próxima reunión de la semana siguiente. Al final, Clovis me felicitó de nuevo por mi idea.

Salí del auditorio muy orgullosa, muy convencida de mi idea. Estaba tan confiada que incluso me enfrenté a Débora. Porque ella siempre tiene que estar en primer plano, en el punto de mira de todas las atenciones, y debía de tenerme ahora una rabia inmensa, muriéndose de envidia por los elogios que recibí. Y eso fue lo que pasó. Porque, cuando la reunión se acabó y salimos al patio, ella dio el cante; pero como es una víbora, nunca ataca de frente. Buscó herirme en mi punto flaco: mis amigas. Vio que Cris y Adriana estaban juntas, esperándome, y soltó su veneno, con esa sonrisa cínica y superior:

—Hummmm, por lo que se ve las dos amigas con carencias se llevan muy bien...

—Oye, aquí tú no faltas sino que sobras —le respondí al momento.

No sé cómo tuve el coraje y la presencia de ánimo para pensar eso, pero me puse furiosa al ver que Débora quería atacar a mis amigas sin pensar en nada, hurgar en la herida, en el dolor más hondo de cada una de ellas. Solo por el placer de agredir. Me parece que ella comprendió que era capaz de pegarle, de tanta rabia que sentía en aquel momento, porque se largó rápidamente, sin hacer ningún comentario, como es su costumbre.

Cuando se alejó, Adriana no dijo nada, pero Cris comentó:

—Vaya, ¿tienes la lengua bien afilada, eh? ¡Qué bien le ha estado!... ¡Fue total!

Adriana permanecía en silencio. Salimos del colegio, pero aún estuvimos un rato en la calle, esperando a más gente que a veces tomaba el mismo autobús que nosotros para volver a casa. Algunos alumnos que iban saliendo me felicitaban por mi idea. Incluso el asqueroso de Fabio se detuvo a hablar conmigo; pero claro, para decir estupideces.

—Es decir, que todas las intrigantes del colegio se van a exhibir en ese espectáculo... Tendrá mucha gracia. ¿Estará esa galería de personajes femeninos completa? ¿Estará toda la chiquillería del colegio? ¿También la defensora de los pobres y de los oprimidos? ¿El lorito que repite todo lo que oye? ¡No os olvidéis de la maloliente, eh!

Tenía muchas ganas de ir a por él para darle en la cabeza un golpe con todos los libros que llevaba, especialmente con el de Matemáticas, que es un ladrillo. Pero Cris me cogió del brazo y me dijo:

—Déjalo, Tatiana. No te rebajes...

Y Adriana añadió:

—Tengo miedo de que esto sea solo una muestra de lo que puede sucedernos...

—¿Cómo? No te entiendo —dije extrañada.

—Pienso que te expones mucho, si te comportas así. La gente se puede volver muy agresiva, si piensa que lo único que quieres tú es presumir ante Gilda y Clovis. Como si quisieras estar luciéndote siempre, porque al final tú estás en todas —dijo ella—. Puede parecer que quieres dejar a los demás en un segundo plano.

—¿A quién? ¿En qué segundo plano? —le pregunté—. ¿Puedes explicarte mejor?

—No lo sé bien, Tatiana. Te hablo así porque soy tu amiga, porque quiero protegerte...

—¿Protegerme de qué? Sigo sin entenderte, Adriana...

—No quiero que la gente te tenga rabia, si te metes en todo. ¿No has visto a Fabio?

—Fabio es otra cosa, no tiene nada que ver. Él está rabioso con nosotras desde aquel día en que Cris le pidió explicaciones por lo que dijo de Carla, y ese día estabas tú presente. Yo nada tengo que ver con eso.

—¿Que no? Pues fue contigo con la que habló... —insistió ella.

—Conmigo sola, no. Con nosotras tres.

—¡Venga!, ¿vais a estar todo el tiempo discutiendo a la puerta del colegio? —interrumpió Cris.

Al oír eso, Adriana cortó la conversación:

—Discúlpame, yo no quería discutir con nadie, y menos con mi mejor amiga. Solamente he querido darte un toque.

—¿Y por qué? Todavía no consigo entender...

Ella me explicó con calma:

—Tatiana, no te lo tomes a mal, pero es que tú estás siempre en el escaparate, llamas mucho la atención. Estás en el equipo campeón de voleibol, has ganado una medalla. Eres unas de las cuentacuentos que va al Ana Neri; y te has metido a redactora del periódico del colegio; fuiste seleccionada para el concurso de literatura y te has clasificado para la fase final. ¿Y ahora quieres meterte en el espectáculo de fin curso? A mucha gente no le va a gustar... Te cogerán manía, pensarán que estás de más en muchos sitios; a fin de cuentas en el Anita hay un montón de alumnos que no aparecen para nada.

—¿Como quién, por ejemplo?

—Como la gente que se dedica al baile pero que no sabe jugar al voleibol ni le gusta pasar el día con las narices metidas en un libro...

Eso de «metidas» me sublevó. «Narices metidas en un libro», una expresión salida de la misma boca que segundos antes había dicho «metida a redactora del periódico del colegio». Mi mejor amiga no decía que tenía condiciones para escribir y que me gustaba leer, sino que dejaba caer que en el fondo.... pensaba que yo... ¿Qué pensaba? ¿Que me metía donde nadie me llamaba? No sé, pero me quedé alucinada, ofendida. No conseguí entender lo que quería decir. Me tranquilicé, y decidí pensar con calma en todo aquello.

Mi primera reacción era negar, garantizarle que yo solo quería participar en las actividades del colegio con todo el mundo, como siempre he hecho. Pero Adriana era mi mejor amiga. Siempre me ayudó, nunca dejó de estar a mi lado en los momentos difíciles. Si ella ahora me decía estas cosas, tal vez pudiese tener razón. ¿Sería verdad que yo me exhibía demasiado y estaba perjudicando a los demás? Sin querer, claro, sin darme cuenta... Podía estar molestando a gente como ella, que baila pero que no juega bien al voleibol, y tampoco es muy aficionada a la lectura, por eso nunca le interesaría participar y aportar ideas para el espectáculo que yo había propuesto.

En el autobús, camino de casa, permanecí en silencio. Ellas dos hablaban sin parar y Adriana decía que un espectáculo de danza sería mucho más interesante, divertido, alegre, sin que tuviese ese aire de clase de historia, ni siquiera se necesitaba hacer ninguna investigación... Recordé que ella tenía una coreografía dispuesta para un solo de danza, que hacía meses que ensayaba para presentarla en una fiesta de la academia, y que, además, podía encajar en un espectáculo más general, porque incluso se podía aprovechar el vestuario. Era una pena que no hubiese oportunidad para que la gente de danza se manifestase, porque yo imaginé que el espectáculo tendría mucho texto, pero no danza. Claro, era comprensible, a fin de cuentas yo no sé bailar...

Y claro que no sé bailar, no. Al tiempo que oía aquella conversación, comencé a sentir un malestar que no conseguía explicarme. No era algo físico, corporal. Era como una emoción rara, que no sabía dónde se localizaba, en el corazón, en el alma, en la memoria... El autobús seguía su camino, recorría las calles de siempre, frenaba aquí, aceleraba allí, yo no prestaba atención. Yo estaba volcada en mis recuerdos, como en un viaje interior, recorriendo otros paisajes dentro de mi cabeza. El recorrido de una amistad.

Llegué a casa tan disgustada que ni siquiera quise comer. Me fui a mi habitación, me encerré allí, y me entraron unas extrañas ganas de llorar sin saber por qué. Me ayudó oír música, leer un libro, poner la televisión, hacer cualquier cosa para distraerme. Cuando estaba seleccionando un CD, sonó el teléfono. ¿Sería Adriana que quería explicarse y pedirme disculpas? La culpa de que yo me sintiese así era suya, por los comentarios que hizo, que me chafaron todas mis ilusiones y me derrumbaron. Había salido de la reunión tan animada y ahora me sentía como una basura.

No era Adriana. ¡Era Diego!

—¡Qué bien que ya hayas llegado!

—¿De dónde?

—Del colegio, claro. Cuando pasé en el autobús frente al Anita, te vi en la calle con un montón de gente.

—Sí... Acabo de llegar ahora mismo. Hemos tenido una reunión, y, a la salida del colegio, todo el mundo comentaba lo que había pasado.

—¿Pero ha pasado algo importante?

—No... Solo ha sido una reunión rutinaria para hablar de la fiesta de fin de curso...

—Ah...

Me había quedado sin tema. Y tenía muchas ganas de charlar con Diego, porque me parece estupendo poder hacerlo. Pero no sabía qué decir. Y él seguía callado al otro lado del teléfono; era todo un poco estúpido, y más por teléfono. Por fin él habló, aunque sin mucha originalidad, porque solo dijo mi nombre:

—Tatiana...

—¿Qué?

—Escucha, solo quería decirte algo, pero no sé si debo. Por favor, no me lo tomes a mal...

¡Eso sí que no! ¿También él? ¿Sería que ese era mi día para recibir palos de mis amigos? A veces leo mi horóscopo en las revistas, pero luego no me acuerdo de nada. Debía de haber una conjunción de planetas en mi carta astral de ese día: «Cuidado con los amigos, que hoy pueden machacarte». ¡Qué tontería! Con los amigos no es preciso tener esos cuidados. Los amigos no te machacan.

Pensé todas esas cosas, pero no se lo dije. Así que insistí:

—Dime...

—Te vi hablando delante de tu colegio con un chico que yo conozco. No sé cuál será la relación que tienes con él.

—¿Mi relación, cómo? ¿Qué chico? —repetí, fingiendo que no sabía de qué iba.

—Uno delgadito, alto, que se llama Fabio.

—Ah, sí...

—¿Sois amigos? ¿Es tu novio?

—¿Ese asqueroso? ¡Dios me libre!

¿Qué significaba aquello? ¿Diego me llamaba para

saber si era la novia de Fabio? ¿Quería saber si tenía novio o no?

—Ah, bueno, entonces puedo hablar —continuó él—. Porque quería avisarte de que tengas cuidado con ese tipo. Es un falso.

—Lo sé muy bien, puedes estar seguro. Estábamos a punto de pelearnos de verdad, casi físicamente. Tenía unas ganas enormes de darle con el libro de Matemáticas en la cabeza, pero mi amiga no me dejó.

—¿Por qué? ¿Qué te ha hecho? Si no es muy indiscreto preguntártelo.

Sí que lo era. No podía contárselo sin hablar de la historia de Carla, sin decirle que Fabio había dicho que ella era fea y que olía mal. Además, Carla era prima de Diego. Pero también me parecía una falta de educación si le dijese que me parecía una indiscreción preguntármelo... Decidí ser lo más franca posible, sin comprometerme a nada.

—Diego, discúlpame, pero no puedo contártelo, porque hay cosas que afectan a otras personas.

—No, no, está bien, lo entiendo —dijo él un poco molesto—. No he debido preguntártelo. Solo quería avisarte sobre ese tipo. No merece ninguna confianza. No puedo darte detalles, porque como tú acabas de decir, afectan a otras personas. Pero cuidado con Fabio.

—¿Dónde lo conociste?

—En casa de Víctor. Se pasa la vida allí...

—Ya lo sé.

Diego dejó escapar una risita, de esas que hacen

que me ponga a imaginar su rostro transformado por su sonrisa.

—El tío Vic le puso un mote muy apropiado, pero no se lo digas a nadie, ¿eh?

—¿Tío Vic? ¿Vic Bellini?

—Sí. ¿Has olvidado que es mi tío?

—Lo siento sí que lo sabía, pero... ¿Y qué mote le puso?

—Te lo digo porque veo que sabes guardar un secreto. Fabio conoce ese apodo, pero no sabe que quien lo inventó fue el tío Vic. Piensa que fue el Penumbra.

—¿Qué mote es?

—Fabio Arroz.

—¿Por qué?

—Porque tiene esa manía de estar pegado siempre a Víctor, de estar siempre pegado a los miembros de la banda, de hablar como si fuese «íntimo de Vic Bellini», de querer ser «amigo del artista», esas cosas... Tío Vic le puso ese mote porque dice que el arroz va siempre acompañando pero nunca es el plato principal.

Ahora fui yo la que me eché a reír. Él continuó:

—Hay gente que es así: solo quiere ser amigo del rey. Nunca has leído el poema de Bandeira.

—¿Qué poema? No lo conozco...

Entonces comencé a descubrir el lado más hermoso de Diego. Yo sabía que le gustaba leer. Pero no imaginaba que supiese tanto de poesía. Porque enseguida él me recitó enterito el poema de Manuel Bandeira, titulado *Me voy a Pasárgada*. Después incluso me explicó que el poeta siempre estaba muy enfermo, había tenido tuberculosis en la adolescencia y en aquel tiempo no había antibióticos, y esa enfermedad por aquel tiempo era mortal. Así que él perdió todas las esperanzas, hubo que quitarle un pulmón y se fue a tratarse a Suiza. Después se dispuso a esperar a la muerte y le fueron prohibidas muchas cosas. Vivió ochenta años. Pero en uno de los poemas que escribió, que Diego me recitó por teléfono, Manuel Bandeira inventó ese lugar imaginario y perfecto donde el podía hacer de todo: andar en bicicleta, montar en burro, ir al parque de atracciones, bañarse en el mar, enamorar a quien quisiera, donde quisiera, todo... Porque allí él era amigo del rey, es decir, tenía un amigo con el poder de adivinar sus deseos y de proporcionarle todo lo que desease, todas las cosas que para él eran imposibles, pero que, gracias a ese amigo, no le harían ningún mal.

—El profesor de Literatura me explicó que Pasárgada era el nombre de una antigua ciudad de Persia. En cierto modo, eso de decir que era amigo del rey es más o menos lo mismo que si Bandeira dijese que era amigo de un genio que satisficiese todos sus deseos.

—¿Y qué tiene que ver Fabio en todo esto? —pregunté.

—¿Fabio Arroz? Creo que es de esa clase de tipos que lo confunde todo, de esos que no saben lo que es amistad y que se acerca a los poderosos por puro interés. Gente que piensa que ser amigo del rey es ser enemigo de la ley, gente que quiere aparentar bailándole el agua a los famosos y a los poderosos.

Fue estupendo hablar sobre la amistad con Diego. Porque poco después le conté cómo me había disgustado el comentario que hizo Adriana a la salida de la reunión, y que yo pensaba que Adriana estaba algo molesta conmigo y que me criticaba por causa de Cris, cuando en verdad era ella la que se estaba apartando de mí por causa de Rafaela.

—¿Pero no fuiste tú la que conseguiste que ellas dos volviesen a ser amigas?

—Yo misma, mira tú. Fue el día de la final de voley.

—¿Y ahora te molesta que las dos estén juntas?

—Yo, no... —comencé a decir, pero corregí—. Es decir, solo un poquito, y solo a veces.

—Ya, me parece lógico...

—Pero ella se enfada si estoy con Cris.

—¿Pero a ti te agrada ella o no? ¿Es o no tu amiga? Entonces, ten un poco de paciencia, ella es aún una niña. Deja que corra el tiempo, para ver cómo queda todo.

—Sí..., puede ser...

—Pero hay algo, Tatiana, que mi madre dice a todas horas, y que te puede ser útil.

—¿El qué?

—Todo el mundo dice que en la desgracia es cuando se conoce a los amigos. Pero no es así, sino que es en el éxito. El que es capaz de alegrarse sinceramente con el éxito de un amigo, sin tener envidia alguna, es porque lo siente de verdad.

Era una idea interesante, que nunca se me había ocurrido. Era estupendo charlar con Diego. Le pregunté algo sobre él:

—¿Tienes un gran amigo? ¿No te molestaría si, de repente, él comenzase a salir más con otro?

—Es diferente... Tengo muchos amigos al mismo tiempo, todos muy cercanos, pero cada uno tiene una forma de ser diferente. Creo que solo puede ser así, porque no se puede querer ser dueño de las personas. Nunca se debe obligar a un amigo a que siempre esté contigo.

Continuamos conversando, cada vez más animados, sobre lo que es un amigo de verdad. Y tuve una idea:

—¿Sabes? Va a haber un certamen de literatura en el colegio y necesito escribir un texto. No sabía qué tema escoger, pero ahora ya lo sé: la amistad.

—Entonces te daré el poema de Bandeira. Si es que lo quieres citar...

—¡Estupendo! Muchas gracias.

Me llené de valor y le dije:

—¿Por qué no vienes a mi casa y me lo traes?

Me pareció que él también le echó valor porque respondió inmediatamente:

—¿Puede ser ahora mismo? Así continuamos charlando...

114

—Claro... Y así me ayudas en la preparación del texto. ¿Sabes mi dirección?

—Claro, es la casa de Frajola... Conozco el edificio, pero no sé qué piso es.

Se lo dije, lo anotó, y nos despedimos.

En menos de media hora, Diego ya estaba en mi casa. Mi hermano se llevó un susto cuando vio que Didi entraba y le decía que venía a hacer un trabajo conmigo. Era la primera vez que un chico venía a estudiar conmigo a casa. Y, además de ser amigo, era un chico —incluso guapo, con una mirada interesante y una sonrisa transformadora—. Fui a toda prisa a arreglarme un poco. Apenas tuve tiempo, porque no lo esperaba tan pronto. Pero lo conseguí:

Cuando llegó, me dio el poema, que comenzaba así:

> *Me voy a Pasárgada,*
> *allá soy amigo del rey...*

Tal vez inspirada por los versos de Manuel Bandeira, resolví hacer un poema sobre la amistad.

Casi me volví loca buscando imágenes y rimas. En la primera estrofa conseguí rimar amiga con vida y con olvida, pero a partir de ahí solo se me ocurrían palabras como enemiga, intriga, e incluso aburrida. O me venían a la cabeza barriga, hormiga y otras palabras así, que cortaban cualquier inspiración que pudiese tener.

—También tienes verbos —sugirió Diego—, como siga, diga, prosiga, consiga...

Intenté seguir su sugerencia. Intriga y enemiga eran muy fuertes. Aportaban al poema un aspecto negativo que quería evitar.

—¿Qué tal si intentamos hacer versos más modernos? Sin rima... —propuso Diego.

Era una buena idea. Me sentí más libre, más suelta. Para dejarme escribir a mis anchas, Diego se fue a la habitación de Rodolfo para charlar con él. Más tarde, cuando los dos volvieron al salón, yo aún estaba totalmente liada frente al papel. Había comenzado un nuevo tipo de juego de palabras en el que «amiga», que aparecía en un verso, aparecía como un eco en migaja en otro verso, o en desmigar. Era difícil que me librarse de esas asociaciones negativas. Nunca pensé que fuese tan difícil...

Cuando volvió, Diego se sentó al otro lado de la mesa, cogió una hoja de papel y comenzó a escribir. Poco después, cuando quise saber qué escribía, me dijo:

—Es solo una lista de expresiones que tratan sobre la amistad. Si crees que puede ayudarte, esta es mi modesta contribución.

Me pasó el papel en el que había escrito:

Amigos, amigos, negocios aparte
Amigo del rey
Amigo del león

Amigo-oso
Amigo para todo
Amigo para siempre
Amigo del corazón, hermano, compañero.

—Veo difícil expresar eso en un poema. ¿No crees? —le comenté.

Su respuesta fue una pregunta:

—¿Y quién dijo que tiene que ser un poema? ¿Tú no me has hablado de un certamen de textos? ¿No pueden ser de cualquier tipo?

—Tienes razón.

Y así fue cómo cambié de idea otra vez. Decidí entonces escribir esta historia en la que entran mis amigos como personajes, usar algunas expresiones de la lista de Diego y otras que yo misma descubrí, narrar detalladamente lo que nos sucede, mientras vamos construyendo nuestra amistad.

Tengo que hablar, además, de los últimos acontecimientos, de cómo me enfadé cuando descubrí que Adriana y Rafaela le habían enseñado a un montón de gente una foto mía durmiendo en Santa Helena, ridícula, despeinada, con la cara hinchada y la boca semiabierta con el aparato de ortodoncia a la vista. No sabría contar cómo sentí mi intimidad invadida y yo traicionada en esa foto, cómo les pedí que la destruyesen, cómo ellas se habían echado a reír, cómo se

117

habían burlado de mí y cómo me dijeron que yo no tenía sentido del humor y que no sabía soportar una broma.

Pero no era nada de eso. Dentro de mí tengo la certeza de que una amiga de verdad, a la que le importasen mis sentimientos, a la que le agradase, no haría una cosa de esas. No me lo merezco. Es una injusticia querer criticarme por haberme sentido ofendida y haber reaccionado por eso.

Puede ser que solo sea una chiquillada de Adriana, y, en este caso, ella misma se dará cuenta y me pedirá disculpas; si es así, podremos seguir unidas por muchos y muchos años. De lo contrario, habrá que hacer frente a los hechos y reconocer que Adriana no era esa amiga maravillosa que yo pensaba. Tendría que apartarme de ella; en mi memoria quedaría como hermoso recuerdo perdido en mi infancia. Como un juguete o aquel osito de peluche que yo siempre llevaba conmigo. Una persona con la que me equivoqué, que me había gustado mucho, pero que fue capaz de herirme por una tontería. Y de hacerme llorar mucho, solo para divertirse y echar unas risas. Como si no diese ningún valor a todo lo que pasamos juntas, y que fue tan bonito. O tal vez el error fuese mío, por dar más valor a alguien que no lo merecía.

Antes, yo no conseguía ver las cosas de esta manera. Pienso que es así porque ahora estoy creciendo, madurando. Y no es solo porque el tiempo pase: tal vez sea por las conversaciones con Diego, que es mayor que yo y ha leído mucho más. Es probable que lo que más me ha ayudado a madurar y a comprender mejor esta situación haya sido el hecho de haber escrito sobre todo esto que pasó. He tenido que ordenar mis ideas, considerar mis emociones, intentar organizarlo todo. Con certeza, el hecho de escribir me ha ayudado mucho.

Si esta amistad va a durar o no, solo el tiempo lo dirá. Pero una también tiene que ayudarse. Por eso, ahora que veo el texto acabado y corregido y que ya puedo ponerle punto final, acabo de tomar una decisión que no esperaba tomar. Pienso que no puede ser de otra manera y espero que estéis de acuerdo conmigo.

He sido muy sincera. He contado todo lo que sucedió tal como lo recuerdo y desde mi punto de vista. Sé que puede haber otros, como, por ejemplo, los de mis amigas. Y no sé si a ellas les gustará ver esta nuestra historia al alcance de los demás. Más que eso: sé que no tengo derecho a contarlo todo y exponer de esta manera a las personas a quien quiero.

Por eso he decidido que no voy a presentar este libro al certamen de literatura del Anita. Es lo mínimo que puedo hacer por mis amigas, aunque me haya llevado un montón de tiempo escribirlo. No puedo dárselo a leer a nadie. Como máximo, puedo enseñárselo a alguien con quien esté comenzado una nueva amistad, como vosotros.

Tal vez algún día pueda cambiar algunas cosas, disfrazarlas, mezclar episodios, inventar personajes nuevos, hacer algo muy diferente, y entonces sí, podré publicar el libro. Aunque dejaré cosas para que ellas, mis amigas, puedan reconocerse en él y vengan a hablar conmigo, pero con la suficiente habilidad para que nadie más consiga identificar quiénes son. O si no, guardo este texto en el ordenador, y ya veremos qué hago; tal vez dentro de muchos años volveré sobre él. A mí me hubiese gustado mucho ganar ese certamen. Pero conservar la amistad de mis amigas es más importante que cualquier premio.

Diego citó el otro día una frase de una gran escritora brasileña llamada Clarice Lispector, que dijo en una entrevista: ¿Literatura? Vale más un perro muerto.

No lo sé bien, pero creo que ella quiso decir que lo más importante de todo es la vida, incluso la que hubo en el cuerpo de un animal muerto. Una simple señal de vida, por leve que sea, vale más que todo, incluso que el arte.

Puede ser que, si yo fuese una gran artista, pensara de forma diferente. Dicen que un artista debe tener el coraje de ir al fondo de lo que vive y siente, y arriesgarse de verdad. Pero no soy una artista. Y tal como soy hoy, me parece que no tengo que hacer nada de eso. Estoy de acuerdo con Clarice Lispector. O bien consigo algún día transformar esta historia en otra y así podré publicarla, para que otros la lean, o, de lo contrario, todo se acaba aquí. Si quiero presentarme al premio del certamen literario del colegio, tendré que escribir otro texto. Aprovecharé todo lo que he aprendido con este, y haré un relato cortito sobre la amistad, por ejemplo.

No por conseguir el premio de un certamen, voy a exponer a mis amigas. Por ellas, incluso aunque nunca lo sepan, me dispongo a modificar el refrán que abría la lista de Diego:

Amigas, amigos..., conservarlos es un arte...

Porque yo quiero que las personas con las que vivo una amistad puedan tener la seguridad, en todo momento, de verdad, sinceramente, de que puedo ser una persona vulgar y sin importancia, pero un amigo mío es un amigo del rey.

Índice

Si te ha gustado este libro, también te gustarán:

Chicas enamoradas, de Jaqueline Wilson

Gran Angular, núm. 211

Ellie tiene un problema con los chicos. Aunque tal vez sería más correcto decir que no tiene ningún problema, porque no existe casi ningún chico en su vida hasta que aparece Dan, y entonces lo que tiene es un dolor de cabeza. Sus mejores amigas: Magda y Nadine comienzan a tener sus propios planes y una vida social interesante, así que Ellie no quiere quedarse atrás.

Chicas con imagen, de Jaqueline Wilson

Gran Angular, núm. 212

Una revista intenta descubrir a jóvenes modelos. Magda y Nadine no dudan en presentarse a la selección; pero Ellie comienza a pensar que le sobran quilos por todas partes. Las tres amigas pasan por una etapa en la que no se sienten satisfechas con su propia imagen.

Chicas que llegan tarde, de Jaqueline Wilson

Gran Angular, núm. 213

¿Hasta qué hora te dejan salir por la noche? Ellie, Magda y Nadine siempre se meten en problemas por el mismo asunto. Tener una cita con un chico estupendo no es excusa y tampoco ir al accidentado concierto de su adorada estrella del *pop*.

Zapatos de cocodrilo, de Alfonso Suárez Romero

Alerta Roja, núm. 33

Paula y Raquel estaban convencidas de que eran las mejores amigas. Se creían casi idénticas. Al creerse tan parecidas, Raquel y Paula nunca se habían dado cuenta de los abismos que las diferenciaban, y todo por culpa de un chico.

Alerta Roja